CW01468501

CYBER CELL

A DETECTIVE BROGAN NOVEL

ANGELA ARCHER

TYG PUBLISHING

A TYG Publishing publication.

First published in Great Britain in 2020 by TYG Publishing.
Ebook first published in 2020 by TYG Publishing.
Paperback published in 2020 by TYP Publishing.
Copyright © TYG Publishing 2020.

ISBN 978-1-9160397-3-5

The moral right of Angela Archer to be identified as the author of this work has been asserted by her in accordance with the Copyright, Designs and Patents Act 1988.

All the characters in this book are fictitious, and any resemblance to the actual persons living or dead is purely coincidental.

All rights reserved. No part of this publication may be reproduced, stored in a retrieval system or transmitted in any form or by any means, without the prior permission in writing of the publisher, nor to be otherwise circulated in any form of binding or cover other than that in which it is published without a similar condition, including this condition, being imposed on the subsequent purchaser.

Cover art by Stuart Bache at Books Covered.

To Christopher, this book isn't for you.

* * *

Books may look like nothing more than words on a page, but they are actually an infinitely complex imaginotransference technology that translates odd, inky squiggles into pictures inside your head.
–Jasper Fforde

CHAPTER 1
PRESENT DAY – MONDAY, 24 SEPTEMBER 2057

The pitch of the woman's scream still echoed in his mind. Brogan nudged the door open with the muzzle of his gun and slid inside. With his back to the wall, gun held ready, he scanned the apartment. It didn't take long to look around the shitty little box of a room, like his on the floor above. The only other door led to the bathroom.

A mess of auburn hair on the floor poked out from behind a tech-cluttered desk. He strode over to the bathroom, busting the door back on its hinges to whack anyone lurking behind it. *Bathroom's clear.*

He rounded the desk. The body of a young woman lay curled on her side. Blood seeped across the laminate. Her glassy green eyes stared at three words painted on the wall, her own blood used as ink. Using the universal method for checking for signs of life: he nudged her with his boot. Nothing. *Dead.*

Brogan holstered his gun then fished out his e-cig and took a long drag. He tilted his head as he took in her bloody scrawl. Funny, how people can drop all the bullshit when they need to; why say ten words when three will do? If only more people were like that. Maybe that's why people avoided him at work, maybe that's why Katie finally left him. Maybe he should get his mind back on the job.

Stepping over the woman's body, he turned to the desk and sat down to survey the scene. Not much of a disturbance. The couch cushions were dislodged, a blue vase and a picture frame had been smashed. Digi-pads, stack extensions and a couple of early-style smart watches lay abandoned on the desk. Nothing seemed out of place. He glanced at the formatic chair under the gallery window. The usual cybernating setup all looked intact. *If this was a botched burglary, what were they after?*

The sirens of the rapid response team bounced off the cityscape as they approached; the girl's life-extinct alarm had automatically alerted them. Brogan hooked up a drive scanner to the woman's computer stack. While it copied the drive data, he rummaged through the clutter on the desk but found little of interest. The drive scanner bleeped its completion and he shoved it into his jacket pocket.

Heavy footsteps rumbled down the corridor, then stopped. He'd recognise that sound anywhere: adrenalized thugs with guns, at least one Metal Mickey by the sound of it. Bruisers disguised as the local Peacekeeper unit. Unmoved, he took out his badge and waited with the arrogance of a man who knew he had absolute authority over anyone who walked through the door.

No one entered. A muffled argument started outside the door.

Brogan huffed. 'Oh for pity's sake.' He strode over to the

door, then flung it open. 'Where the bloody hell have you lot been?' Appearing suddenly before a bunch of twitchy, gun-wielding, half-witted 1st Division Peacekeepers is always a bit of a gamble, but it gave him the buzz of the old days. 'What are you doing? Playin' Rock-Paper-Scissors or something?'

Two slack-jawed officers jumped back, aiming their guns at Brogan's forehead.

'Don't bother, lads.' Brogan halted them with a flash of his badge. The glare from it alone was enough to stop them.

'Detective Brogan, 5th Division. Well? Where the heck have you been?' Brogan stuffed his badge back in his pocket. 'Who are you?'

'D-Divison One, sir. I'm Deacon.' He nodded towards the other guy. 'And this is Heston.'

'Which one of you is the Metal Mickey?'

'I am, sir.' Heston proffered his right leg, hitched his trouser leg up and revealed the titanium prosthesis.

'Have you forgotten the regulations? Switch the actuators back on. Christ, I could hear you clomping down the corridor a mile away. What do you want, a fucking fanfare?' Brogan shook his head. 'Get on to Control, this is a murder scene. Get forensics down here, set up the secure-door, and more importantly, get out my way.'

The pair of Divvies looked relieved when they realised they didn't have to sweep the apartment. Their look reminded Brogan of the relief he felt after the first sip of beer at the end of a very long day. He had hoped it wasn't going to be one of those days, but that hope was fading.

As the Divvies scurried about securing the scene,

Brogan glanced around the room once more. It looked like a classic burglary gone wrong; but something niggled him, something wasn't quite right. Apartment buildings were pretty secure these days, what with bio-scan security and CCTV systems everywhere. You'd have to really want something to get in uninvited.

He didn't linger. Forensics would record the details and he could peruse them later. Crime scene analysis was all done by computer these days, crime having changed in many ways. Nowadays, the honest folk were the ones you had to watch, largely because there were fewer of them. Brogan took the view that everyone could be corrupted and it was only a matter of time. That kind of cynicism didn't develop overnight, it had to be nurtured over decades.

Reaching the street, he took another drag on his e-cig. He let the morning sun warm his face and the traffic whizz by above him. His comms-watch buzzed and the nicotine rush vanished. He rolled his eyes and tutted.

'Brogan,' he snapped.

'Marcus, it's me, Katie. Although you'd know that if you looked at the display.'

'I'm working, Kate. What is it?'

'Yes, that's why I left you. Anyway…' Brogan opened his mouth to cut her off but she beat him to it. 'It's Mikey, he's cybernating again.' Her tone wavered.

'What? How? I thought we got rid of the pod? We paid a fortune to sort out his gaming addiction. How could you let this happen?'

'Don't you dare lecture me, you haven't been here…'

She ranted on. Brogan tuned out and stared mindlessly

at a delivery-bot negotiating a kerb. He tuned back in when her voice softened and the anger had run its course.

'...his grades were good, he seemed happier. He said he could control it and, well, he promised, so I let him keep it.' She seemed meek now. Brogan took pity, since he did still love her.

'How long for?' He took another drag of nicotine.

She hesitated. It was a bad sign. 'Six weeks.'

'Bloody hell, Katie!' He blew up. 'What was he thinking?' Brogan shook his head. 'I'm coming over!'

The investigation would have to wait. Six weeks. Six weeks hooked up to a machine, feeding through a tube and shitting into another. For what? Living – if that's what you call it – in some made-up virtual reality, or whatever reality you choose except for the real fucking one. Some cyber bullshit life where you can be a twat in two worlds instead of one. Brogan sighed, stashed his e-cig and hailed an aero-cab.

* * *

Two months previously – Thursday, 19 July 2057

'Clayton Mace?' The bland, digital tones of the prison computer interjected into Mace's re-education programme. 'You have an interface request from Miss Amber Hausman. Do you accept or decline?'

'Accept,' said Mace, in mind only, his bodily needs dealt with by the prison's caretakers and safely locked away at His Majesty's pleasure. The screen in his mind flicked from laborious prison reform propaganda to the image of a woman. Bustling ginger hair lying seductively on her shoulders, a dusting of freckles drawing the eye to pink lips then up to emerald eyes. Amber had aged better than wine when compared to the adolescent years when Mace had known her.

'Amber, I'm so happy to see you! It's so lonely behind bars. I mean, two years and you're my first visitor. It's been like, what, ten years since I last saw you? You look great, by the way.'

'Oh, thanks. Yeah, it's been a while hasn't it.' Amber tucked a lock of hair behind her ear. 'Look Clay, I...' She faltered and gazed down. 'I'm only calling because of Pete. He'd want you to know...'

'Know what, Amber? What's your crazy brother been up to now?' He grinned. 'I miss that lad.'

'Clay, he died. I'm so sorry.'

'What? When, how?' Mace screwed up his face. His prison-issue avatar just made him look cross-eyed.

'He was on his way to a gig...' A tear formed in the corner of her eye and she quickly wiped it away. 'Some kid on an old-school motorbike ran him over.' She pursed her lips. 'It was four months ago, Clay. I'm sorry no one's told you before now.'

Mace stared at the clock on the wall behind her. *Pete*. Even though his body was in stasis, his heart ached for his only childhood friend.

'Look, Pete wanted to come see you. He really did. But he was advised by his PR team to cut ties with you, you know, when the charges became public.'

'Amber, I didn't kill eighteen kids, I couldn't. I wouldn't. I was framed.'

'I'm sorry, Clay.' She shrugged. 'I wanted to tell you sooner but, well, there are a lot of people who think you should be dead already for what you did.'

'I didn't rig those kids' pods. I'm telling you the truth.' He wanted to reach out of the screen and grasp her shoulders. 'Please, please tell me you believe me, Amber. You know me. It's not in me. I'm a computer geek, nothing more.' The opportunity to get Amber on-side felt like it was slipping away. 'Two years I've been locked up in a cyber cell. I've only got three left before they terminate me.' The government judged that five years was a long enough cooling-off period before the finality of death couldn't be changed in light of new evidence.

'I don't know what to think, Clay. I know you're more than a geek. You're a hacker, that's way cooler.' She gave one of her trademark sultry smiles and Mace wondered what had become of the men she'd perfected it on. The brief moment of adoration flicked off. 'Look, I've got to go, Clay. I'm supposed to be working. I've done what I promised Pete I'd do. I'll be seeing you.'

'Amber, no, wait… Please? Chat with me a while longer? How's your mum, how's work, how's your love life?' The eyes in his mind subliminally pleaded with her to keep chatting, praying that the clunky, outdated avatar pixels would do him justice.

'Hmm.' She glanced down at her watch, bit her lower lip, looked at something off screen, then focused back on Mace. 'One minute. Mum's, well, she's as good as can be expected given the circumstances. Work's okay, new job and all. Love life's non-existent.'

'Oh, new job?' Mace's ears pricked up.

'Yeah.' She fidgeted in her chair. 'It's okay, you know the usual corporate marketing stuff I've always done…' She chewed her lip again.

'Yeah, who for now?'

'Please don't be mad?'

'Why would I be mad?' Mace tilted his head, aiming for a confused look.

'Well…' she started.

'Oh shit. It's Novanoid, isn't it? Otherwise you wouldn't be stalling.'

'They're big business, the pay's good and the fringe benefits… well, a girl's gotta look after herself.'

'Shit! You watch your back working for them. Be very careful. Don't trust anyone.'

'I think I'm pretty safe working in marketing, Clay.'

'I mean it Amber. I was framed by those bastards. It wasn't me. Please, please believe me?'

She wouldn't look at him. If he couldn't convince her then he might as well die for the murders he didn't commit. He had fought for the truth for so long, his hope was ebbing away like the last grains in an hourglass.

'Amber?' His voice softer now. 'Amber, you know me. I used to say sorry to a snail if I accidentally trod on one, and do you remember the summer before Pete and I went off to secondary school? When Pete was going to kick the shit out of a scrawny kitten and I wouldn't let him? I rugby tackled him and we had that big fight. You grabbed the kitten and ran home. Amber?'

'Yeah, I remember.' A small smile stretched across her face. 'I also remember Mum wouldn't let me keep it and I found it dead in the gutter not long after that.'

'Help me. Please?'

'You need a lawyer for that, not an up-and-coming marketing exec.'

'Say you'll visit me again then?'

'Look, I've got to go. I'll think about it.' Amber clicked off before Mace could reply. The prison system kicked him out of the e-vid-link area and back into his main cyber cell dash panel. He stood and stared. If he were in the real world, he would have sagged into a chair. If this plan failed then he might as well be dead already. *Amber, you're my only hope.*

CHAPTER 2

PRESENT DAY – MONDAY, 24 SEPTEMBER 2057

B rogan flagged an aero-cab, the blue rim of its underbelly highlighting a static advert for the latest AR lenses. The cab door glided open and Brogan ducked in. He spat out the coordinates for his old place. The familiar words rolled off his tongue without much thought. Making himself comfortable, he pondered the dead woman's scrawl:

I aM atone/

It was as if she'd run out of time to finish her sentence, but why not write something helpful, like whodunnit or where she kept her will?

Brogan liked puzzles, but not bloody cryptic ones. They involved serious thinking, and he only dealt with everyday thinking. He liked your everyday criminals, largely because he was one – just one that stood on the right side of the legal system. No, it was clever criminals that really got his goat. The sneaky ones who thought they could outwit him. He'd always get them in the end.

He was settling into his thoughts when the aero-cab finished setting its course and rose abruptly to the third-level traffic stream. His stomach remained at ground level, and he groaned and pressed his hand to his stomach as he waited for the sensation to pass. He didn't have to wait long, as a new sensation filled him when the aero-cab jerked him into the back of the seat as it accelerated to join the traffic stream. He did his best to avoid getting sucked in by the continuous reel of adverts on the cab's TV. He couldn't give a toss about wellness plans for the over-forties.

The Cambridgeshire skyline spread out like an infected fly bite, the city's sky-trax routes formed a chequerboard across the sky.

As the cab descended outside his old place, nothing seemed to have changed: a red-brick detached with a driveway and no car. He was about to walk straight into the house, but realised that the bio-scan lock, above the door, hadn't acknowledged his presence. She'd deleted him from the security register. He sighed and reached for the intercom.

'Hi,' she said as he walked in, 'why is it only now we're divorced can you drop everything at work to come home?' She was bitter and there was no sensible answer to this that wouldn't lead to another argument. He opted for silence. It didn't work, but it was damage limitation.

He noticed she'd redecorated. To his dismay he liked it.

Damn it, he missed her, missed her scent, missed the way her blond curls bounced as she walked, missed the way her nostrils flared when she was pissed off, like now. He couldn't escape the feeling of emptiness hitting him in the stomach like a sledgehammer. He distracted them both from her rant with a question about Mikey.

'So what was Mikey up to before he hooked himself up?' His voice soft and enquiring. Interview techniques had their uses.

'As I said, he's cybernating. I left for work thinking he'd head off to college as usual, and I came back to this…' She opened the door to Mikey's bedroom. His pod – the Plexus Pro G – sat in the corner, with him lying there, in-state, touchable but unreachable except through a series of noughts and ones. Brogan stared at his son's body, all trussed up like he was in some space-age hospital. The gentle hum of a cooling fan whispered in the background. Katie reached into her pocket, pulled out a digi-note and handed it to Brogan:

> Sorry Mum,
> I'm not designed for an analogue life.
> I'm nobody in reality.
> I'm somebody in the Grid.
> It's where I belong.
> LM x
> P.S. Please don't be mad.

They retreated silently to the living room, where Brogan sunk back into the sofa. Damn, it was a comfy sofa. 'Shit!' It was the best he could come up with. 'Have you spoken to his frien—'

'He has no actual friends. He lives online. The teachers say he keeps to himself, his grades are average, average at everything really except computer sciences.'

'Look, they've improved the safety features since all those kids died. It's been, what, two years at least. He'll be fine… well, until he unplugs and I get my hands on him!'

Katie gave herself a hug. She looked small and unsure.

'Look, if you're still worried, I'll have my guys look him up, keep an eye on him. If that will make you feel any better?' *I'll feel better too.*

'Okay, yes. Thank you.'

'Right, I've got to go. I'll let you know if I hear anything.' He scrolled through the apps on the watch, stabbed the blue halo logo of the sky-trax cab company, and by the time he got out to the street an aero-cab was descending in front of him. He'd been ignoring the buzz of his comms-watch and glanced at it to see four missed calls from his boss, Kane. He didn't bother calling him back.

Chapter 3

As soon as he stepped out of the aero-cab, Brogan's ears were assaulted by the chants of a mob. *Oh bollocks. Protesters.*

The throng of protesters were banging and clattering their way across the plaza. Office workers scurried around the edge of the crowd as armed responders tried to herd the rebellious cattle away from the Peacekeeper HQ entrance. *Why-oh-why didn't I get dropped off on the upper platform?*

He stared up at the twentieth floor, the corner precipice cut out to allow aerial access to the building. Peacekeeper HQ was a building unencumbered by architectural beauty. It stuck out, a solid and immovable lump like a rock in a hard place.

Brogan usually enjoyed the short walk across the plaza, the chance to taste synthetic nicotine, and the delay in getting back to his desk. Not today, though. He was on a collision course with the protesters. A mix of 1st Division Peacekeepers, hovering drone units and, out of sheer tradition rather than anything else, seven officers on horseback rode the line.

Brogan squinted at some of the slogans: 'My life, not yours,' 'Change the system not the climate,' 'Data mining sucks.' Brogan shook his head. *Any chance to moan and they all come out.*

Someone threw a rock, and Brogan dodged backwards to avoid it. The culprit was instantly subdued by a drone tranquilliser dart, his comrades shuffling him away into the angry swell. The rock landed a few paces in front of Brogan. He picked it up, turned it over in his hands. It was a weighty chunk, smoothed by years of erosion. It had a stencilled message scrawled on it: *'They're watching you, always.'* It ended with what looked like a grid address. Brogan glanced back towards the crowd. *Muppets.* He abandoned the stone in a planter at the front doors of the HQ.

The 5th Division Peacekeepers took up the whole of the sixteenth floor. Two thirds of the old basement car park had been converted into prisoner holding cells, reserved for the more violent clientele. There were more cells on the ground and first floors, the latter having access to medical care should they have sustained injuries in the course of their transgressions.

The rest of the floors below his were split amongst the lower-ranking Peacekeepers, departments moved around in motivational reshuffles. Brogan never kept track of who was where. He didn't really care.

He entered the airlock, the only way into the lobby. The green landing-strip lights of the security tunnel followed his progress and the automatic doors at the other end slid open. The lobby was empty. It's funny how busy officers can get when there's trouble on the doorstep.

Brogan poked the button for the elevator. The din from outside drowned out the little space he had for thinking.

'Good morning, Detective Brogan. What floor do you require?' Paysos, the force's AI, had been given a particularly cheery persona.

'Where's James Anders, 4th Division?' Brogan stepped inside the shiny metal box.

'Mr Anders is currently on the ninth floor.'

'Good, take me there.' Brogan didn't see the point in being polite to a machine. The elevator confirmed the destination and ascended. Relief washed over him as the yelling faded away.

Stepping out on the ninth floor, Brogan looked out across the busyness of the open-plan offices of the 4th Division. These were the go-to guys and gals for all things science and tech: cyber-crime, forensics, psychological profiling, the lot.

Brogan approached Anders. The man had three screens and a visi-wall behind him. Anders was known for his computer wizardry. He had a reputation for reading and writing code like he was one of them, a machine. Brogan recognised bits of code but had no idea what it meant.

'…well, this is the third time it's happened and the third time I've had to call! It's simply not good enough… No, no, is there someone else I can speak to?' Anders looked up, rolled his eyes at Brogan, then went back to speaking into his comms-watch. 'No, I'm at work right now, I just need it sorting otherwise I'm switching providers'. He hung up and rolled his eyes at Brogan. 'Glitchy network provider.'

'How's the analysis on the Hausman case?' Brogan dispensed with the small talk.

'I've not long got back from the scene, sir. Just running the usual battery of tests...' Anders was good on the ground, but only after the crime had happened.

'Anything stick out to you?' Brogan valued his opinion. Not as much as his own, of course, but Anders was reliable, and occasionally insightful.

'What, apart from the bloody message and the amateurish attempt to make it look like a struggle?'

'Mmm, my thoughts exactly. Let me know if you find anything.'

'Will do. I've requested the security logs and I'll make a start on analysing her stack.'

Brogan nodded. 'Keep me posted. By the way, you wouldn't do me a favour would you? Would you have a look and see what my son's up to? Not official business I know, but he's cybernating and, well, you know... the ex is worried.'

'Sure, I'll take a look, unofficially of course, sir.' Anders ran a hand through his thick black hair, it was so glossy you could almost see your face in it.

Brogan gave a little nod, then he headed back to the elevator. This room was full of super-nerds, eugenic successes that gave Brogan the creeps. He wondered if Kane would be around, and if he could make it to his desk before getting yelled at.

CHAPTER 4

TWO WEEKS AGO – SUNDAY, 9 SEPTEMBER 2057

'Hey.' Mace's skin tingled when Amber appeared on-screen. 'How are you? I'm so glad you're back. I didn't think you'd come.'

'Yeah, I'm okay thanks.' She tugged a ringlet of hair.

'You don't sound certain?'

'It's just that I told Mum I'd spoken to you and she went a bit mad.' Her face crinkled but her eyes smiled. 'She still says you were born rotten.'

'And you? What do you think, Amber? You're my only hope of getting out of here alive. Please, tell me.'

'Clay, I don't know.'

'You know me, I haven't changed. Honestly. You must know that, you must, otherwise you wouldn't have called again.'

'I believe you… I think.' She twisted a lock of auburn hair around her finger.

'Amber, I need you to trust me. I need your help and I

need to trust you too. I don't know what else I can do to make you believe me. I hope, maybe, deep down you do?'

'It's the thought— oh Clay, those poor kids.'

'Exactly, Ams, those poor kids.' Mace jumped on this new angle to get her on-side. 'But it wasn't me, and that means whoever did kill those kids is still out there. They're free to do it again. Amber? You know I'm right. You know it in your bones, otherwise you wouldn't have called again.' There it was again, the lip-biting. Damn it was sexy. Mace let his words sink in.

She appeared to think it over. 'Okay, I believe you, but what can you do?'

'I have a few ideas.'

'Clay, I don't want to get into anything illegal. Mum's had enough to deal with.'

'You won't, I'll see to it. I only need a small favour and I'll do the rest. I can't really say any more here, I can't even think without it being recorded. If my pulse rate goes up they know about it.'

'But where else can we talk? You're in prison, remember?' Her mouth curled into a smile on one side.

'Yeah... call me again this time next week then, but before you do, go check out a really cool grid page called "Vintage Knits r Us". There's some really *useful* knitting patterns on there from the 1970s.'

She tilted her head at him. 'It won't get me into trouble will it? I mean, that's the last thing Mum and Dad need right now.'

'You can't get into trouble for clicking on an ad. Go to the page marked 1971, there's an advert that looks *really* out of place, click on it.'

'Okay, fine,' she huffed. 'But I'll curse you if my feed fills up with ads for knitted cardigans.' Her face grew bigger on Mace's screen as she leant forward to terminate the video call. 'See you next week.'

Mace grinned. His plan might work after all.

CHAPTER 5

PRESENT DAY – MONDAY, 24 SEPTEMBER 2057

'Brogan, my office.' Superintendent Kristoff Kane's gravelly voice rumbled across the open-plan office. Several heads turned in Brogan's direction. Kane glared at Brogan as he limped through the maze of desks to his greenhouse of an office in the far corner.

Brogan hadn't made it anywhere near his own desk. He took a deep breath and followed Kane. Their conversations usually ended with Brogan wanting to land him one. 'Sir?'

'Explain yourself,' Kane barked before Brogan had even closed the door.

'You're going to have to be more specific, sir.' Brogan took up a defensive position in the middle of the room.

'How was it that you were first on the scene at Hausman's?'

Brogan shrugged. 'Because I live there, sir.'

'With Hausman?' Kane's face creased like an old man's scrotum.

'No, sir.' Brogan clenched his jaw. Tedious questions

gave him a headache. 'It's an apartment building. I live in the apartment above.'

'And what, you accidentally got off on the wrong floor?'

'What's this about, sir? D'you think I killed the girl?'

'We all know you have anger management issues. So you need to start talkin'. I need a darn good explanation as to how you got there faster than Rapids and *before* the girl's biochip fired off a life-extinct alarm.'

'As I said, sir, I live on the floor above. I was getting ready for work, heard a scream, went to investigate.' He shook his head. 'The girl was a goner before I arrived.'

'Did you check for vital signs?'

'Didn't need to, sir. Her vital signs were all over the floor, if you catch my drift.'

'What?' Kane threw his hands out and leant forward.

'Sir, I've seen enough death to know what it looks like.'

'Oh, what, so you're a medic now are you?'

'No, sir, but during military serv—'

'Detective Brogan.' Kane stuck his palm out to silence him. 'I don't give a shit about your time in the military this, and your time in the military that. What I do care about is avoiding cock-ups and having to defend the actions of one of my officers. That woman was still alive when her security system logged you entering the room.' Kane raised his eyebrows to a whole new level. 'So, you leaving a woman for dead is what I care about.'

'How long?' Brogan took a stride towards the desk. His nostrils flared, the red mist descending.

'What?'

'How long after I entered did her biochip report life extinct?' He tilted his head.

'About a minute.'

'About? We're talking specifics. Get specific.' Brogan's fingers twitched.

'Forty-three seconds.'

'Right, so let's say what, fifteen seconds to sweep the apartment, another fifteen to twenty seconds to locate the medi-kit. That leaves seven seconds for the initial work-up which, in my experience, is usually at least a minute, by which time, well, she was all out of time.

'I estimated she'd lost at least five pints of blood, her heart rate would have been through the roof and all that adds up the fact that she was fucked. There was nothing to be done.' Brogan glared at his boss, daring him to waste any more of his time. 'It'll all be in my report, sir.'

'You bet it will. I'm giving you the case. If it gets out that an officer left a citizen for dead, there'll be uproar. It's bad enough outside already. We don't need to give the media any more fodder.'

'Fine. Then don't let it get out.' Brogan had reached his limit, and headed to the door.

'You fucked up, Brogan. You can fix it and I'll be watching you. I want your prelim report by Wednesday.'

Brogan refrained from smashing the smirk off Kane's face, 'Sir.' *What a way to start the week.*

At his workstation, a coffee was waiting for him. *Clarkson.* She was a good detective, and coincidentally an even better soldier in his old unit. She knew how he liked his coffee, and better still she knew to leave him the heck alone until he'd finished it.

He fired up his stack. The visi-wall, a divider between

the desks, flicked into life and the royal crown that was the Peacekeeper logo span nonchalantly.

'Paysos, open case files relating to Amber Hausman. Assign me as the lead detective.'

The blue, androgynous face of Paysos, the force's AI, changed into the case file icon.

'Right, Ms Hausman. Let's have a look at you.' He tracked to her birth certificate.

Born: Amber Gemelia Hausman, age 26, date of birth 27 October 2028.

Parents: Jacinta Hausman (nee Stringer), Dalton Hausman.

'Paysos, complete the standard background search on Amber Hausman and her family.'

'Certainly, detective. Processing.'

Brogan sipped the lukewarm coffee. Synth caffeine was not the same as the real deal. You never got the same hit with this stuff. The World Health Alliance took all the fun out of living.

'Miss Hausman has no criminal record, no infringements or fines. She appears of average general intellect but scored highly on emotional intelligence. Studied English at Kings College Cambridge. Registered as employed by Novanoid Corporation as a junior marketing executive. Do you require further information?'

'Nah, save it for later. Just upload the parents' address to my comms-watch.'

'Hey, finished that coffee yet?' Selina Clarkson's perfume arrived before she did.

'Hey, cheers Sel.' He clutched the mug and dipped it in her direction, then gulped down the dregs and suppressed a shudder.

'So, what's new?' She perched on his desk.

'Not much.' As much as he liked her, she had an unreliable mouth and he wasn't about to fuel it. 'You?'

'Kane seemed pretty pissed at you.'

'Kane's always pissed at me.' *What's she fishin' for?*

'Listen, some of us are heading out for drinks on Friday. You in?'

'Nah, probably not.' Brogan shifted and focused back on the visi-wall.

Clarkson leant in. 'Still doin' the whole lone wolf thing then?'

'Something like that.' A grumble of irritation grew in Brogan's stomach.

'It wasn't your fault, you must know that. You were cleared of all charges.'

'Yeah, but it still doesn't stop 'em callin' me the Baby Killer, does it?' He tutted. 'Just leave it, Sel.' *In other words, fuck off.*

'Ignore them. You were just doing what you trained for.' When Brogan didn't reply she added, 'It is only Monday, there's time to change your mind. When you're done with all that guilt-trippin' shit, come and join us for a pint.' She stood and adjusted her skirt.

'Cheers for the coffee. I've gotta go.' Brogan grabbed his jacket.

Clarkson stepped aside. 'See ya later then.'

Brogan's only reply was to show her the back of his head.

* * *

The sky-trax platform, on the twentieth floor of Peacekeeper HQ, was a carousel of aero-cabs. He didn't recognise any of the faces getting in or out of the cabs. There was no brotherhood here, but it was better than facing another round with the protesters. The chilly autumn air, mixed with the wind tunnel through the platform, made him fasten his jacket.

It wasn't a long wait for the aero-cab to hover in through the corner precipice. This was a particularly classy looking cab, sleek black sides with a panoramic view through a tinted glass lid. The machine was a thing of beauty, if your definition of beauty involved painted metal and flashy lights. Brogan couldn't care less. The doors swished open and he stepped into the plush interior. This was one of the newer models. It didn't matter where you sat, a screen would appear opposite you and pump adverts into your eyeballs until you either went blind or mad.

'Take me to this address.' Brogan flicked his watch and the Hausmans' contact card uploaded to the cab.

'Destination accepted, Detective Brogan. Estimated journey time is twelve minutes. Would you care for any refreshments?'

'No. Enable silent mode.'

'Silent mode enabled.'

Brogan avoided watching the infomercial about life

insurance for the over-forties, and opted for rummaging in his pocket for his e-cig. The tip barely touched his lips.

'WARNING: This is a smoke free vehicle. Smoking is in contravention of World Health Alliance recommendations. Contravention will result in transport termination.'

He was so tantalisingly close to a delicious drag. The craving would have to wait. Instead, he flicked the screen on his comms-watch and the in-cab display changed to his home screen.

'Open emails.' He scrolled through the usual diatribe of work memos, an appointment reminder for an epilepsy review, but nothing else caught his eye.

'Send message to Mikey.' He waited for the computer to catch up. 'Mikey. It's Dad. You'd better have a bloody good explanation for cybernating again. Six weeks, Mikey. What were you thinking? You've upset your mother and I'm none too impressed. Dad. Message ends. Send.'

He pinched the small screen on his comms-watch and the in-cab display returned to yet another infomercial, this one about dating. The bastards knew everything about you these days. Every fart recorded, in case of some farting-related pandemic or greenhouse-gas-related propaganda series. Next it would be an advert about men over forty contributing twenty per cent of today's gas emissions, or the methane release of meat-eaters compared to vegans, purifying the planet with their vegetative expulsions.

'Display news channel.' Brogan looked past the display and out at the boring Suffolk flats. Dense traffic headed in the opposite direction, towards the city. The flickering sunlight had a strobe effect. *Bloody epilepsy.* Brogan looked away. They were travelling in the third-level traffic stream, the motorway stream. He felt the cab descend. Sky-trax had both vertical and horizontal slip roads.

They levelled off in the second stream, the slow lane. Bullet-loaders – the wagons of the sky – dominated this stream. Hooking a right and down into the first level, the local level. People on the ground were clearer at this level, scurrying about, concerned only with the business of their own lives.

'Two minutes to destination arrival.'

Brogan closed his eyes. Grieving parents were hard work. *Grief is a shitter.* Meteor's face circulated in his mind, the last image of his sergeant and best mate, before their captors shot his face off. His stomach churned and shuddered the memory back into its box. The cab slowed and descended to street level.

'You have arrived at your destination. Please exit safely and have a nice day.'

Brogan stepped out and squinted against the bright sunshine. The tinted windows of the aero-cab were darker than he'd realised. This was an odd part of Cambridgeshire. Technology wasn't exactly embraced, but it wasn't exactly rejected either. He looked up and down the street. The few front doors he could see didn't have the telltale security bulkheads over the doors. They had old-fashioned palm panels and fish-eye cameras.

Number twenty-seven, the left side of a semi. *Here goes.* The green front door had seen better days, the palm-panel security system easily hackable. Curtains closed. *Not a good sign.*

He placed his hand on the ID panel and waited.

'Hello?'

He stepped back to make sure his face was in the camera frame and proffered his badge. 'Mrs Hausman? Detective Brogan. I'm here about your daught—'

'Really? Right now? One of your lot just left.'

Hmm, probably family liaison. 'Yes, Mrs Hausman. I'm terribly sorry but this is a murder investigation, and time is of the essence.' Brogan fiddled with his shirt collar.

'Not for us it isn't!'

'I'm sorry. I know this is difficult.' He tilted his head as he looked into the camera.

'Do you? Do you really?'

The mechanical whirr of the lock drew Brogan's gaze to the door. It creaked open and a shell of a man appeared.

'I'm sorry about my wife. Please, come in. Whoever did this needs to be caught. I'll do my best to help.'

'Thank you, Mr…'

'Dalton, Dalton Hausman. People call me Tone.'

'I really don't want to intrude, I know this is a difficult time for you.' The man didn't reply, he just turned, left the door open and headed into the pit of the house. Brogan followed.

As they entered the cramped living room, several cards on the mantelpiece caught Brogan's eye. 'Sorry for your loss', 'Thinking of you', 'Our deepest sympathies'. *The girl's only been dead half a day…*

'Can I get you a drink?' Tone's voice was devoid of life, like the rest of him. He sort of hovered, like he was there but he wasn't.

'No, no thank you.'

'I'll go and get my wife.'

As Mr Hausman disappeared, Brogan stepped over to

the mantel, picked up a card and read it: 'Pete was a great friend.' Another: 'I can't imagine the pain of losing a son.' *Crap.* Brogan remembered the news. Pete Hausman, lead singer of some band Mikey was into, had been killed in a motorbike accident.

'Don't touch those.' Jacinta Hausman brought an icy blast of tension into the room with her.

'Sorry. I had no idea.' Brogan replaced a card and turned to the two hollowed-out faces blinking back at him.

'Two children, gone, never to come back. Never to walk through those doors again.' Tears streamed down Jacinta's face. Dalton put an arm around his wife.

Brogan remained silent and hoped his face displayed the correct emotion. He didn't have room to feel anything much for them.

'Shouldn't there be two of you?' Dalton gestured for Brogan to sit.

'Just me, I'm afraid. We're short-staffed. The drone units know I'm here.'

'Well, isn't that reassuring.' Jacinta spoke with venom. 'Go on then. Ask your questions if you must.'

'Sit down, won't you.' Dalton gestured again to the crusty leather sofa.

The old thing swallowed Brogan up, tipping him backwards. There was an awkward moment while he readjusted, bum shuffling to the edge and regaining composure. 'When was the last time you saw or spoke to Amber?'

'Saturday. She phoned. She said she was really busy, something to do with work.' Daltone pursed his lips. Cracks were appearing in his brave face.

'Work for Novanoid, you mean?'

'Yes, she loved her new job. She spoke highly of her new boss but he made her work hard. She spent that much time there, Pete thought they were dating.'

'Was she involved in anything? Did she mention having fallen out with anyone?'

'No, not our Amber. She's the—' He stopped himself. '—*was* the sensible one.' Tone squeezed his wife's hand. She was sobbing. 'You will get them, won't you?'

'I can assure you the force will make every effort to bring the perpetrator to justice.'

The couple nodded, clinging to each other, holding each other up. Brogan gave them a moment of silence. There was nothing else he could give.

'What was she like, what was she into?'

'She had the laugh of a warehouse worker but the smile of a princess. She had her own lifestyle brand, you know? She liked gaming, music, reading, anything that made her think. She liked writing, poetry mostly, I think.'

'Do the words "I am atone" mean anything to you?'

The Hausmans gazed at each other, almost searching each other's memory banks. Both shook their heads.

'There is something. We fell out, a few weeks ago.' Dalton clutched his wife, his bottom lip trembled as he glanced at her. 'She told us she'd been to see that murderer, the cyber killer. Clayton Mace. They grew up together, you know. Thick as thieves they were. The three of them, Pete, Amber and him. Always thought he was a bad egg, that one.'

'And do you know if she'd had any contact recently?'

'She promised us she wouldn't see him again. She said

she only went to tell him about Pete because they're not allowed the news in prison.'

'Okay, that's helpful. My contact details are logged in your system. Call me if you have any questions or if you think of anything else that might be useful. The department offers its condolences, and rest assured we will do everything in our power to see that justice is done.'

'Your condolences? Is that it? Is that all we get?' Jacinta's hackles were up. 'We're very sorry, we're doing all we can, goodbye? Two children dead within six months of each other and that's it?' She pulled herself to the edge of the sofa. 'You try it, detective. You try burying a child and then tell someone how sorry you are. You're going to walk out of here and carry on with your life. Your life hasn't changed, you haven't got to deal with it, you don't have to wake up every day remembering your children are dead. You live it and then say you're bloody sorry. Sorry isn't going to bring them back, is it?' Frothy white spit formed at the corners of Jacinta's dehydrated mouth.

'No. I am sorry I can't do more, but I will do my best for you and Amber.'

Neither parent stood, they stayed huddled together on the sofa. Brogan saw himself out. He needed a walk after that. *That was intense.* His muscles loosened with every step he took away from the house. A rock formed at the back of his throat. Mrs Hausman was right. His life would carry on as normal, whatever that was.

He strolled to the end of the road. This was a quiet area, the dense traffic streams off in the distance, the undisturbed sunshine and the occasional birdsong filtering through Brogan's mind. What was it about this botched burglary that niggled him? The fact that nothing seemed to be stolen, the message on the wall… had they fled because they were disturbed? No, he got there pretty quickly after the scream. She wouldn't have let someone in uninvited, or someone she didn't know, unless it was a service guy or maintenance. He made a mental note, then his stomach rumbled. *Food o'clock and meds time.* He patted his pockets, found his epilepsy tablets and took two. He had a knack of pooling enough saliva to swallow them without water.

CHAPTER 6

TWO WEEKS AGO –
WEDNESDAY, 12 SEPTEMBER
2057

Wednesday evening, and Amber had been going round in circles. It had been three days since she'd last spoken to Mace, and three days since she'd been able to focus on anything else. *What if he is innocent?* She couldn't stand the thought of someone she knew, someone she had feelings for, being put to death for something they hadn't done. *But what if he did it?* What if all the beatings from his alcoholic father had taken their toll, what if he wasn't the gentle giant she once knew. *I've not helped him yet, I've not done anything wrong. What could be in this stupid link anyway?*

She pulled on her second-skin gloves and lowered the headset over her eyes. The Grid loaded. She was facing her dash panel. A carousel of her favourite sites to the left. Her message boards across the bottom and the news channels to the right. She swiped to the search page and entered the Grid address Mace had given her.

Her finger hovered over the link to the Vintage Knits Grid page until curiosity got the better of her. She selected the link. The site was littered with old-fashioned models wearing chunky cardigans, a man in a knitted burgundy waistcoat stood with his chest puffed out and his belly sucked in. Knitted tea cosies and Christmas decorations all vying for the viewer's attention. Ads popped up here and there, mostly dating sites. She'd have to stop looking at those, it was getting depressing. She found the menu bar and clicked '1971'.

Not much caught her eye. There was a very fine woman modelling a knitted scarf and hat set. An ugly crocheted handbag dangled off her shoulder. *Jeez, this is so last century. It can't be making a comeback, surely?* She scrolled a little further down the page. Knitted socks. An ad for wool. A dating site ad. An ad for pepper spray. She smiled. Mace. She clicked on the advert.

A flutter in her stomach grew as the page loaded. She had no idea what to expect. It was taking a while to load, and she was almost ready to disconnect when the image of a door appeared. A plain, internal door, nothing flash, just a white door on a battleship-grey background. Her heart beat a little faster. Then she did what anyone does when faced with a door: she tapped on it.

Suddenly the door opened and rushed towards her. Instead of falling down a rabbit hole, she was being swallowed by it. The display warped, her world twisted, her stomach churned, and then she was standing in a log cabin.

There were only three walls to the cabin. The end wall was a picturesque view of a lake and pine-covered mountains.

'Glad you could join me.' Mace's avatar appeared

behind her and made her jump. Even though he couldn't physically touch her, she was still on edge.

'Couldn't have used a standard portal entry like everyone else? Jeez, I thought I was gonna vomit.' She gazed around the barren cabin. 'What the heck is this place anyway?' *Where've I seen this place before?*

'Welcome to my little piece of paradise. Do you like it?'

'Erm, it's beautiful... but I didn't think you were allowed out the prison mainframe? That's what cyber cells are all about isn't it? Keeping you locked up body and mind.' She hugged herself. *He's out of his cyber cell. What else could he do? Kill again? No. He wouldn't.*

'Think of it as my dream, and you're visiting.'

'Except it's not, and you've escaped and broken God knows how many laws. You've effectively broken out of prison. Oh God! I'm helping an escaped criminal.' Her gaze darted to the exit.

'No, calm down. You're not. I'm very much aware that I'm still in prison, and so are the guards.'

'Then what is this place?'

'Call it an extension... I'm still in prison, Amber. I haven't left.' Mace took a few steps towards her.

'So how come you're here?' She glared at his avatar, the sensors in her headset doing a pretty good job of recreating it.

'Always asking questions. You haven't changed.' He grinned.

'Clay, if you want help you'll have to give me answers.' She crossed her arms. If she were wearing a full sensor-suit she'd be tapping her toes now, too.

'Okay, fine. Back when I was working at Novanoid, they gave me a job to update the prison security software and…'

'And what?'

'…and, well, I installed a back door. I didn't think for one minute I'd need it, thought I'd maybe sell it at some point.'

'Did you?' Her nostrils flared. 'Did you sell it?'

'Nah, I hadn't got round to it. Then the shit hit the fan so I kept it quiet. You're the only one that knows.'

'So for two years you've been in prison but you've been roaming the Grid freely?'

'Clever, eh? It would be cool if I wasn't on death row.'

'You can go anywhere on the Grid?'

He nodded. 'Pretty much.'

Amber's gaze zigzagged the view of the valley outside. *Is this a joke?*

'Amber, it wasn't me. I didn't kill those kids, but I'm damn sure it's got something to do with Novanoid.'

'Oh, Clay. I want to believe you, really I do. But…' she gestured around her, '…this is… just, well, you can see what it looks like can't you?'

Mace sighed and hung his head. 'What about this? Can you see what this looks like?' With a swish of his hand the lakeside scene turned into a wall of articles, news clippings, images of the dead cybernaters, faces of Novanoid employees, scribbled notes and lines that crisscrossed them all like a spider's highway. Amber stepped closer, taking in the new scene, her head tilted to one side.

'This is what I've been working on for the last two years, Amber.' He moved to stand next to her.

Her eyebrows creased. 'My name's on there. Why?' Heat built up inside her.

'Because you work at Novanoid.'

'In the marketing department!' She bent closer to the entry on Mace's board. 'It's dated before I came to see you.' She span round to face him. 'You knew. You knew I worked for Novanoid. You knew Pete was dead. No wonder you didn't seem upset.' Tremors rippled through her body.

'Well, yes. Sorry.' Mace grimaced.

'Why, Clay? Why would you do that? What were you thinking? Do you think I'm in on it? This is a ridiculous obsession. Christ, I feel like a fool.' She grabbed her avatar and moved to the exit.

'Please, it's not what it looks like. I'm sorry. I can explain. How could I have told you about the back door when the guards record everything. C'mon, Amber. I was going to tell you. Honestly.' He moved to try and block her exit. 'Please help me, you're my only hope. I love you. Always have, always will. Please? Don't go?'

She stood still for a moment, then turned to face him.

'Great! Now I'm angry and confused! You need to give me some space, Clay. I don't know what to think, what to make of all of this, of you.'

'Fine. You believe me though, right, Amber? I was framed.' He stepped closer but she edged back. 'Look, I can't leave the link open for long. If you don't come back by midnight on Sunday, I'll know your answer.'

'Goodbye, Clay.' She didn't look back at him before stepping through the doorway. As soon as she did, her avatar's legs stretched out in front of her. It looked like it was being pulled through the eye of a needle. Just when the effect couldn't get any worse, her avatar started spinning. She closed her eyes but the visuals fucked with her senses. When she opened them again, she was staring at a knitting pattern for socks. She yanked off the headset and gloves.

What a prick.

Chapter 7

The chat was buzzin' as the Ranger, a recruiter, entered the milieu of a game called *Xenon Fire V*.

'Hey, have you seen this?' Minty beckoned to the Ranger.

'No, I've been analogue. What's been going down?' The Ranger sat his avatar down next to her.

'Holy hell balls, you've missed the single most ingenious takedown, like, ever. The Nomads only went and joined forces with the friggin' Cluster Cruzers and took out half of Sector 18.'

'No way.'

'It lasted two days.'

'Oh man, I've gotta watch the replay.' The Ranger swiped his screen and loaded the replay. A fleet of battle cruisers dominated space. He turned and grinned at Minty. 'I can't believe I missed this.'

'Where've ya been, anyway?' Minty glanced over to his screen. 'Oh, this is a good bit.'

'Ah, had to look after Mum and earn some creds.' Six huge battle-class ships came into view. Thousands of smaller fighter jets took off from the mouths of the ships.

'So she's no better then?'

'Nah, sometimes I think she'd be better off…you know…' He glanced towards the screen, at a fighter being blasted to smithereens.

'Oh, don't say that. Look, I've been thinkin', I'd like to move on to the final stage of the trial. I'll give you some of the creds, it'll be way more than I need, and you can buy the meds your mum needs.'

'No, you don't have to do that for me.' *Yes. Nice one. Reel 'em in nice and easy.*

'No, I want to, honestly. Ooh, don't miss this bit.' She poked her avatar's hand towards his screen. The lead battle cruiser had blast holes on all sides. Then the port-side engine took a massive hit and the explosion ripped through the ship.

'Sweet.' The Ranger leant in towards the screen. 'You sure about this?'

'Yeah. I'm sure.' Minty's avatar was pretty androgynous but she had a sweet smile.

'Nice one. I'll set it up.' The Ranger sat back to face Minty. 'Thanks.'

She nodded. 'Cat. Hey, Cat?' Minty stood and waved to someone over the Ranger's shoulder. 'Catsanga's here.'

'Yo peeps.' Catsanga strolled over.

'I've just agreed to do the final stage of the trial.'

'Seriously?' Catsanga's gaze darted between the two of them.

'Yep.' Minty seemed triumphant.

'You're gonna be rollin' in the creds.' The two girls giggled.

The Ranger eyed them. *This is too easy.*

* * *

The Ranger carried on pretending to enjoy the rest of the 'epic battle' while actually scanning his dash panel and the source code. Catsanga's source code. He looked her up on the Grid. *This girl really likes cats. Not much online presence, though.*

He found some family photos, the usual forced awkward smiles, drab unstyled attire, hair like a swarm of angry bees, but underneath it all a pretty little thing resided. Petite frame, striking eyes that looked like they could see straight through you. He checked her academic background (just above average), bank details (family debts coming out their ears).

He dug deeper. *Now this is interesting.* She used to be a top gamer but fell from grace after being caught cheating. A diagnosis of anxiety and depression, according to her medical record. She had it all, then disappeared.

She seemed ripe for the taking. Minty was already in the bag – getting another new recruit so quickly would be purr-fect. He grinned.

* * *

Nine Days Ago – Saturday, 16 September 2057

. . .

During his two years of incarceration, the last three days had been the longest and most painful. Nothing held Mace's attention for long. Amber consumed every corner of his mind. If his body weren't being fed through a tube, he would have stopped eating. His appetite for breathing wasn't much better. It probably would save a lot of trouble if he stopped that too, save the prison some money. How could he have been so stupid as to leave her name on his research board? Why did he tell her he loved her if he wasn't sure it was true in the first place? Round and round his thoughts went, on an infinite loop of misery.

Mace didn't care for the time right now. He didn't know it was noon until a message popped up across his display: 'WEEKLY REFLECTION'. A chance to reflect on the things you've learned in the week, a chance to make up shite about how you're a better person before they terminate your sorry death-row ass. Mace clicked the link and his mind was instantly transported to a room full of other inmates, their prison avatars barely different from his own.

Twenty minutes into a tedious discussion about one man's neglected childhood, an icon of a little door appeared in the corner of Mace's display. It disappeared seconds later. *She's there, she's in the cabin.* He suppressed a smile. His body felt lighter for a moment but it gave way to a growing itch. *Another twenty-five minutes of this shite.*

He considered leaving his prison avatar where it was, like an empty shell, to go and see Amber, but it was too risky. The therapists liked to keep everyone engaged by asking questions at random. *Please wait, Amber. I'm coming, I promise.*

* * *

Mace was gone as soon as the therapist closed the session. He went straight to the cabin. He knew she was still there because the little icon on his display would have flashed again had she left.

He couldn't help but smile when he saw her. She was busy pawing over his research, and hadn't noticed he'd arrived.

'I'm so glad you came back.' A lump formed at the back of his throat. All was not lost.

'I did.'

'Does this mean—'

'This doesn't mean anything other than the fact that, if you're telling the truth, then someone else killed those kids and we need to find them.'

'Right, right. So, what do you make of my evidence?' He nodded in the direction of his research.

'What evidence? All you've got is a bunch of assumptions.'

'But doesn't it make more sense than a lone wolf on a killing spree?'

'It's speculation, Clay. Nothing more. I'm sorry.' The pity in her eyes leached out from her pixel face.

Mace's gaze sank to the floor. All his research. All his time. Occupied by thoughts of freedom, of justice, of revenge. All dismissed. He valued her opinion, it was the only other opinion he'd had, but it was not the opinion he wanted. It was the truth.

'Help me get it, then? You're so good with puzzles.' *Reel her in, easy does it.*

'Get what?'

'Evidence, of course. Real, solid, proper evidence.'

'No, no way, Clay. I'm not doing anything illegal. I'm already risking everything by coming here!'

'I know. Thank you.' Mace paused. 'It would just be a phone call? There's nothing illegal about that.'

'No!' She folded her arms.

'Then why do you keep coming back? Amber, I know I keep saying this, but you're my only hope.' Mace watched her. She had that look she always had when she was trying to solve a puzzle.

'Look, all I'm asking is that you accept a call from me while you're at work. That's all.' He bobbed his head down to get in her eye-line.

'Yeah, and then what?'

'Well, then I think I can bypass the security protocols and access the mainframe.'

'Oh my God, you're crazy.' Her eyebrows disappeared off the top of her head. 'Are you serious? I would be an accessory. No. No way.' She shook her head.

'Not if it were a genuine emergency.' Mace had to be careful. He didn't want it to seem like he'd been planning this since she'd got her job at Novanoid.

'You've got to be kidding?'

'Hmm, no. What if I become suicidal?'

'But you're not!'

Mace didn't reply.

'Are you?'

'Frequently,' he admitted. 'I'll tell my therapist I've found a way to kill myself in my cyber cell and I'll do it if I don't get to speak to you. They'll call you up, at work, and

I'll do what I need to. You'll look like an innocent bystander.'

'So I'll look like you used me, like you are now?'

'Why are you here, then?' This was harder than he'd expected.

'Honestly, I don't know. I did love you once, when we were younger. Now, with all of this, I just don't know.'

He'd often caught her staring at him when they were younger, but he'd thought that was what girls did, or she was staring at the bruises his father had given him the night before. 'I'm still the same boy.'

Amber turned her back on him and faced his research. Mace waited.

'I thought you were a hacker. Why haven't you hacked in already?'

'I've tried for two years. No one's been able to do it... but I think I've finally found a weakness.'

She pressed her lips together. Closed her eyes and took a deep breath. 'Okay.'

'Okay?' Mace lit up.

'Yes, Clay. Okay, I'll do it.'

'Great. Amber, honestly, I can't tell you—'

'Just tell me what you need me to do and when. As much as I like to know everything, this is one occasion where the less I know, the better.'

'Right, well, I need a couple of days to set everything up...' He didn't really need them, it was already set up, but he didn't want her to think she was a foregone conclusion. 'Let's say Wednesday?'

'Why a weekday? Can't it be the weekend?'

'No, there'll be more traffic on the servers on a weekday, I'll stand a better chance of hiding in all that noise.'

'So, Wednesday it is, then. What if something goes wrong, or I need to say something?'

'Use a code, you know, like we did as kids.'

'Are you sure this will work?'

'I'm sure. I'm also sure you won't get into any trouble. I wouldn't do that to you, Amber.'

'Okay, till Wednesday then.' She left the cabin. Alone, Mace changed the display wall to lines of code and set about checking every detail. This had to work.

* * *

Present Day – Monday, 24 September 2057

Brogan's comms-watch buzzed. He swiped the screen with his free hand. 'Brogan.'

Anders's clean-shaven face hovered in the air just above Brogan's wrist. 'Sir, I've found a couple of things you might be interested in.'

Brogan chewed through a faux chicken sandwich then swallowed the lump. 'Hmm, don't tell me. I'm in the mood for guessing… Could it be Ms Hausman has been in cahoots with the nefarious cyber killer Clayton Mace?'

'Oh, you already know. How?'

'Her parents. They rowed about it and told her not to see him.' Brogan took a swig from a can of Jive, the fizzy bubbles popping like miniature fireworks on his tongue.

'So how did you know she had?'

'It's called having kids. So what contact did she have with him?'

'The data from her stack says she last contacted him at the prison two weeks ago, via vid-link. I'll keep checking but it doesn't look like there's been anything since.'

'Okay. What else did you find?'

'I've downloaded the CCTV footage from the apartment building. I'm sending you a clip now. Take a look.'

Brogan glanced around the little community garden he'd found not far from the Hausmans'. No one seemed to be paying any attention in his direction, mostly mums herding toddlers and old boys out for a stroll. He pinched the display on his comms-watch and opened the secure link. He stared at the blank space for a moment before the footage appeared.

'So, this is from outside the building, pointing south.' Anders's face formed a tiny square in the bottom right corner as the CCTV footage loaded. 'Here's the victim, she looks to have been jogging.'

'Freeze it, rewind to when she's reaching for the door.' Brogan squinted at the small display.

'Sir.' Anders froze the screen and rewound it a few frames.

'There. She looks like she's talking to someone. Is there another camera?'

'No, sir, just this one.'

'Move it on a few frames. Slow-mo.'

Anders swiped the footage on.

'There. She's definitely talking to someone. I can see a hand. It looks like it's reaching for the door.'

'These types of camera are programmed to rotate, but

this one doesn't. It stops at ninety degrees to the building, then once she's inside and out of shot it does the full sweep.'

'So it didn't pick up who she's talking to?'

Anders shook his head. 'No, and it doesn't get any better from the inside.'

Brogan sighed. 'You'd better show me.' The sandwich was gone, so Brogan made a start on a chocolate brownie.

'This is the footage from the foyer.' Anders looked off screen and a few seconds later a still image of the foyer appeared on Brogan's screen.

'Here's Amber, entering. You can almost see someone holding the door open for her.'

'But not much else. What's that, a pair of legs?' The screen pixelated. Brogan screwed his face up. 'What happened? Where's the footage?'

'Told you it got worse. I'm not sure yet, sir, but it happens in the elevator too.'

'Shit. Is it a corrupted file?' Brogan squinted at the pixels on his screen.

'It's unlikely, watch…' Anders continued to play the footage. In a fraction of a second the pixels disappeared and the image was crystal clear, although the foyer was now empty.

'It returns to normal when they leave the shot? I don't get it.'

'My working theory is some kind of scrambler, sir.'

'Are they on the open market? We used them in the military, but only for blocking radio waves.'

'I need to check the data logs but I can't see anyone being able to tamper with the footage before we acquired it.

It would take too long. They also knew the rotation of the external camera and blocked it somehow. I checked the people walking past, and no one approached that didn't vanish. It's weird.'

'Right. Then there was some premeditation involved. Damn it, I hate it when I'm right.' He grinned. 'Kane's going to have to swallow this one.'

'Looks that way.'

'Who the hell would have it in for a junior marketing exec? Double-check the files, will you? Be absolutely sure. Then tell me it wasn't just a glitch or a badly timed software upgrade or something.'

'Okay, I'll be a couple of hours.'

'Fine. I'll head back to HQ now.' *Scramblers? Who the hell is selling digital scramblers?* 'Anders, before you go, who was logged as the last person she spoke to on her stack?'

'The last logged call was to Elliott Parker, CTO at Novanoid Corp.'

'Right then, I'll check out this—' Brogan's comms-watch gave a double bleep. 'How convenient. It looks like he's trying to get hold of me. Anders, I'll catch you later.' Brogan didn't wait for a reply. A little tone told Brogan that Anders had disconnected, so he swiped his watch and opened the new channel.

'Brogan.' His standard snap response to any call was more like a reflex than a thought. The screen on his comms-watch turned black with a large golden N in the middle. This was an audio call.

'Hello, Detective Brogan,' the voice was too cheery to be human. 'I have a connection request from Mr Elliott Parker of Novanoid Corp. Do you accept?'

'Yes.' Brogan rolled his eyes.

A series of unnecessary little bleeps told Brogan that the call was being put through.

A photo of a man who'd only recently left puberty appeared. 'Detective Brogan. I'll get straight to the point—'

'Good,' Brogan cut in. Some people irked him immediately, some built up to it. This kid fell into the former.

'I've just been made aware of the devastating news about Miss Hausman. I have information regarding the circumstances that I think will help further your investigation rather expediently.'

'Okay, I'll hear you out.' Brogan glanced around the park. The busyness of lunchtime was fading.

'It would be better to speak in person.'

'Right, fine. I'll come to your office tomorrow at 09.30 hours.'

'Thank you.' The connection went dead.

Brogan didn't know the lad, but he did know he didn't like him.

CHAPTER 8

LAST WEEK – WEDNESDAY, 19 SEPTEMBER 2057

Amber had been unable to sleep last night, her mind a carousel of unanswerable questions. Mace was due to call in a few hours. She sighed, hauled herself out of bed and got ready for work.

She drifted through the usual myriad of faces on her commute. Everyone seemed to look like Mace. At her desk, she stared at the list of emails and e-vid messages she'd received overnight. *Some people still haven't heard of work/life balance.*

She'd made it as far as mid-morning on caffeine alone. Every time her phone rang, her stomach churned a little more. Another trill bleep in her ear and her heart raced. She took a deep breath and tapped the comm-switch on her earpiece.

'Miss Hausman, I have a call for you from Dr Simms of the King Henry Rehabilitation and Remand Centre. Do you accept the call?' Even ANNA, Novanoid's Advanced

Neural Network Assistant, sounded judgemental. Amber shook the idea away. *It's just ANNA.*

'I accept.' She shuffled in her seat and sorted her hair. Cameras were good for one thing, at least. After a little bleep Amber started to speak, but her mouth had dried up and she sounded croaky. 'Hello, Novanoid Corporation, Marketing Department, Amber Hausman speaking. How can I help?' She forced a smile as Santa appeared on-screen.

'Hello, Miss Hausman. Thank you for taking my call. My name is Dr Simms, I'm a psychiatrist. I have a rather delicate but urgent matter to discuss with you. Is it okay to talk?'

'Oh, right, yes. Is he okay?' Amber tried not to sound like she was expecting the call.

'You know I'm calling about Mr Mace?'

Drat. 'I… I figured it was, he's the only criminal I know.' She flashed a smile. 'And, to be honest, he didn't seem quite himself the last time we spoke.' She almost started chewing her lip again, but checked herself and rubbed her thigh instead. *Can they read minds, can he tell I'm nervous?*

'How do you mean, he didn't seem himself?' Simms looked impassive, like someone trying not to look judgemental and working hard to hide the fact that they were actually assessing you.

'I'm not sure I can put my finger on it.'

'Well, what sort of things was he saying? Did he seemed troubled, did he express any thoughts of harming himself or others?' The man's eyes were like blue probes.

Shit. Amber squirmed. She'd only expected to speak to Clay. 'Well, it had been a few years since I'd seen him and, well, I can't imagine it's fun being on death row.'

Simms nodded. 'No, that's very true.'

'I got in touch with him to tell him my brother had died. They were best mates growing up.'

'I'm sorry for your loss.' Simms pressed his lips together in that sympathetic way people do.

'Thanks.' Amber had never really known how to respond when people said that, she always felt it was like asking what the weather's like. 'They didn't talk, Clay and Pete – I mean, after Clay was arrested. I think it hit them both very hard.'

'I can imagine. How was he after you told him about your brother?'

'Well, he seemed all right on the surface.' Then she remembered Clay telling her about all the interactions being recorded. 'But it was as though the spark had gone out of him. He's been lonely, and personally I think he's lost hope. I mean, he's still adamant he's innocent and now, well, he's getting desperate.'

'Desperate for what?' Simms stroked his grey beard.

'For someone to listen, or to be taken seriously, I guess.'

'Okay, thank you Miss Hausman. Mr Mace has some suicidal ideation, he tells me he's worked out a way to kill himself despite being in a cyber cell.'

'Well, given his conviction I could quite believe him.' Amber leant on her elbow and twiddled with the hair on the back of her neck.

'Indeed. He is requesting to speak to you as a matter of urgency, he says unless he does he *will* terminate himself.'

Amber took a sharp intake of breath. 'Oh.' Her gaze darted around her desk. *I can do this, I can do this.*

'Now, we don't usually give in to these kinds of

demands, but as you rightly pointed out, we aren't quite sure what he is capable of so we have agreed to his request. That is, if you're willing to take his call?'

'Right. I guess. Not sure I'll be much help but…'

'As you said, all he needs is someone to listen to him. Miss Hausman, I am legally obliged to tell you that your conversation will be recorded. Is that okay?'

'Okay.' She really wanted to say *no*, but she was in too deep now.

'Thank you for your cooperation, Miss Hausman. There's a glitch with Mr Mace's avatar so it's only audio. The next voice you hear will be Mr Mace.'

The line was silent for a moment. Amber's heart beat out of her chest. She glanced around the office, sure that the Peacekeepers were on their way to get her.

'Amber? Is that you?' Mace sounded dead already.

'I'm here, Clay.' Amber impressed herself with her acting ability.

'I'm done. I wanted to say goodbye. I'm going to meet up with Pete.'

Flippin' heck he's believable. She shuddered. 'Clay, I know things are bad, but please don't talk like that.'

'I just wanted to hear your voice one last time. Talk to me Amber, please?'

Amber heard the instruction loud and clear. She wasn't sure if she could still be seen on the camera, so she let her grief for her brother trickle out and a tear escaped. 'Clay, you must stop talking like that, please. Pete wouldn't want that, Pete would want you to fight. I know he wasn't allowed to speak to you after your arrest but he was advised badly and he really did want to see you, I know he did. He told me so. And with his PR company and Mum and Dad on at him not to— well, you know what they're like. We miss him, we all do, but look, please don't end your life. I don't want to lose you too, I don't want to lose another brother.' *I'm rambling. Stop rambling.*

Clay let out a long sigh. 'Is that how you see me? Like a brother?'

Oh shoot. 'Yes, Clay. I love you like a brother.'

There was silence between them. Amber stared down at her desk.

'I hoped we could have been something… more?' Clay sniffed.

'Clay?' *Damn.* She could almost hear the psychiatrist tutting. What had she said? She wasn't sure herself now – was Clay actually suicidal or not? 'Clay, listen, there was a time that I loved you in that way, when your father's beatings were at their worst. I wanted to hug you and take it all away, but Pete and Mum – well, you know, Mum in particular – said we'd be no good together. I wish I'd not listened but, well, I just can't let myself fall in love with a man who's in your situation. I've lost Pete, I can't go through it again.'

'I understand, really. Who could love a monster anyway, eh?'

'I'm sorry. Don't ask this of me, Clay. You're not serious are you? You're not going to kill yourself are you? I mean, have you really found a way of terminating yourself from your cell?' She imagined Simms giving her a thumbs up for that question.

'Maybe. What's it to you?'

'If you do it you'll look as guilty as hell, you know that don't you?'

'I'll be dead, what will I care?'

'Then people will know for sure that you had the technology to kill those cybernaters and you used it on yourself. That'll leave the real killer to roam free.'

'No, no, no! I'm innocent. I've told you, Amber. I can't keep saying it, I was framed by the pricks at Novanoid. If you don't believe me then what hope do I have, what will it matter if I'm dead because no one believes me anyway?'

'I want to come and see you. In the flesh, I mean. Not over the uplink, not over the phone, but in person. Will you see me?' This wasn't for the psychiatrist's sake, this was for her own.

'Do you remember that summer we went up to the lakes with your brother? We fished until it was too dark to go home and everyone was looking for us.'

'I remember. I remember you pushing me in, the water was so cold. We found a cabin…' *Oh.* Amber could see where this was going.

'I'd love to go back there for just one more day.'

'I think I have some photos of that cabin somewhere. I'll send them to you if you like?'

'Thanks. Do you promise you'll come and see me? Did you mean it?'

'Yes, Clay. I'll come and see you, are you free this weekend?'

'Hmm, depends on your definition of free?'

'Haha, sorry.' She slapped her forehead.

'You have to submit a visitor's request.'

'Okay, I'll do it, but only if you promise not to do anything stupid like killing yourself.'

'It might be too late for that…'

'What do you mean, it might be too late?'

'I've a history of doing stupid things. I got in at Novanoid for starters, now look at me.'

'Oh, I see. Well, make sure you stay out of trouble then. I've got to go, I've got a meeting to get to. I'll see you at the weekend.'

'Sure.' Mace sighed. 'Thanks for your help, Amber.'

Amber hung up quickly. *Man, that was exhausting.* She didn't want to risk having to chat to the psychiatrist again. She tried to get back to work for a moment, but the aftershock of adrenaline gave her the jitters. She headed to the kitchen for a drink. She gazed out over the botanical gardens. A bird swooped into a tree and disappeared.

A hand tapped her on the shoulder. She froze. 'He's called?' The voice whispered in her ear.

'Yes.' Her gaze fixed on the point where the bird disappeared and she envied it. 'He got in, didn't he?'

'Yes.' Footsteps and the smell of aftershave faded.

What have I done?

* * *

The Ranger logged in and his avatar strolled over to the console. Computers within computers. *Mental.* He sat near the cat – or the girl with a cat's head and tail, anyway. Now he'd done his research he knew his angle. He manipulated the console to display a particularly popular battle that was going on. Despite his total lack of interest in these games, the quality of the graphics and the skill level of some of these guys was immense. They should be good, they put in the hours, days, weeks and years.

He looked up and clocked the cat-girl staring at him. He gave his trademark eyebrow-flash, head nod and a one-sided smile that was like winking with your lips, and went back to pretending to watch the action. The cat strolled over to him. *Showtime.*

'Hey.' She slid elegantly onto the seat next to him.

He flashed a bigger smile and returned his gaze to the console. *Don't look too keen.*

'Ah, the League of the Doomed have got this.' She added a little purr at the end.

'Oh, and you know because...?' He gave her some cheeky side-eye.

'Call it feline intuition.'

'Or the voice of tactical experience?' He dangled a complimentary carrot.

'I played once or twice.'

A massive explosion drew their attention to the action.

'Must have been more than twice. Man, you're good.'

'Not any more, apparently.' The Ranger didn't reply. Superficially, he was watching the League of the Doomed battleships doing some sort of victory celebration in a formation of a giant L and a D. Internally, he was letting Catsanga dwell on her obsoleteness, leaving the thought dangling between them like a fly in a spider's web.

He swished at the console and the holograph zoomed out to show the digital universe. Planets, gas clouds, distant galaxies and clusters of battleships defending bits of cyberspace and hiding from real life.

'You could be good again?'

'Nah, too old. Can't get the sponsors.'

'Oh come on, you read the tactics just now as if you could see the future.'

She pulled on one of her cat-ears. 'No one's interested in a has-been.'

'I doubt it. Besides, there are other ways to regain notoriety, to be a legend.'

'Oh, what makes you think I was notorious?'

'Just guessing. But I mean, what if you were the first to do something incredible, the first to marry a robot, or earn more creds than you knew what to do with, ooh, or the first to live forever…?'

She laughed at him. It was a cute laugh and it worked, the tension between them eased. 'Laters, funny man.' She slinked off the chair with a grin on her face.

Plant the seed, water it a bit and watch it grow. The Ranger watched her go.

CHAPTER 9

PRESENT DAY – TUESDAY, 25 SEPTEMBER 2057

The Ranger held out his avatar's hand. 'Are you ready?'

Minty looked at it then took it in her own. The uplink tagged them together. Her avatar would go wherever his went.

The Ranger inputted the Grid address. The transition was smooth. Jumping straight from one program to another can be a bit jarring, even if you're expecting it. The lofty clinic room, where she'd been before, faded into view. Both avatars were frozen momentarily and they delinked.

The mocked-up clinic room was light and airy. Minty headed straight for the window. The first time she'd come, the whole wall was given over to a view of the Milky Way. The second time, it was of the ocean. Now it was a mountain range. Despite knowing it was a projected image, Minty couldn't help getting lost in the views, awed by the quality of the graphics and the scenery.

'It's Vermont. Do you like it?' The avatar of a young woman in a lab coat appeared at Minty's shoulder.

'It's amazing.' Minty turned to the woman. 'Hi.'

'Hi, Minty. Nice to see you again. I'll be with you in a moment.' The woman had one hand on a palm-port and the other was swiping and tapping a mid-air display screen. Minty looked on.

She twisted her fingers together. If avatars could look nervous, then Minty would be even paler than she was in real life. 'What's this stage about? When will I get the credits?'

The woman turned and smiled. Her avatar graphics were top notch, even her eyes smiled. 'Now, don't worry,' she said with the gentleness of a mother, 'your credits will be transferred to your online account as soon as the program is completed.'

'B-u-t... I-I-I'm not really sure about this.'

The woman glanced over at the Ranger, who shrugged.

'I've done my bit. Minty, I'll see you later.' He tapped out before either woman could reply.

'I don't want you to do anything you're not comfortable with. The program won't hurt you, but it will make you the most famous person in the Grid. Don't you want that, doesn't it sound good?'

'Yeah, but...'

'And think of all the easy credits you'll earn for taking part. You'll be a true pioneer. You'll go down in history.'

'Okay, but, well, how long will it take? I've gotta be in class at one p.m.'

'Oh, don't worry, it'll take less than an hour. We have the very best systems and portal speeds you wouldn't believe.'

The woman went back to the palm-port and keyed something in, then gestured for Minty to place her hands on it.

'Okay.' Still a little unsure, but driven by the desire for fame and money, Minty placed her hands on the palm-port.

'Very good. Are you ready?' She gave the reassuring smile of someone about to give an injection under the promise it wouldn't hurt.

Minty nodded, and the doctor hit the .exe command.

For a moment, Minty's consciousness was still present in the chat room. She could see her avatar's hands on the portals but they started to appear transparent. The clinic room fuzzed. Everything blinked in and out of focus like a flickering light. Her mother's smiling face appeared. Then she was outside, looking down at a pair of pink handlebars, then the sensation of falling and a pain in her wrist – the time she fell off her bike and broke her wrist. Her mind flitted from one memory to the next. Her primary school teacher telling her off. Chasing her friends in the playground. The memories came faster, flashes of the past, her grandfather's face, his funeral, her pet dog, her best friend Lucy. The speed of them was sickening, like being on the waltzers.

Minty tried to pull her hands off the portal but she couldn't. The images were a blur, glimpses of life spinning in a vortex of the past, losing grip on reality. She couldn't come up for air. She willed it to stop but it didn't. She was going to throw up, she had no idea how long it had been, she wanted to cry, in her mind all she wanted to do was curl up into a ball. She tried closing her eyes but it didn't work, she could still see. Memories swarming into and out of her consciousness, faster and faster, it was too much.

'STOP. No more,' she screamed in her mind. Her heart beat a few more times before it realised the signal from her brain had switched off.

The doctor stared as Minty's avatar remained motionless, frozen pixels like a game on pause. Then the avatar that was Minty disappeared.

'Shit, shit, shit! Where'd she go?' The doctor stabbed at the console, frantically checking the data. No vital signs. Nothing. *Not again.*

Chapter 10

Brogan sat at his desk, staring at the visi-wall. He scanned over the notes from his interview with Hausman's parents. Paysos appeared on the face of every screen. The hum of life in the office died away.

'A female life-extinct alert has been received. There is an indication that the female was cybernating at the time. The Rapid Response team have been deployed. No further information is currently available.' The screen returned to the report he was working on. Brogan's skin prickled. *Mikey.*

Kane appeared from his office. Some heads looked up, most kept low and pretended to be busy. Kane eyed his team.

'Clarkson, my office.' Brogan rolled his eyes. *Damn, the kid's still not learnt to dodge the boss's glare.* He shook his head and stood up.

'Sir, with all due respect—'

'With all due nothing, Brogan. You've got the Hausman case. Deal with it.'

'But, sir, Hausman's death is relevant. She knew Mace and she worked at Novanoid. If this kid died cybernating then there's a connection, I know it.'

'Let it go, Brogan. You've got nothing solid and you know it, the cases aren't even remotely related. Hausman's death was nothing more than a burglary gone wrong.' Kane headed back to his office. Clarkson gave Brogan an apologetic smile.

'But sir…'

'No. Clarkson, with me.' Kane curled his finger towards Clarkson.

Brogan followed them. 'Sir, I think it's a mistake. You should give me the case. No offence, Sel.' He glanced at her, then back to Kane. 'Hausman worked for Novanoid, she knew Mace. She saw him last week, for Christ's sake. She could have been working with him to help start another killing spree. My guess is something went south and she paid the price. Maybe Mace ordered her termination.'

'Brogan. This is all guesswork, speculation, a fairy tale based on a hunch. No, I've heard enough. Out.' Kane was an antique but he still managed to whip his arm out and point it like a shotgun.

Brogan's nostrils flared. *Wanker*. Sel kept her gaze on the carpet tiles as he left Kane's office. He clocked a few smirks from his co-workers and his lip twitched. He glared at them. He sat back down at his desk and drummed his fingers heavily. Blood bubbling over.

He checked his messages. A message from Katie scrolled

across his comms-watch. She'd not heard from Mikey. Neither had he. *Shit*.

Clarkson strode across the office. She focused on her desk, shut down her stack and grabbed her jacket. Brogan grabbed his and caught up with her at the elevator.

'What did Kane say?' His body was still thrumming.

'He said not to tell you anything.' She glanced at him then rummaged in her bag as they both stepped into the elevator.

'We both know I'm right, there *is* a connection. I just can't prove it. Yet.'

'Look, we follow orders, that's what we do, that's what we've always done. If it'll make you feel better I'll give you a heads-up if there's a sniff of a connection with this victim, but do yourself a favour and stop pissing Kane off.' A little smile crept across her lips.

'Ha! The man's a prat, another Charlie not to be trusted.'

'You don't trust anyone.'

'Can you blame me? They hung me out to dry in that court-martial.'

Clarkson rolled her eyes and shook her head. 'No one blames you except you. You followed orders. You did your job.'

'Yeah, cos everyone signs up to kill pregnant women.' Brogan's body stiffened.

'She was a known terrorist.' The elevator pinged open and they stepped out onto the sky-trax platform. The wind whipped up her hair. 'Where are you off to, anyway?'

'Novanoid Corp. The CTO has some intel, apparently. Seemed pretty keen to tell me in person.'

'Well, I'll catch ya later then.' She ducked into the first

aero-cab and Brogan waited for the next one to pull up. His thick rug of hair barely flinching in the gusts of wind racing through the tunnel.

* * *

Brogan stared at the glistening glass mountain that was the Novanoid headquarters. The aero-cab took him over the top and descended into a central ring. Brogan had never cared to get this close before, but the botanical gardens they'd planted in the building's central core provided a green oasis he'd not anticipated. Trees and plants grew on just about every balcony, on every level. It was a well-manicured jungle. It looked good, but it felt like showboating.

Inside the glass atrium, Brogan spotted a human receptionist and made a beeline for her. He was cut off by a securatron. Bloody do-goody robotic security guards. 'Good afternoon, sir. May I access your identity details.'

'Permission denied. My name is Detective Brogan. I have a meeting with Elliott Parker.'

'Welcome, Detective Brogan. I have notified Mr Parker of your arrival. He is expecting you.'

'I should bloody well think so.'

'I sense you are in no mood for small talk. I shall refrain from offering you the complimentary commentary as we pass through our magnificent building. Please, follow me to Mr Parker's office.'

Brogan looked around. The place was like being inside a glass termite colony. Activity going on everywhere, it was exhausting just looking at it. Man and machine scurried around doing important tasks, feeding the relentless machine of consumerism.

It was a bit of a trek to Parker's office. From what Brogan could work out, they were halfway around the circumference and twenty storeys up. Every door and every wall was made of glass. The view of the jungle was, to be fair, quite impressive.

Trees protruded from balconies, every level a wildlife habitat, bugs and birds thriving in this unique microclimate. Brogan thought he heard birds chirping at one point. He spotted the youthful face of Parker sitting at his desk.

As if poked in the ribs, Parker looked up and saw Brogan's approach. He stood and strode over to the door, hand outstretched.

Cocky prick. There was just something about the way the man bounced on his toes when he walked that made Brogan want to punch him. At least his impression over the phone was still right.

'Detective Brogan. Good of you to come.'

'Well, we appreciate the support of the general public.'

'Sure, sure, come in. Take a seat.' Parker gestured to the sofas and coffee table set near the window. 'Drink?'

'No thanks. Impressive view.' Brogan mustered the smallest bit of small talk he could. God knows why.

'Thanks. I don't want to take up your time. We're both busy men, I'll get to point.' Parker poured himself a glass of water and joined Brogan on the opposite sofa.

Brogan reached for his comms-watch. 'You don't mind if I record this, do you? Standard practice and all that.' He watched the man carefully. Parker glanced at the watch but there was no sign of a twitch or a tell. *Cool as a cucumber, this guy.*

'No skin off my nose. Where would you like me to start?'

'Hang on a sec...' Brogan stabbed at his comms-watch. 'Interview with Elliott Parker regarding the Amber Hausman investigation. Persons present, Mr Elliott Parker and me, Detective Brogan.' Brogan nodded towards Parker. 'Right, Mr Parker, from the beginning if you please.'

'Okay. Well, Amber started working here in January this year. She was in the marketing department and she was pretty good at it. I got to know her through a product we're launching and she was going through some of the design features.' He paused.

Brogan waited. He wasn't interested in a sales pitch.

'So, it was a couple of weeks ago now, but one afternoon she came to me somewhat troubled. She was worried, really worried actually. She wouldn't tell me what it was at first but asked a bunch of questions like, if you knew someone was doing something wrong but you loved them would you try to stop them even if they got into trouble? You know, that kind of vague girl stuff.'

'Yes, I know. Go on.' This guy clearly liked the limelight.

'Then last week she came and told me everything. Turns out she knew Clayton Mace and she'd been to see him.'

Brogan kept silent. People liked to think they were giving you new information. This kid seemed to want to be really helpful.

'Apparently they grew up together. She saw him recently, e-interfaced with him to tell him her brother had died. It turns out Mace already knew. And he knew she'd got a job here.'

'That's relevant because…?'

'Because, Detective Brogan, prisoners are blocked from the Grid, they can't get outside the prison network.' Parker sat back. He seemed pleased with himself.

'So, couldn't someone else have told him?' Brogan shrugged.

'No, he's not had any visitors since his incarceration. She said he gave her a link.' He sat forward again, getting closer to Brogan and the microphone. 'That link took her to somewhere outside the prison system, somewhere in the Grid.'

'What? Is that even possible?' Brogan glanced at his watch to check it was still recording.

'Apparently so. I have to hold my hands up here. When Mace worked here, he was one of the best programmers we had. He worked on the prison security protocols, network encryption, he was the best and we needed the best. It was prison security, after all. Amber said that's when he installed a back door. He planned to sell it, but then it turns out he needed it for himself. I mean, that was a stroke of luck right there.' He laughed but stopped when Brogan didn't join him.

'Okay, let me get this straight then. Both Amber and yourself knew that a prisoner, in a cyber cell, had unrestricted access to the Grid.'

'That's right.' Parker's brow creased.

'And neither of you thought to alert the authorities immediately?'

'It was Amber. I wanted to raise the alarm but Amber convinced me not to.' Parker ruffled his hair.

'That's convenient, blame the dead woman. So what is this link? Where is this place on the Grid, Mr Parker? I need evidence.'

'Amber told me he'd digitally constructed a log cabin, he told her to think of it as an extension but he was still in prison. He had a display wall with all the cybernaters' deaths on there, all eighteen. And my name and personal details, Amber and her details, and countless other Novanoid employees. He asked Amber for help to prove his innocence but it sounded more like he was planning his revenge. That, and to kill again.'

'What help did he ask for?'

'He wanted help gaining access to Novanoid's mainframe.'

'Did he get it?'

'Well, Amber came to me in time and we came up with a plan. She would help Mace and we'd let him have a look around our system, only we made a mirror system so he would think he was looking at our mainframe. He had actually been looking around what is essentially a clone of our mainframe, like I said – a mirror system.'

'And you have evidence of this?'

'Oh yes. Every detail logged, every file he's looked at.'

'Why? Why did you agree to this happening?'

'Because ever since the cyber-deaths, Clayton Mace has been attempting to defile the reputation of Novanoid Corp. We lost a lot of revenue and our reputation has been seriously damaged. We do not wish it to happen again.'

'Yes, I can see how damaging it's been for you. Can I have a copy of the logs?'

'I can have them transferred over to you today.'

'And the link? What do you know of that?'

'Amber said that Mace was going to delete it. I don't know what or where it is.'

'Right. But why would Mace have her killed?'

Parker rubbed his chin. 'She'd served her purpose, I suppose. I don't know, maybe he thought it was too risky that she knew about his back door. I don't think he knows about the mirror system.'

This kid's got an answer for everything. 'Well, this has been most informative. Thank you, Mr Parker. Interview terminated.' Brogan stabbed his comms-watch again. 'If you think of anything else, please let me know.'

'Sure.'

'Straight away this time?' Brogan stood and headed to the door.

'Yes, yes, certainly. Like I said, it's what Amber wanted.'

'As you say.' Brogan strode out the office and was collected by a securatron. *I knew Mace was in on this. Kane is going to love swallowing his shitty words now. Gotcha.*

Brogan walked on air as he left Novanoid and hailed a cab. Mace was as guilty as sin, again. Could he feel any more smug?

'Secure uplink to Kane.' While the connection was going through, Brogan glanced out the window of the aero-cab as Novanoid's jungle fell away.

'What now, Brogan?'

'Well, sir, it turns out that Hausman did a little more than chat with Mace. She assisted him in hacking

Novanoid's servers. I have their CTO on record and they're sending the data logs over for analysis.'

'Is the evidence strong enough to hold up? We can't afford to cock this one up.'

'Sir, it's solid, and better still it also implicates Mace in today's cybernater death.'

Kane's glassy stare penetrated the screen. Brogan noticed the guy's craggy neck as he gulped. 'I'll submit Mace's temporary extraction pending further investigation. I need you to approve it and formal charges need agreeing.'

'What's his motive?'

'Mace had Amber killed because she blabbed about the back door he'd installed in the prison network.'

'How?'

'He paid someone.'

Kane seemed to be considering this. 'How do you know?'

'Well, the guy's in a cyber cell but he's got a back door into the Grid, he could have hired anyone.' Brogan knew where this was going.

'That's circumstantial evidence, you know that. I need to see proof, dates, names, transactions, interactions. You know how this works.'

'Yeah, and I know that a kid's just died because this fella's been able to wander freely around the Grid. I know enough to know I can charge him for breaching his prison terms. I know if he's not hooked up to the Grid, then no more kids have to die. I know I can add to his charges following further investigation. Sir.'

Kane stroked his chin. 'The governors aren't going to

like it. Keeping someone locked up without shoving them into a cyber cell costs money, you know.'

'Okay, give him unlimited access to the Grid and let him carry on killing, then. That's your call.'

'Fine.' Kane leaned into the screen until his face filled it. 'But if you're wrong, it's your neck on the line. Get on the Vortrax and interview him. I'll clear his extraction.' The connection went dead.

'Cab, reroute to the Vortrax station.' Brogan sat back. *Not a bad morning's work.*

He checked his messages. Nothing from Mikey. If he was trying to let the heat out of the fire by ignoring his emails, he was only stoking it. *Shit.*

He swiped at his comms-watch and called Anders.

'Anders, have you had a chance to check on my son?'

'Only quickly. His location puts him in a game called *Squadron Survivor.*'

'Oh, so he's too busy playing games to reply to his dad.'

'You probably won't get him until he's out of the game. They disable in-play messaging from external sources, it's a bit of a con to keep players invested and stops them from getting distracted. Best way to get him is to get inside the game yourself.'

'I can't get drawn into that. I haven't hooked up since I was discharged, it can trigger a seizure.'

'I didn't know you were epileptic.'

'Yeah, too much bastard time hooked up as a drone pilot. Still, no sympathy from the government.'

'Oh, I thought it was because of the inci—'

'Let me know if Mikey pops up for air, won't you?'

'So Ka. Will do, sir.'

'Cheers.' Brogan disconnected. *So ka?* Brogan shook his head and disconnected his thoughts too.

* * *

The Vortrax station was filled with people, and they were filled with their own self-importance. They battled through legions of others to get into or out of the station. Brogan strolled through them, staring dead ahead, people dodging around him like a rock in the stream. He selected Cardiff on the ticket machine, and then swiped his watch against it. His watch bleeped and displayed a message.

Destination: Cardiff.

Journey Time: 40 minutes.

Depart: Platform Two.

He grabbed a sandwich and waited on the platform.

A voice came over the tannoy. 'The 11.30 train to Edinburgh has been delayed at Luton due to a faulty airlock. We apologise for any inconvenience—'

Brogan tuned out. *Bloody frictionless travel my arse.*

Chapter 11

A message flashed on Mace's dash panel: *Cell extraction in five minutes.*

'What? No. Not now. I'm not scheduled.' He scrambled to save the data he'd scraped off Novanoid's system.

His neural link powered down. The brainwave modulators dialled down and he slowly became aware of his body. His synapses reconnected with muscles as actual physical sensation crept back. The cool air tingled as he breathed in. Then the hum of electricity buzzed into his mind.

He knew all too well not to open his eyes or try to move too soon, since even the dimmest light could be blinding and the slightest move could see you on the floor. The formatic bed adjusted his position and he began to feel the cool surface that was supporting him. As he began twitching back into his skin, a shuffling sound warned him of the presence of one of the caretakers.

The removal of various orifice tubes was best done

while still slightly groggy from the sedative effects, but this was prison and dignity was the least of your worries. The guy was heavy-handed and disconnected Mace's hygiene tubes in a way that was sure to cause bleeding and resentment.

Mace rubbed his wrists, flexed his arms and rolled his head from side to side as though he was trying his body on for the first time. A sudden strong grip around his wrists was quickly followed by a socket-wrenching heave of his body. Two men hauled him up to standing, and the oppressive reality of the prison walls brought him back to himself. In the grimness, a shiny buckle was the first thing he was able to focus on. It strained around the waist of a thickset guard. His head was heavy, but Mace traced the line of buttons upwards until his eyes fell upon a man's face. He had the look of a discarded saucepan.

'Visitor.' The guard whipped out a pair of cuffs and slapped them onto Mace's wrists with all the pomp and ceremony of a dog pissing up a lamppost. When the guard judged Mace was able to move, he yanked the cuffs in the direction of the door. After a wobbly ten feet or so Mace found his rhythm, his brain remembering how to handle this walking thing, and it allowed his conscious mind to ponder other things.

'Who's the visitor?' Mace's voice sounded croaky and dry, his larynx not used to the exercise.

'I dunno, but they brought your extraction forward from Saturday, so I'm guessing you've pissed off some big dick.'

They trudged along an endless corridor, punctuated every few metres by a dark grey door, each with eight prisoner numbers on. Eight inmates stacked and racked up in cells designed to house four conscious prisoners.

The corridor eventually led to a secure door at the end, which led them into an airlock. Two other doors led off the airlock and the computer would only open one door at a time. The secure door to the right swooshed open. Mace was dragged through one more set of doors, where he was confronted by a row of booths cut in half by a wall of glass. The visitors' room. In his two years inside, Mace had never seen this room.

The guard seemingly couldn't be bothered to walk any further. He heaved on the cuffs, pulling Mace past him and sending him on a trajectory towards one of the middle booths. He hadn't realised how much the guards had been propping him up until his knees almost gave out.

He fell into a chair. From the other side of the glass, a man was studying him. The two men stared at each other for a moment. Mace couldn't be bothered to speak. The walk had taken it out of him. It had been about six months since he'd taken his last step.

'I'm Detective Brogan, 5th Division Peacekeeper. Assuming they extracted the right person, that makes you Clayton Mace.'

'Yeah, what of it?'

'I have some questions that require your response.' Brogan held his gaze.

'Whatever it is, it ain't to do with me.' Mace waved his cuffed hands at Brogan.

'A young girl died this morning. She died cybernating. Her death bears a striking resemblance to your previous handiwork.'

'What? Like I said, it wasn't me. It's someone at Novanoid, I'm sure of it. So they waited two years to strike again. I always knew they would.'

'Who's they? Give me names.'

'Jaro Dax, for one.' Mace's skin prickled at the sound of the slimy bastard's name.

'The CEO?' Brogan smirked. 'Don't waste my time.'

'Don't waste mine either, then.' *Two can play at that game, pal.*

Brogan leant towards the plexiglass. 'Tell me about Amber Hausman.'

'Grew up together, didn't we. Me, her brother Pete, and her.'

'Why did you have her killed?'

Mace sat bolt upright. 'What?' His head jerked back and his eyebrows knitted together. 'What did you say?'

'I said, why did you have your childhood friend murdered?' Brogan's gaze was unrelenting.

Mace clenched his jaw. His eyes flitted around the stark room behind Brogan. His mouth fell open but no words came out.

Brogan rummaged in his jacket pocket, unrolled a digi-note, and an image appeared. He stuck it up to the glass divider. Amber Hausman, curled up on the floor, drenched in her own blood.

Tears welled in Mace's eyes, his nostrils widened as his heart beat faster. 'Take it down.' He buried his face in the crook of his elbow. *Amber.* Mace kicked at the table. He would have fallen off the chair had it not been screwed down. He wrestled with his cuffs, trying to pull them apart, but they bit into his skin. Tears rolled down his cheeks.

'You didn't know, then?'

'Course I didn't fuckin' know.' Mace's mouth foamed. He wiped snot on his sleeve.

'Then who would do such a thing? I know that you know more than you're telling me.'

'Do your fucking job and find out.' Mace stared at Brogan. The man looked like he was trying to solve a crossword. Then he pressed a tab on the smart-paper and a different image appeared.

'Know anything about this?' He held up the image of Amber's last three words.

Mace tipped his head to one side. *I am atone.* He pressed his lips together. 'No. Nothing.'

'So, let's be clear then. You know nothing of Hausman's murder, or the death of the cybernator this morning?'

Mace flung himself into the back of his chair. 'How many more times. No. I know nothing about either of them.'

'Okay, shall I tell you what I know?' Brogan didn't wait for a reply. 'I know about the cabin. I know about the back door in the prison mainframe. I know you've had access to the Grid since you've been in here. I know you asked Amber for help accessing Novanoid's servers. And, I know you've been data mining their system. Still innocent, are we?'

Mace went numb. *Fuck.*

'You won't be returned to your cyber cell, you'll remain in quarantine, with no access to anything more advanced than a spoon, until your court hearing. Given the circumstances, I think that will be sooner rather than later.'

Brogan stood, looming over Mace. 'You had a chance. You blew it.' The big man walked away.

Mace stared at the empty chair opposite him. He barely noticed the two guards dragging him off to a one-bed cell. The metal door slammed as he sat on the edge of the thin mattress and stared at the flaky, pale grey wall three feet away from him.

What have I done?

Chapter 12

'Hey, Cat.' The Ranger sat his avatar opposite Catsanga. 'You heard the news?'

'Who hasn't?' She barely looked up from her console in the chatroom.

'It's pretty shit. Do they know who it was?' The Ranger swiped through the sectors on his console, and stopped at a skirmish between a supply ship and a handful of fighter jets.

'Word is some girl in the States.'

'Oh. Where's Minty?' The Ranger watched her reaction. There wasn't one.

'It's not her. She sent a message saying she had to go analogue for a few days, some trouble with her stack or somethin'.'

'Oh phew. I'm relieved she's okay.' He grinned inwardly.

'Everyone's pretty bummed, though.'

'What's the latest conspiracy theory?'

'Some say it's Russia. Some say it's China perfecting a virus. With what's-his-name Mace out of the loop, it's anyone's guess. What's your guess?' Catsanga turned to him.

'Me, I think virus. I think Mace developed it and someone else has got their hands on it.' He scanned her face carefully. Her nose twitched a little. *She's a closed book sometimes.* 'Minty did well at the trial, apparently. I got my finder's fee this mornin', so she'll probably be rollin' in the creds.'

'Oh that's good.' Catsanga pawed at something on her console.

'Yeah, it means I can afford Mum's meds this month.'

'How is she?'

'Ah, not great. They're still not sure what they're treating, and there's not really enough research.'

'Shame.' She did that sympathetic head tilt thing.

'You seem distracted?'

'Well, despite this death… let's just say I think I'm better off hanging out here than I am at home.'

'Ah.' He let the silence linger between them. 'Let me know if I can help?'

'Maybe, but I need to think about it some more.'

He nodded. 'Okay. Wow, someone directed an asteroid strike at the Invictus ship.'

'Ooh, what sector?'

'Sector Eight.'

Let her dwell, don't push. Maybe another message from 'Minty' will help.

* * *

Present Day – Wednesday, 3 October 2057

Shackled and wearing a baggy blue jumpsuit, Clayton Mace stepped up into the dock. Prissy jobsworths scribbled down their judgements for the rest of the world to make theirs. Mace scanned the faces that were staring at him; he was being fed to the lions. His mouth dried up.

The judge walked in and the chatter in the courtroom settled.

'Court hearing No. 67918, Clayton Mace verses the Crown, eleven a.m., Wednesday 3rd of October, 2057. Will the defendant confirm his identity? Are you Mr Clayton Mace?'

'Yes, Your Honour.'

The tippy-tap of fingers and pens on screens perforated the silence. *What are they writing?*

'Be seated,' ordered the judge. 'You are accused of a very unusual crime, Mr Mace. Never before have I had to judge a case whereby the accused has escaped prison whilst simultaneously being in prison. You have been charged with breaching your prison terms, acts of cybercrime, and the vicarious murder of Miss Amber Hausman.'

'No! I didn't kill Amber. I didn't kill anyone.'

Jeering swept across the courtroom.

'Order! Order!' The judge banged his gavel.

'I will set the trial date for six weeks hence. Given the nature of the charges against you, Mr Mace, you will be held without access to a digital network of any kind. You will remain confined to a standard cell from now until the conclusion of your trial.'

Mace opened his mouth to speak, but what could he say? *Should never have trusted Amber.* He hung his head, staring into the face of hopelessness. *I'm done. There's no point any more.* Sensing someone's eyes on him, he glanced up. He locked eyes with Detective Brogan. The man didn't blink but twitched his head to one side like an eagle eyeing it's prey. *Smug twat.* A guard jerked Mace's cuffs, pulling him out the dock. His gaze hitting the floor once more.

* * *

Dr Deborah Tempest sat at her desk in the lab. The fifteenth floor of the Novanoid building was dedicated to all things bio-tech, from her brain–machine interface to bionic body parts and cancer-killing nanobots.

She pressed her fingers onto the security pad. The bio-scan confirmed her identity, her stack booted up and the visi-wall blinked into operation.

'Initiate Security Protocol 9.' She stared blankly while the protocol ran: secure communication lockdown, stack isolation from the mainframe, encryption and tracer-scrubbing activated.

'Display subject file nineteen, body map.' A life-size holograph of the recently deceased teen appeared in front of her. The latest recruited to the trial and the latest one not to have survived. Another failed test. She sighed. *What are we missing?*

She studied the hologram for a moment then zoomed in, meticulously checking each of the major organs in turn, ruling out possible alternative causes for the sudden death. She isolated each organ, rotated it and inspected it from every angle, right down to a cellular level. She cross-referenced what she could see with the stats screen: liver, kidneys, lungs, heart functions all showing normal ranges, and bloods were normal too.

'Display brain and brain stem.' A hologram of the girl's brain appeared.

'Split view. Show pre- and post-death.' She studied the two images.

'ANNA, overlay with the electrical activity. Start ten minutes before death until one minute after death, speed up times two.' Tempest still got a kick out of the intricate workings of the mind and the advances in technology to visualise them. The brain floating in front of her changed colours as different areas of electrical activity lit up, faded, and lit up again. The girl's brain showed intense activity in the amygdala and frontal lobes just after the program started to run. The same as the others, then it just switched off.

The smell of freshly brewed coffee percolated in her mind. She stepped away from the hovering brain and made a beeline for her vintage coffee machine. Pouring a fresh mug of hard-to-come-by organic coffee, she inhaled deeply.

'Dr Tempest. Jaro Dax wishes to make a secure connection. What are your instructions?'

Tempest sighed. 'Uplink agreed, ANNA.'

'Deborah.'

'Jaro.' The elephant had entered the room.

'Two years. Two years you have been working with Parker to fix the program. You both assured me it would work this time.' His face seemed sympathetic, but his steel-grey eyes said differently. 'No doubt this failure and its consequences have been on your mind?'

'Yes. Yes they are.' She clutched her mug, pulling it in to her chest and letting the warmth comfort her.

'What went wrong this time?'

'I don't know yet. I'm working on—'

'You need to work faster. We need answers. Mace has provided us with a brief respite but we need this code to work.'

'We can't risk another life. I'm trying to figure it out, Parker's working on it too.'

'Damn right he is.' The facade of sympathy didn't last long.

'I'm just not sure it's possible anymore.'

'It is possible, and you and Parker are going to make it happen.'

'Look, I'm not sure I'm right for this project anymore. Perhaps you'd be better getting Gerhart or Tundi, they're better suited to this kind of work.' She cleared a tickle in her throat, glanced at Dax then to the door.

'Gerhart and Tundi are not an option. You are not giving up on this project, doctor.'

'But—'

'How is your daughter?'

Tempest's pulse quickened. 'She's stable at the moment.'

'Good. We wouldn't want that to change, now would we? We wouldn't want the plug to be pulled on her?'

'No, no, I-I wouldn't want that at all.' She glanced at her daughter's smiling face in the photo on her desk. The last photo taken before the accident.

'Then remember why you're doing this, Tempest, and

find the solution. What is causing them to die? Do we have another candidate lined up, or should we use your daughter?' His eyes narrowed.

'What? No. The Ranger tells me he has another candidate, he's working her now.' *I hope.*

'Fine.' Dax disconnected.

Her screen went back to displaying today's schedule.

Tempest sat back and stared at her colleagues through the glass wall. Some were chatting, others were engrossed in whatever happy little world they were in. Her stomach tightened. *Julayha.* She swiped the privacy panel on her desk, waited for the glass to go opaque, and then sobbed.

She was no further forward with the research, despite being responsible for yet another death and failed experiment. Tempest sat and stared at the glee in her daughter's photo. *A whole year since I last saw you smile like that.* 'ANNA, hold all my calls will you? I need to go and do something.'

'Certainly. When can I say you'll be available again?'

'I'll be about an hour.' Tempest logged out of her stack and silenced her comms-watch. She headed to the elevator. Wrapping her arms around herself, hugging herself tightly, she waited forever for the elevator to arrive.

A handful of people filed out, lab techs mainly. She nodded politely then ducked inside and pressed the button for the basement. No one else got on, so she sagged against the wall, glad that she wouldn't have to make small talk.

The basement was dark and empty in contrast to the upper, light-filled levels. Servers and storage took up the first basement level. The second floor below ground was given over to specialist labs, some for high-security military equipment. Some required low lux levels, others thick layers of concrete and blast doors. At the far end, almost a quarter of a mile away, were the high-tech medical bays, tucked away as though healthcare was an afterthought. A perk for Novanoid's employees, they were manned by the most advanced medical team in the country, and not one with a heartbeat. There was only ever one human, an auxiliary to tend to the tasks that the computers and robots could not perform.

Tempest stood in range of the bio-scanner at the door and it bleeped its permission to allow her entry. The beds were all full, as they usually were. Some patients were conscious, others were not. She nodded to the auxiliary and headed past all the beds to a plain door that could easily have been mistaken for a cleaning cupboard.

Her heart began to beat faster as she waited for another bio-scan to bleep and unlock the door. She pressed her palm against the door, took a deep breath, and pushed it open. The tears welled before she crossed the threshold.

In a soft blue glow, her daughter's body lay still and alone. Kept alive by machines, pushing oxygen into her little lungs, feeding it with nutrient-packed liquid and keeping her muscles in shape through small electrical currents that caused intermittent contractions to ripple through her seven-year-old body. *A whole year of this.*

Tempest stood next to the bed, watching her daughter's chest rise and fall. *A living death and a living hell.* She leant forward, stroked her daughter's little cheek, and neatened up the locks of hair poking around the skull cap. Most of her blond locks were covered by a haystack of wires and electrodes.

She kissed her warm cheek, inhaling deeply as though trying to breathe in her little girl's soul. She pulled up the chair and sat down, resting her head on the bed next to her daughter's, hoping that somehow her daughter would smell her perfume and know she was there. A tear trickled down her face and her heart ached. She stroked whatever part of the little body wasn't covered in wires. That wasn't much, even her small hands were gloved.

Steeling herself, Tempest turned, reclined the chair and took the ocular set that hung on the wall. A little light flashed and then stayed on, indicating it was ready for use. Tempest took a deep breath and slipped it over her head and eyes. She settled her body, letting it twitch about a little until she was comfortable. It was better to be as still as possible for a smooth uplink.

The golden N logo revolved before it blinked onto another screen that read, *Uplink processing…*

She waited…

'Hi, baby.' Tempest gripped the arms of the chair. It was all she could do to stay strong.

'Mummy!' Julayha's avatar bounced with the energy of any normal seven-year-old.

Tempest smiled at her daughter. 'What have you been doing today?'

'I've been at school. Mr Jenkins put a sticker on my record for asking good questions. He said to always ask questions about things we don't understand.'

'Well done you. What did you ask questions about?'

'About why lots of animals have all died and we can't see them anymore.'

'Oh.'

'Yes, Mr Jenkins said that our great-great-great-grandparents were mean to the planet and made a lot of mess. It upset the animals and now we have to pretend like they're there but really they're only alive in a computer.'

'Yes, it's very sad isn't it.'

'Why did they do it, Mummy?'

'Well, I don't think they did it on purpose. Not to start off with, anyway. I think it took a long time before they realised the mistake and even longer to do anything about it.'

'Mummy, when can I wake up?'

Tempest felt a tear roll down her cheek and a lump form in her throat. 'Oh, darling. Your body is still very poorly and needs time to rest. The doctors and I are working very hard to fix it, I promise.'

'But I want to hug you and smell your hair, Mummy.'

'I want that too, very much. Bodies are complicated things and we can't be sure what will happen if we switch off the machines that help you breathe.'

'You mean I might die, Mummy? Mr Jenkins told us about that.'

'Oh, he did, did he?' *Maybe I'll have to have a word with this Mr Jenkins.*

'But I might?'

'We don't know that. Try not to worry about it, okay? Let Mummy worry about it.'

'I don't want to die, Mummy.'

'I don't want you to either. Listen, try and think of happy things, okay? Do you remember the time I took you to a real zoo and—'

'—and a monkey did a big wee on another monkey,' she giggled, 'then we went for ice cream and cake.'

'Oh yes, I felt so sick afterwards. Now, do you remember I picked you up and gave you a big kiss and told you how much I love you? We were right by the polar bear.'

'Yes, Mummy.'

'Good. Keep remembering that, try and remember all the little details, my arms around you, my hair blowing in your face and how much we laughed and how happy we were.'

'Okay, Mummy.'

'I have to go back to work in a minute. I came just because I missed you.'

'No, Mummy. No. Don't go. Please?'

'Sweetheart, I'm sorry. I have to get back to work, we're working on a way to fix you up, okay?'

'I don't want to be on my own.'

'I'll be back tonight. We'll read some books together, I promise.'

'Mummy, no, Mummy!'

'I'll see you later, I love you.' Tempest quickly closed the uplink before the heartbreak won and she hooked in permanently with her daughter. She knew her daughter would not survive if they took her off life support, and neither would she. She had to find the way forward. The code was her only glimmer of hope.

Chapter 13

The Ranger clocked the time. *Better log out for the day.*

A chat request appeared on his dash panel. *Tempest.* He sighed and opened the chat.

'Ranger, I need to know when you'll have another test subject ready?'

'Hello to you too, doctor.' *Should've ignored her.*

'Hello. Look, I'm sorry, but we're running out of time and I need to run another test. Dax is threatening to use my daughter.'

'Well, why not?'

'No. No way. Not until we're sure it works. Look, do you have someone or not? What happened to that Catsanga kid?'

'I'm working on it. You can't rush these things.'

'So how much longer?'

'I'm not sure…'

'You'd better get sure, because I know who you are and where you work.'

'I seriously doubt that, doctor. Please, do not make threats like that, otherwise you can find yourself another recruiter.'

'Just get me another subject.' Tempest ended the call.

You're in no place to be making demands. Still, it won't hurt to check in on my little friend. The Ranger swiped his dash panel, found the *Xenon Fire* hangout, and linked in.

No Catsanga. He hung around anyway. Checked the console and the general chat, then left. Instead of unhooking, he hacked Minty's email and typed.

Hey Cat, how are ya? I'm spending my creds on a new pod. Should arrive in a couple of days. I had it modded to the max. Hope you're okay? Spk soon. Mint x

That should do it. He unhooked from the Grid, grabbed a quick shower and headed to work – in the real world.

* * *

Present day – Friday, 12 October 2057

Mace lay on a crusty, thin mattress, staring at the ceiling of his cell: the mouldy corners, the peeling paintwork, the dim bulb shedding its judgemental light over his prone body. His back ached but he didn't care. No one cared. He spent his wakeful periods thinking of ways to die, willing his heart to stop. If only he could be bothered to go through with it.

'Mr Mace, you have what we call a reactive depression.' When no reply came, the voice of Dr Simms, the psychiatrist, continued. 'We are treating you under Section

Three of the Mental Health Act, and we want to start you on antidepressants.'

The words passed through Mace's mind like tourists streaming through a cathedral. He was vaguely irritated by the distraction but thoughts of death prevailed, resenting every breath he took. A prisoner in his own mind. Dying the only escape.

'Mr Mace, we are going to start injecting you with a drug called Seromelanine. I have a responsibility to tell you that the side effects may include hypotension, blurred vision, sickness and diarrhoea, and hallucinations, among others. These, however, are the most commonly reported.'

Mace didn't even notice the prison nurse, and he hardly felt the sting in his arm as the drug was injected.

'It might take a few days before we see even a small improvement. Please, alert the staff if you feel unwell.'

Mace remained consumed by emptiness.

* * *

A few days passed. Mace moved. He didn't know what caused it, but he suddenly had the urge to sit up after what had felt like an eternity lying down. His body jerked like a vintage robot. His head hung low, the weight of its contents too heavy for his neck muscles. He stared at his lap and at the hands clutching the frame of the bed. They were his, but they didn't feel like it. His brain was devoid of any happiness, stained with the image of his swaying soul hanging limp from a rope tied around a tree branch. Death lingered in every crevice.

* * *

Two more days passed.

'We are pleased with your progress, Mr Mace,' said Dr Simms. 'Your REM sleep is improving, as are your diet and fluid intakes.'

Mace grunted, raising his head a little. Then he saw it. His opportunity. His gaze fixed on Simms's pocket.

Leaning back on his hands, he pushed himself up the bed a little more. Dr Simms, standing next to him, adjusted his position slightly to accommodate the move.

In one swift lurch, Mace grabbed the pen protruding from the doctor's pocket. Clasping it in both hands, he rammed it into his own throat.

'Shit. No. Shit.' Dr Simms slapped his panic alarm, then grappled with Mace.

Mace tried to pull the pen out. He was gargling and gasping, eyes wide, blood oozing from around the pen. The two men fought, Mace desperate to have another stab at death.

'Oh no you don't.' Dr Simms prised Mace's hands away from the pen still sticking out of his neck. The men fought, both full of adrenaline, both fighting for life at opposite ends of the scale.

Mace, surprisingly strong given his physical condition, fought his corner and dislodged the pen slightly. Blood spurted in a satisfying arc across his chest. 'You. Will. Not. Die. Like. This.' Dr Simms gritted his teeth as he held Mace at bay.

A guard rushed in and immediately helped with the restraint.

'We need to stem the blood.'

Mace writhed on the bed, but with the added manpower he was being overwhelmed. The guard grabbed Mace's left wrist and elbow and pressed them down onto the bed. Dr Simms used his leg to pin Mace's right arm then grabbed a handkerchief, wrapped it around the pen, and applied pressure. Blood soaked the handkerchief.

Mace gargled and coughed up blood, the taste of iron as refreshing as beer. His world swirled and faded. Aware of activity but outside of it.

Three more guards appeared in the small cell.

'Get a medical evac team in here.' Dr Simms was sweating now.

'I'm on it.' A guard barked orders into his radio in the background.

Mace could feel the weight of the men pressing down on him, he could feel his own strength slipping away, and reality faded into peaceful nothingness.

CHAPTER 14

PRESENT DAY – THURSDAY, 18 OCTOBER 2057

B rogan sipped his morning coffee at his desk. He'd only just fired up his stack when Paysos patched a call through.

'Brogan.'

'Ah, Detective Brogan. Dr Simms. I'm led to believe you're leading the investigation involving Clayton Mace.'

'I am.' Brogan reached across the display and expanded Dr Simms's contact details. *A psychiatrist. Great.* He shuddered at the memory of his previous encounters with that special breed of human.

'I have the unfortunate news that Mr Mace very nearly managed to kill himself this morning.'

'What?' Brogan leant in close to the camera, his face filled the screen. 'How?'

'After his trial hearing he developed an affective disorder, to the point of near catatonia. He had marked somatic symptoms including psychomotor retardation and loss of appetite. He—'

'Dr Simms, I understood about three words there. Not one of them included words that gave me a clue as to what you're talking about.'

'Right. Sorry, detective. Mr Mace has been experiencing a major depression, to the point where he felt suicide was the only option.'

'I see.'

'Due to the decline in his physical and mental well-being, we started him on a pretty potent antidepressant. Unfortunately, it gave him the energy he needed to attempt to take his own life.'

'Excuse me? It sounds like what you're saying is that he couldn't be bothered to kill himself until you gave him drugs?'

'It's not like that. When people become so depressed, as in Mace's case, we have to act in their best interests, and despite his circumstances we believed it was not in his interests to allow him to starve himself to death. The dilemma is that when we give someone who is suicidal antidepressants, where previously they didn't have the energy to attempt to take their own life, an antidepressant will give them that little boost of energy but the suicidal thoughts remain. Therein lies the risk. Mace saw an opportunity and chose to take it.'

'I see. And what was that opportunity?'

'He grabbed a pen from my pocket and stuck it in his throat,' Dr Simms said, sheepishly.

'Ah, so you gave him the means and the method?'

'Look, there will be an internal investigation but I can assure you our intentions as healthcare professionals are not malevolent. I managed to stem the bleeding long enough to keep him alive. He's currently in our specialist medical care facility here at the prison.'

'How long will that be?'

'He'll be there until he's medically stable. It'll be at least a month, then he'll be transferred back to the psychiatric unit.'

'Fine. Will I be able to speak with him?'

'It's not clear what long-term damage he's done to his voice-box—'

'But he can use a headset, right?'

'Yes, but the terms of his sentence negate that use.'

'I know the terms, doc, but that man's got questions to answer and he needs to spill the beans one way or another.'

'Well, you'll have to take that up with higher powers.'

'Oh, I intend to. In the meantime, I need to be kept updated on his condition.'

'I'll get the hospital to call you if anything changes.'

'Good.' Brogan cut the man off. Sat back in his chair and stared at a stylus on his desk. His face tensed with effort as he tried to understand how anyone could stab themselves in the throat with one of those.

I need a sounding board. 'Paysos. Where is James Anders?'

'Mr Anders is at his desk on the ninth floor.' If Anders were a mechanic, he'd be elbow-deep in grease. As it happened, he was eyebrow-deep in programming code. Brogan had no hesitation in disturbing him.

'Mace tried to kill himself this morning.' Brogan sat on the edge of Anders's desk.

'No way. Really?' Anders glanced to his screens and flicked them off.

'Yep. I don't know about you, but something hasn't sat

right with me since this whole business with Hausman began.'

'What tipped him over the edge?' Anders leant his slender frame back in the chair. Considering he spent most of the day sat at his desk, there was barely a crease in his navy suit.

'He was diagnosed with depression.'

'That's not surprising, but it is pretty desperate.' Anders nodded as though he agreed with Mace's act.

'What is?'

'Not the diagnosis, I mean Mace trying to end it. He must have been desperate.'

'Desperate to avoid another trial.'

'No, desperate to be understood, to be listened to. I've analysed loads of suicide notes. They all say the same thing if you look deep enough.'

'So, Mace was desperate to be heard… and the only one who was listening was Hausman?' Brogan pursed his lips. His gaze followed the small cleaning-bot as it made its way around, hoovering under desks.

'He didn't have contact with anyone else.'

'I wonder if she knew she was his last hope? If she did, then her message *was* meant for Mace.' Brogan rubbed his face. 'Paysos, split the screen. Bring up the image of Amber Hausman's body. Zoom in on the writing on the wall.'

Paysos responded and the men stared at the bloody message.

I aM atone/

· · ·

'No one writes "I am atone/" as their last goodbye.'

Brogan and Anders stared at the blood-smeared image waiting for divine intervention, or at the very least a thought.

'Sir, we are assuming that the last character is the unfinished letter *d*, but what if it's not?'

'Well, what else could it be?' *Smartarse.*

'Sir, I've looked at some of her handwriting. Like a lot of people, she starts the letter *d* at the top of the circle, here.' Anders indicated the midpoint on the screen. 'The smear in the image starts at the very top.'

Brogan stared at the image, head to one side like a dog watching a magic trick. He could see the man's point, and his heart beat a little faster.

'Paysos?'

'How can I assist you, detective?' The way she looked at them was creepy in Brogan's mind.

'Give me everything you can find on the phrase "I am atone".' Brogan never used manners where AIs were concerned, and hardly ever when humans were concerned.

The image of Paysos looked up and to the left. She'd been programmed to reflect the body language of a human deep in thought.

'I have returned over 40,000 results based on the search criteria. How would you like to proceed?'

Brogan looked over at Anders, who spoke before he had been able to form any words with his mouth, let alone his brain.

'Paysos, please sort the data into the following categories: definitions, synonyms and antonyms, classical/religious references, popular culture, historical references, and finally cross-match any references with the name Amber Hausman. Then, please display the top ten matches for each category.' Clearly this was not the first time Anders had dealt with a shitload of data.

'Thank you, Mr Anders. Please wait a moment.'

The visi-wall morphed from the face of Paysos to a screen displaying six tabs, each labelled with the categories.

'Let's look at the cross-match with the name Amber Hausman definition.' Brogan shifted, unnerved by Anders's efficiency. The tab opened. Paysos was always listening. The first result read:

No results found.

Brogan sighed. 'That would have been too easy. Right, Paysos, show results from the definition category.' The visi-wall blinked and read the following:

The word Atone *is a contraction of the words* at *and* one, *the verb means reparation for an offense or wrong doing. To be at one or to make peace with someone or something. In a religious sense it means to repent for sins.*

The two men stared at the text in front of them. The silence of two men thinking was actually quite loud.

'An admission of guilt, of sorrow for something, an apology?' Anders had a habit of thinking aloud.

Brogan tapped his forehead. 'Paysos, show results for popular culture.' Neither man looked away as the screen displayed the new content:

- *Daxtarr to atone for crypto-cash blunder… data leaked… personal caches now vulnerable…*
- *Rasika Atoné… murder trial continues as mounting evidence…*
- *The Atoner… The vintage remake sees Hayden Maddingly return to famedom as murderer Hank Steele…*
- *Rome atones for selling centuries of psuedophilia… murderers, paedophiles and profiteering…*
- *Refined Almoxatone approved for use in children with…*

'Paysos, give me the synopsis of the film *The Atoner*. Gotta start somewhere.' He glanced at Anders.

'*The Atoner*, directed by Daniel Zealand, produced by Plasmatonic Productions Ltd. The film starring Hayden Maddingly and Memphys Ramone…' began Paysos as Brogan lazily stared at the visi-wall and Hausman's message still occupying the bottom right corner of the display. His head lolled to one side, quizzical dog mode. As if pulled by some invisible gravitational force, he drew nearer the screen. He had been pretty good at Scrabble and other word games during his down time in the drone wars. He began encircling the letters and shuffling them around.

'Sir?' Anders was silenced by Brogan sticking a palm out in a *talk to the hand because the face is thinking* kind of a way. Brogan must have looked in pain because Anders broke the silence. 'Paysos, list all words containing these letters.' Anders used his fingers to highlight Hausman's sentence. Paysos converted the letters into a text format and a new screen appeared.

Brogan sighed, disappointed that his flow had been interrupted. They both roamed the new screen, a jumble of words containing such things as *Mania toe, Atone aim, mean oat I, mean iota, eat I moan, a team I no,* all pretty meaningless. *Tea amino, Eat Naomi.* The spark of a breakthrough ebbed away from Brogan's grasp.

Anders sagged a little and tugged at his tie, then swiped to the next page of results. A depressing list of more nonsense. As they scanned, hope leaving them, both men seemed to settle at the same time on the final word in the list: *metanoia.*

They looked at each other.

'We assumed that the sizing of the letter *M* was an accident, given the circumstances. But what if it is supposed to be capitalised?'

'Go on?' said Brogan.

'Well, sir. What if the letter *M* is the start of the word. What if it is an anagram?'

Both men stared at the word. If they'd been vintage clocks you would have been able to hear the mechanisms whirring. It was the only single-word result that Paysos had found.

'Metanoia.' Brogan felt the sound of the word as though he was tasting a new food. 'Met-an-oia.' He looked over at

Anders, who also appeared struck by the presence of the word on the screen.

'Paysos, define the word *Metanoia*.' Brogan's pulsed raced a tad. The display fuzzed and Paysos read aloud the definition that was now before them.

'*Metanoia*, first known use dates back to between the sixteenth and eighteenth century. The etymology of the word is Greek, from *metanoiein* "to change one's mind, repent", from *meta-* and *-noein* to think. Theologians have traced the word back to the King James version of the Bible and is translated as "repent", but more common connotations suggest the term means "repudiation, change of mind, repentance and atonement..."'

The word *atonement* stuck in Brogan's mind.

'...but "conversion" and "reformation" appear more frequently.

'In Christianity, the term became used to express a fundamental change in behaviour or way of living. In classical Greek, metanoia is not a confession of sins but a change of mind, a transformative change of heart, especially a spiritual conversion.

'In the nineteenth century, American philosopher and psychologist William James used the term to describe the fundamental change in human personality. Taking the ancient Greek form of *Metá* (meaning beyond or after) and *noeō* meaning perception or understanding or mind, James used the word to describe a stable change in an individual's life orientation. Subsequent usage by Carl Jung used it to define the process of an attempt by the psyche to heal itself of unbearable conflict by melting down and being reborn into a more adaptive form...'

'Paysos, stop.' Brogan read and re-read the text.

'Could be a coincidence, sir.'

'Really? An anagram of Hausman's message throws up only one possible single word amongst a ton of nonsense. Two words that also link by the similarity in definition. Nah, it feels too thought out to be a coincidence. Don't you think?' Brogan paced around the room, rubbing his stubbly chin, the sensation focusing his thoughts. They were close to something. They had to be, because they had little else.

'What could she have meant? Either she was sorry for something, or she'd changed her mind about something, something she lost her life for.' Anders was looking at the screen as he was thinking aloud again.

'I'm not sure but I'm betting there's one man who does know.'

'Sir? Do you think Hausman's death *is* related to the cyber deaths?'

'Yes, Anders, I do. She worked at Novanoid and so did Mace. He knows something, and for whatever reason he's not telling.' Anders looked as though he wanted to say something else but Brogan cut him off. 'I'll be in the conference room.' He turned and left like a dog who'd just snatched a bone.

* * *

'Paysos, put me through to the hospital wing dealing with Clayton Mace.'

'Certainly, Detective Brogan. I'll patch you through.'

Brogan waited. The stupid plinking sound as Paysos made the connection really grated on him.

'Putting you through now.' Paysos sounded cheery even during a terrorist attack.

'Good afternoon, Detective Brogan. My name is Dr ATAC, I am at liberty to inform you that I am an AI medic but come well equipped to deal with any queries you may have.'

'What happened to Dr Simms?'

'Dr Simms is in charge of Mr Mace's mental health care. I am in charge of his physical health care. How may I be of assistance?'

'I need to speak to Mr Mace.'

'Unfortunately that is not possible at this time. Mr Mace is unable to speak due to the damage he inflicted upon himself.'

'I'm aware of that, but you must use an uplink to communicate with him about his care?'

'You are correct, but unfortunately your request cannot be granted. There is a restriction on his access to the network.'

'I need to override that restriction. I need access to speak to him immediately.'

'This is not within my protocol—'

'Then put me in touch with someone who can help.'

'Certainly. Please hold.'

The tinkly music again. *For fuck's sake.*

'Hello, legal department, Louis speaking. How can help you.'

Why is nothing ever simple? 'Hello. I need clearance to speak directly to Clayton Mace.'

'And who might you be?'

'Check your damned uplink data. I'm Detective Brogan

and I'm running out of patience. I need to interview Clayton Mace immediately.'

'I'm sorry, Detective Brogan. There are protocols to follow. Please hold while I check your clearance. It won't take a moment.'

Brogan rolled his eyes. Bureaucracy was not high on his agenda.

'Your identification has been confirmed. Your permission has been granted. I will shift you to the secure channel. You will have to wait while the medical team connect Mr Mace to the system.'

'Fine.' Brogan paced the ninth-floor conference room. Waiting was not his strong point. He was staring out the window, down towards the plaza. There were still protesters there, but definitely fewer in number than a month ago.

A bleep caused Brogan to spin around. The visi-wall displayed a message: *Audio connection in progress.* A prison photo of Mace appeared on the right side of the display.

'Mace? Are you there?'

'Unfortunately.'

'Right, let's recap so we're on the same page, shall we?' Brogan couldn't get involved with the guy's emotional baggage. 'We both know you had contact with Amber Hausman just before she died. We know that you created yourself a handy little back door out of the prison system. We know about the cabin, and we know that you hacked into the Novanoid mainframe. Now, given that I'd say your situation is pretty fucking serious, you need to start doing some straight talking.'

'No small talk then?'

'I'm not here to talk about the weather, Mace. That stunt you pulled with the stabby pen has landed you in a whole heap more trouble and made you look ten times guiltier. So, I'd say now's the time to start talking, because I'm in the mood for listenin' but only to the truth, and believe me, I can smell bullshit.'

'If you know all these things, then why have you called? You've got your evidence, I've been charged, it's a slam dunk.'

'Because I like to get to the truth, the real truth, and so far you've not been entirely honest with me.'

'You're gonna pin all this shit on me anyway, why should I bother?'

'If I remember rightly, you've touted your innocence to anyone who'd listen. Right now, I'm the only one who's listening and this is your only chance to tell me your side. I might not be in such a listening mood tomorrow and once that ship has sailed there ain't no telling when it might come back.'

Mace was silent. If he were a computer it would display that annoying rotating egg-timer. There was something calculating behind the silence.

'Where shall I begin?'

'Wherever you want.' Brogan glanced out across the ninth-floor offices. Anders appeared engrossed in his work again.

'I worked at Novanoid—'

'I know that.'

'I thought you were listening?' When Brogan remained silent, he carried on. 'Parker, he was my boss, we gelled. You know, not best buddies or anything but, well, he knows his shit when it comes to programming. Anyway, I accidentally showed him up at a meeting in front of Dax—'

'The CEO, Jaro Dax?'

'Yeah. After that Parker went ice cold. Froze me out like I didn't exist. We'd started sorting things out when I was arrested for the cybernater murders. They found the files on my stack, but I swear it wasn't me. I'm pretty sure Parker was involved.'

'How so?' Brogan sat on the desk at the front of the conference room and focused on a join in the carpet tiles.

'Not sure. He went from being all nicey-nicey to cold-hearted bastard and then, all of a sudden, he sidles up to me again. It didn't ring true but I didn't really think about it much at the time. Plus, whoever planted the files did it without a trace. They knew what they were doing.'

'So you created this back door, and thought you'd do what?'

'Nah, I created the back door to the prison to sell to the highest bidder. Turns out that was me. I only ever used it to help prove my innocence.'

Brogan replayed the words in his mind. The digital voice took all of the nuance out of Mace's words but there was still something genuine about them. 'And Hausman, what did she have to do with it?'

'I'd been looking for a way back into Novanoid's mainframe. Pete's death and Amber's visit gave me an… an opportunity, let's say.'

'Right, keep talking. That doesn't explain why Hausman paid the ultimate price.'

'I don't know why either. Honestly. I wouldn't have asked her to help me if I'd known she would get hurt.'

'She got more than hurt, I'd say. So you used Hausman to get access to Novanoid's mainframe. Then what were you going to do?' Brogan stared at Mace's shabby image on the screen. Something about the way his eyes cast downward, off camera, didn't fit right with a serial killer.

'Look for evidence, of course. Look for a clue, for anything that would clear my name.'

'And Hausman believed you?'

'She didn't at first, but she came around in the end.'

'How do I know you weren't trying to get revenge?'

'I thought you could smell bullshit, detective?'

'So why try and kill yourself?'

'I lost hope. Now I can't access the Grid, I can't prove my innocence.'

'But you know what it looks like? Another cybernater death puts you back in the hot seat.'

'I am not responsible. I have no idea who's behind it or how it's happening. All I know is that Amber found something out and was trying to send me a message.'

'What message?' *So you knew that scrawl was meant for you.*

'*I am atone/*. It wasn't anything to do with her being sorry. It was code. She was great with puzzles, especially anagrams. She used to tease me all the time with little notes and word games. She found out about something called *metanoia*.'

'What do you think she meant?' Brogan tilted his head.

'The last character was a forward slash. That has a lot of uses in coding. I can only think she used it as a file name separator. So maybe she was trying to tell me about a file named Metanoia. I searched Novanoid's system, not knowing it was a cloned system, but I couldn't find anything. Only an archived email from Dr Tempest that had some redacted text that was followed by the word *code*.'

'Hmm, the Metanoia Code.' Brogan scratched his chin. 'What do you know of Dr Tempest?'

'She works at Novanoid. She's the star lady, she helped scale up the neural interface and worked on the bio-stasis programming. It was pioneering.'

'Okay, so maybe there's a full moon or something and I give you the benefit of the doubt. I'll check out this doctor but, man, if any of this turns out to be bullshit I'll be joining the crowds and clapping at your termination.'

'I'm not bullshitting you, detective. My life is on the line.'

'Yeah, and you tried to end it the other day.'

'Hope is the fuel that drives the engine of humanity, and I'm running on empty.'

Brogan nodded. 'Hang in there, kid.' He wasn't quite sure why he said that. There was something about him, something likeable. 'Brogan out.' He terminated the uplink and checked his watch for the time. *Just enough time for another trip to Novanoid.*

Chapter 15

Brogan was striding back to his desk to grab his jacket when Paysos sounded an alarm.

'A fatality has occurred. This person was cybernating at the time the life-extinct alert activated. Rapid Response have been dispatched.' The visi-wall displayed a thumbnail map in the corner.

Brogan's mouth dried up. *I know those roads.* 'Paysos, zoom in on location.' Clarkson came over and stood next to him. Brogan's eyes darted down to her feet, then back up to the screen.

'That's... that's... Mikey...' *No, no, no.* He couldn't think. He turned to Clarkson. His heart pounded in his chest, heat rose from the ground up.

'I-I-I'm sorry Brogan,' was all Clarkson managed.

Brogan stared at back at the map, his old place – dead centre. A file name appeared at the top of the screen. Eyes wide, nostrils flared, shallow breaths came in quick succession as his mind tried to take in what his eyes saw.

. . .

*INVESTIGATION No. G3994P: Michael Rowan Brogan –
Deceased.*

The world stopped. The office went silent. The air froze.
The sickness grew like fire in his blood, coursing through
his veins to every cell, every fibre of his being, burning. It
filled him, consumed him. There was no controlling it, no
taming it. His lungs exploded and the sound that followed
was a guttural roar of emotion that filled the room, the
corridors and into the bones of every man and woman on
the floor.

He flipped the desk next to him. People shuffled away.
No one tried to stop him. He picked up a chair and
slammed it against the wall, then against a desk, then, as he
recoiled to launch another blow, he lost his balance,
momentum spun him around, and he slung the chair down
the office narrowly missing Kane, who'd come to see what
the commotion was. Their eyes met. Brogan made towards
him, anger fuelling the pulsar within him. He had to get
out, he had get to Katie. He had to see her. Kane had the
sense to move out of the way.

* * *

'Take me to Kathryn Brogan.' He flicked the contact card on
his watch and the cab's onboard computer confirmed the
destination.

When Brogan arrived at his former home, Anders was

already there, along with another tech-investigator who had her head in a laptop. He didn't recognise her, but right now he didn't care.

Anders sat up. 'Upstairs, master bedroom.'

Brogan headed upstairs and found Katie sitting on the bed facing the window.

'Katie?'

She turned towards him, her tear-streaked face hollow and worn. Brogan choked. Neither spoke as he made his way over to her. He was beyond numb, because to be numb meant there were feelings there, but there was nothing.

They sat together. He tried to comprehend the incomprehensible. Tried to find the sense. *It's not real.* Mikey was only out, he was late back, he would come home any minute. He never would. Forever in the next room, never to come in, never to be reached, touched or heard.

Katie turned to Brogan. He shifted and stretched his thick arms around her. Their tears fell, silently at first, then growing louder and more painful, each tear a falling memory, each tear hurting more than the last.

He didn't know how long they'd been crying. Then Katie leant back against his embrace, stared at him momentarily, and out of nowhere she clenched her fists and pounded on his chest. 'You bastard. You bastard.'

He grabbed her forearms and tried to pull her back into him. She wrestled her way free and clutched the duvet by her side.

'Why? Why! You bastard! You should have saved him, it's all your fault, it's your fault he's dead. You were supposed to be keeping him safe.' She cried into her hands.

'Get out, go now, I don't want you here.' She pulled away from him and lay on the bed, sobbing.

'Katie, I...' No words could fix this. He stared longingly at the back of her head. 'Katie?' he pleaded.

'GET OUT.' Her voice was muffled but the message was clear. He lingered for a moment then forced his body to stand.

When he reached the door, he spoke. 'You don't have the monopoly on hurt.' He didn't look back. Across the landing the secure-door was already in place. He couldn't even go and sit in Mikey's room, couldn't smell his teenage stink, couldn't hold his things as though they were his newborn son.

A couple of scruffy 1st Divisioners were on guard duty. He passed them on his way out and noted that a few cables already hung on the garden fence. They were tied in a figure of eight, the infinity loop, a sign of mourning and respect from fellow gamers and the like. *Jeez, how'd they know already?*

* * *

'Dr Tempest?' ANNA's gentle tone cut through Tempest's concentration. 'Mr Dax is requesting an urgent conference call. Do you accept?'

'Is there much choice?' Tempest didn't take her gaze off the visi-wall. *Peacekeeper's son dies cybernating*, read the headline. Tempest froze, her body tingled. *How could that be?* Her mouth dried up. 'Accept the call, ANNA.'

Her display split between the faces of Dax and Parker.

Parker looked pale, Dax looked as though he was made of stone.

'You've both seen the news, I expect? Why was I not informed of another test… On a Peacekeeper's son, of all people.' Dax had a stare that could penetrate lead.

'Because…' Tempest bit her lip, she glanced away. *He'll have to know.* 'Because it wasn't us. We didn't run the test.'

'What? How can that be?' Dax leant in closer to the camera, his face filled the screen.

'I-I don't know.' She glanced at Parker.

'Parker?' Dax snapped.

'I don't know either, sir.' Parker had that deer-in-headlights look about him.

'One of you is lying. One of you thought you'd take the code for yourself. And one of you will pay.'

'No. It's the truth.' Tempest clutched her hands together.

'Maybe it was stolen?' Parker's eyes had a wild desperation about them.

'Come on, Parker. A level nine file? Really?'

'Maybe.' Parker shrugged. 'I mean, Mace found a way in. Maybe it was him?'

Silence. Dax stroked his chin. Tempest couldn't move. She spotted Parker's gaze darting between the two of them.

'Okay. Find the evidence, or you'll find yourself as the next test subject.' Dax cut off the call.

Tempest stared at the blank visi-wall. Her body trembled. *I need to get out of this.* She rubbed her face and headed down to the medical bays in the basement. *Julayha.*

* * *

Brogan found his way to a booth in the back of an underground bar and slumped into the corner.

'Wadd'ya want?' The waitress interrupted the emptiness in his mind.

'IPA, a pint.' He didn't bother taking his gaze off the old lines and wrinkles on his rough hands. Hard to believe that Mikey's little hand once fitted in there.

'Which one? Our guest ale—'

'You choose, I don't care.'

Moments later he was sipping a pint. Autopilot had been switched on. Only his body was present.

Brogan stared at the little bits of froth on the side of the glass. His only movement was the slight rise and fall of his chest. He was trapped in a bubble, the sound of life around him disconnected. He was in transit, not in this life, not in this reality but passing through it, on his way to hell. Although he couldn't see how it could get any more hellish. This *was* hell.

He sank the pints. Three, maybe four. None of them washed away the lead weight of pain in his chest. Halfway down the fifth pint, he started to look at the people in the bar. A couple having a cocktail were all over each other. Brogan remembered being in that bubble with Katie. He swallowed that memory down with the remainder of his pint and beckoned for another.

'You sure you want another, mister?'

'As sure as hell is hell.' His gaze lingered on her youthful face. It worked, although she did little to hide her disapproving look before she turned back to the bar.

When she returned, she slid the beer wordlessly onto the table. Brogan didn't bother to thank her, he merely grunted and took another gulp. His gaze fixed on the grain in the wooden bar, stained and scratched and knotted and warped. *This whole fucking thing is warped.*

* * *

The days morphed into a relentless blur. He was at the bar most of the time, whatever time it was until they kicked him out and he'd wander off to find another one. He'd not showered, not changed his clothes, his beard was growing, he stank of piss. At some point he'd fallen or got into a brawl or something. The screen on his comms-watch was smashed, his knuckles were swollen and grazed and crusty flakes of blood caked his hair and ear.

'Here you are!' Clarkson sat down in front of him. The sickly smell of her perfume made him gag. 'I've been looking everywhere for you.'

'Yeah, well, ya found me. Now you can piss off again.' Brogan went to pick up his pint but a hand appeared and lifted it away. Clarkson had taken it, stretched her arm out, and put it on the table behind her.

'Give it back.' His voice was like steel. He thought about twatting her one, but his body didn't respond.

'No. It's Mikey's funeral tomorrow and you need to be there.'

'What's the point, he ain't gonna know if I'm there or not.'

'No, probably not, and clearly you don't give a toss about anyone else right now, but I know you'll regret it forever if you don't go. Maybe not today. Maybe not tomorrow or next week. But one day. The Brogan I know, the Brogan I served under and followed into the mouth of hell and came out the other side, that Brogan, that Brogan would want to be there and that Brogan would regret missing it.'

Brogan stared at her, or stared through her. An echo of the past sparked in his mind, the Brogan in uniform, the Brogan with balls, the Brogan commanding his unit, the brotherhood. The death. The loss. The torture. He shuddered. To this day his missed his mate Meteor. So many dead.

'Just give me my pint back.'

'I never took you for a quitter.' Clarkson reached around, grabbed the pint off the table and slid it back in front of him. 'His funeral is tomorrow. Be at Katie's for eleven hundred hours.'

He grunted, not lifting his gaze from the amber in the glass. His body rigid, his skin crawling, his jaw tightened. *She needs to leave.*

'I can see you've no fight left, Captain.' Clarkson slid out from behind the table and disappeared from his view. '*Alis aquilae*, sir,' she whispered as she walked away. Her perfume left shortly after.

Captain… Captain…What are your orders? What do we do?

We stand, we fight, not for king, not for country, not for the poxy government but for each other. Fight for Dixie because she's got a kid at home. Fight for Russo because he's only a young 'un. Fight for Meteor because who else can we take the piss out of? We fight for each other and forget the rest. We stand where others fall… His speech to his unit when they were led up the garden path into a trap. *Alis aquilae… On an eagle's wings we will find strength.* He stared down at the tattoo on his wrist.

The wings of an eagle. The mark of his unit. He slumped back, staring at his pint.

* * *

Present Day – Tuesday, 30 October 2057

'Nice to see you've sobered yourself up for the occasion.' Katie glared at him as he stood on the steps of his old house. He could see the strain in her eyes and was about to speak when she stepped past him. 'He's here.'

Brogan turned to see the black cars, his son's coffin in the first one. Katie had had a bouquet made into an infinity symbol. Brogan pressed his lips together, swallowing the tears. *Mikey would have approved, not the flowers but the symbol.*

They sat in the back of the hearse, Katie on one side, Brogan the other. The gulf between them was a poignant reminder of their loss. He so desperately wanted to reach over and hold her hand, but she sat arms folded, as though cradling their little boy. Neither of them spoke as they followed their son on his final journey.

As they approached the crematorium, a gathering of media vultures stood eagerly at the gates. The cortège turned through the gates to a storm of camera flashes. He glanced down, hoping it wouldn't trigger a seizure.

The pit of his stomach swirled. His jaw clenched with the effort of holding back the tears and not breaking down in public. The cars rolled to stop, and Brogan looked at Katie, whose tears seemed to fall in limitless supply. Brogan had seen pain, but looking at her face, none had ever matched the pain on a mother's face before she buries her child.

'Ready?' he asked gently.

'No.' She held out her hand and Brogan took it gladly. He gave it a squeeze as the funeral director opened the car door. From somewhere they found the strength to get out, to stand among family and friends and follow behind the coffin of the boy they had loved and cherished.

The lump in Brogan's throat swelled, every step harder than the last. He wanted it to be over, he wanted not to feel like this, he wanted this not to be real, he wanted his son. His chest tightened. His nails dug into the palms of his clenched fist. *I should've done better. I should've been there. Whoever did this is gonna pay.*

He couldn't look at the people in the pews as they passed them. He could only look forward, his stare boring into the coffin and his imagination finding his son, sleeping. Katie had organised everything, but where she found the strength to do that he had no idea. He was never good enough for her. No wonder she left him. He didn't even know what clothes she'd decided to bury him in. *A hoodie and jeans, probably.*

There were several cameras set up inside the crematorium. The service was being live-streamed, access by invite only, and well over a thousand people had asked to attend the service remotely.

Katie had somehow managed to write a eulogy, a tribute to her clever Little Pickle. Katie's sister read a poem but Brogan couldn't recall a word of it. As the service was coming to a close, Katie walked up to the coffin. She placed one of Mikey's favourite teddy bears on the lid and kissed the wood. Brogan had not prepared anything of the sort. He stepped up to the coffin anyway. Feeling the grain of the wood under his fingertips, his heart ached at the touch and the memory of Mikey's curly hair.

'Night, son,' he managed as he leant to kiss the wood too. The dam was breached and the tears fell.

The wake was a blur of conversations, of sympathy and sorrow, of relatives coming out of the woodwork for the free food and disappearing again, only to reappear at the next funeral, relieved it wasn't them in the box.

Brogan gazed at the people in the room. *The Hausmans were right.* Their lives would carry on as normal. They would go back to work, back to whatever, while he was left trying to fill an unfillable hole. The beer called his name.

* * *

'Are you sure you want another, mister?' How many times had she asked him that recently?

'Yeah. I am.' Brogan glared at her, swaying slightly. His stare lingered long enough to motivate her to move. As he sat nursing his empty pint, a sudden quietness spread over the bar. He looked up at the TV. The news was on. He tilted his head, the blurry image on the screen looked familiar. A clip of Mikey's coffin and then one of Katie and him getting out of the car. The image froze on his face and his name came up across the screen. Whispers spread like a summer breeze, faces turned and stared, at him.

'Yeah! What you fuckin' looking at?' Brogan banged a fist on the table and glared around the room. The whispers died away. The news channel moved on and so did everyone else.

The waitress set his pint down. She didn't get too close to the table, as if he was going to bite. She gave him that sympathetic look, the one that people hope is sympathy but actually comes across as pity. Brogan allowed himself to imagine slapping it off her face. The angry beast was bubbling beneath the surface. He took another slug.

A tramp came and sat at his booth. Brogan felt the man's eyes upon him.

'Piss off.' Brogan didn't think at all, he didn't even raise his gaze.

Unmoved, the tramp ordered water from the waitress. When it arrived he took a long swig, leant forward and spoke carefully.

'I'm sorry about Mikey.'

Brogan lunged forward, knocking the drinks over. He grabbed a clump of the man's hair and slammed his head down onto the table. The waitress yelled something in the background. With fury in his eyes he leant over the tramp.

'What the fuck did you say? Who the hell are you to be sorry? What the fuck would you know about my son?' Brogan increased the pressure on the man's head. Saliva dribbled from the tramp's mouth, his eyes failing to blink away the pain. Brogan's stare bore into him.

The burly bar manager approached them. 'You're going to have to take this outside.'

'This is Peacekeeper business.' With his free hand Brogan flashed his badge, and the bar manager backed off. Brogan began pushing his thumb into the tramp's eye.

'Get off, get off me. You're a fucking lunatic!' He squirmed and banged on the table.

Brogan hauled the man up by his stinky threadbare jacket collar. The guy stumbled, jarring the table. He winced.

'Look, mate, I-I don't want no trouble.' He clasped his hand over Brogan's and tried to push it away. His eye watered, still recovering from having Brogan's thumb in his eye socket.

'Too late.' Brogan saw the whites of the tramp's eyes and it fuelled his anger. He pulled his free hand back and thumped the guy under his ribcage. Air spewed out of him in a groan and Brogan let him crumple to the floor. He swung his leg back to boot him but something grabbed his arm, pulled him back and slammed him down onto the tabletop. Pinned, he tried to kick up from behind but they were too fast and he was sluggish from the beer. His arm was being pulled and twisted further up his back.

'Stand down, soldier. You. Get up and get out, now.' A scrambling noise and the scraping of a table punctuated the silence as the tramp hurried away.

Brogan wriggled again. A boot kicked his leg out from under him, the edge of the table bit into his hipbone as his weight fell onto the table. A familiar scent filled his nose.

'Get off me, Clarkson.'

'You're out of line. You're going nowhere.'

Muttering rapidly ascended into typical bar-level conversation. Brogan felt Clarkson relax her grip and release his arm, so he pushed himself up, off the table. He rolled his shoulder around and gave it a rub.

'Sit.' She stood in front of him, blocking him from

following the tramp out the door. 'You'd have annihilated that guy, the mood you're in. Now, sit down.' She raised her eyebrows and dipped her head towards the table.

Brogan's nostrils flared, his jaw clamped shut, and his chest was heaving, like a raging bull. She didn't budge, she didn't even blink. He sat down.

'What the hell was that?' Clarkson glanced around the bar. People were getting back to their beers.

'What did it look like?' Brogan's hand trembled slightly as he reached for his beer.

'It looked like a Peacekeeper about to smash seven bells of shit out of a vulnerable citizen.'

'The guy got in my face. He deserved it.' He took a long swig.

'Oh, so you deserved to lose your son then?'

'An eye for an eye.' He smirked.

'Look, I know you've just buried Mikey and you're still getting your head around killing a pregnant woman, but hell, she was a terrorist. You should have been a hailed a hero with all the crimes she committed.'

'But Annika Estrada's unborn baby didn't deserve to die too, did it?' Brogan shook his head and stared down at the woodwork.

'You were told it was a bomb. You couldn't have known. You followed orders. When will you let that go?' Clarkson leaned in.

'And the sudden onset of epilepsy. That was a convenient excuse, was it?'

'It happens. The medics said it was shit timing. That's all.'

Brogan's head snapped up. 'And Mikey, he just had shit timing too, then?'

'Only in the sense that it throws doubt on Mace's conviction.'

'Mace, that fucking prick… he did this.' Brogan balled up his fist until his fingers went white.

'No, think about it, he couldn't have. He didn't have any access to the Grid.'

'Doesn't matter. I spoke with him and threatened to bring his termination forward, so the vindictive bastard set Mikey up to get to me. He's gonna wish he had killed himself by the time I'm through with him.'

'Now just take a minute to think about it. Yes, he had the back door and accessed the Grid, but since Minty died he's not even had access to the prison system. Mace had no idea you'd be the one investigating Hausman's case, and by then it was too late.. So how could he have organised it?'

'Mmm, s'pose.' Brogan stared at his empty pint glass.

'Well then, he had no MO to set Mikey up, and no time to carry it out. Then he became self-injurous and had no access anyway. He only had an MO after he was denied access to the Grid.'

'He could've had help.'

'He didn't. I checked.' Clarkson shook her head. 'The hospital logged his contacts. No one went to visit, no one tried to call. Not even his own family.' She shrugged. 'Hausman was the *only* one to have any contact with him.'

'So it couldn't have been Mace? But that means…' Brogan's face crinkled like a scrunched-up paper bag.

She nodded. 'Someone else is killing the cybernaters.'

'And Mace was telling the truth all along?' Brogan rubbed his face. *This is messed up.*

'We can't be certain he wasn't involved in the last spate, but certainly these most recent deaths, he looks innocent to me.' Clarkson sat back in the booth, an expectant look on her face.

'Then we've got to find out who the fuck is killing our kids, before they kill any more.' Brogan stood quickly. Too quickly. He groaned. His head span and he sat down again. 'What time is it, Sel?'

'It's time you had a shower and a shave and sobered up a bit.'

'Right. I'll grab a coffee and we'll go and pay the doctor a little visit.'

'We'll go nowhere. It's 20.30 hours and you're tanked. Besides, Kane doesn't want you anywhere near this case. In fact, he doesn't want you anywhere near HQ.' She raised her eyebrows and looked like a mother scolding her child.

'Kane can swivel. Meet me at Novanoid first thing tomorrow—' Brogan landed a fist on the table.

'I don't think that's such a good idea.'

'Look, Sel, I'm only going to have a little chat with a specialist, that's all. You can either leave me to it or come with me and report back to Kane that I was a good boy.'

Clarkson rolled her eyes and shook her head. 'Nine a.m.?'

'Fine.' He rubbed his shoulder. 'You've still got some strength in you.'

'I still train, that's why. It's like my grandma always used to say, "It's not the gettin' old that kills you, it's the sittin' down that does it."' She smiled and stood up. Brogan followed suit, only a little more slowly this time. The adrenaline subsiding, combined with the alcohol and an empty stomach, was not the best combination for a vertical position. *I need food.*

'Have you been remembering to take your epilepsy medication? Katie asked me to check.'

'You've seen Katie?'

'Yeah, well, she called me, said she was worried about you.'

'Oh. Thanks, Sel. For looking out for me, I mean.'

'*Alis aquilae.*' She dipped her head, gave a quick salute, and flashed a smile. She queued with him while he ordered a kebab then bundled him into a cab.

Brogan gave her a wonky salute as the cab pulled away.

CHAPTER 16

PRESENT DAY – WEDNESDAY, 31 OCTOBER 2057

His tongue felt like sawdust, his head hurt like an IED had exploded, and his body hardly felt like his own. His hands trembled slightly. *Beer, you're a cruel mistress.* He rubbed his face as if it would do any good. Somehow he'd made it to Novanoid, and somehow he'd even managed to be early.

Sitting amongst the greenery of the botanical gardens outside Novanoid, he waited for Clarkson. A gang of joggers in stupid Halloween costumes filed past him, sweating away their youth and knackering their knees for middle age, if they were lucky enough to get that far.

'Mornin'. Coffee?'

Brogan looked up. Clarkson offered him a coffee cup and a smile. He sighed. 'Thanks, Sel.' He took the cup and sat back as she sat next to him. They sat in silence. Clarkson's perfume blended with the scent of the gardens, but it was a bit too sickly for Brogan. He held his mug close to his nose and drowned out the smell with his coffee. Another gaggle of joggers ran past. *Muppets.*

'You know you can talk to me if you need to.' Clarkson leant forward, resting her elbows on her knees and wiping a smudge of lipstick from the rim of her cup.

'Don't, Sel. I'm not going there.' Brogan's pulse quickened. His trigger finger twitched so he buried it into his palm, digging the nail into his skin. 'Come on, let's do this.' He downed his coffee, stood up and made for the entrance, ditching the coffee cup in a recycling bin by the main doors.

Cobwebs hung from the reception desk, black plastic bats dangled from balconies and pumpkins huddled together in corners around the atrium. A helpful securatron, clad in a Frankenstein costume, intercepted them halfway across the foyer. 'Detective Brogan, welcome back. How can I be of assistance today?'

'You're too clever for your own good. We're here to see Dr Tempest.' Brogan never knew where to look at these things. Although they had facial projectors, they never quite seemed to look you in the eye.

'Do you have an appointment?'

'No.' *Why do I tolerate these things?*

'And who is your colleague?'

'Detective Clarkson.' Clarkson bobbed her head forward. She looked like she was going to shake hands with the thing.

'I see. Please wait a moment while I contact Dr Tempest.' The face on the screen looked down, a perfect replica of a real receptionist. He glanced over at the front desk. The real receptionist was actually filing her nails.

'Dr Tempest has agreed to see you. Please follow me.' The securatron rolled off along the corridor. Brogan and Clarkson dutifully followed the lumbering unit.

The building's security system automatically swished the doors open as the securatron approached. Every wall and door seemed to be made of glass, there was so much light in the building that they might have been outside. *I'll bet even the bogs have glass doors.*

The securatron stopped them by a glass door. A dishevelled-looking woman sat at her desk, appearing to be engrossed in something. She looked up as the door glided to the side.

'Dr Tempest, thank you for agreeing to see us. I'm Detective Clarkson, this is Detective Brogan.' Clarkson was straight in there, striding over to the woman in the white lab coat. Brogan had seen Clarkson in action as a soldier, but never as a detective, until now. *She's taking the friends route.*

'Oh man, I wish our office had this view.' Clarkson put her hands on her hips and stared out the window. Tempest's office faced out across the Suffolk skyline.

'It's not bad, I guess. I forget to look.' Tempest glanced out the floor-to-ceiling window. 'What can I help you with?' She swivelled in her chair to face the centre of the room. A formatic bed and a small cupboard with a few books on top were the only other things in the office.

'Hey, is that a nineties coffee maker?' Brogan strode over to the cupboard and eyed it. 'These are rare. You've got the filter papers and everything.'

'You're into the vintage life?'

'Yeah, I've got a Sony Walkman, a vinyl record player

and a few other bits from my grandfather. They all still work too.' Brogan dipped his head towards the black liquid sitting in the jug. 'Can I try some?'

'Sure.' Tempest's face formed a tight-lined smile.

Brogan took a clean mug off the side and poured a drop. The smell alone gave him a buzz. *That's so good.* The crappy synth-caff didn't compare to the taste of real roasted beans.

'We need to talk to you about cybernating. I read your work, oh what was it called… The er… *The Mechanical Mind*, that was it. It was fascinating. Well, the bits I could understand anyway.' Clarkson smiled and stepped towards Tempest.

'Oh, thank you. That piece did result in rather a few accolades.' She blushed a little.

'So we thought you'd be the best person to ask about the resurgence in cybernating deaths.' Clarkson glanced over at Brogan. He didn't flinch. He couldn't afford to.

'I'm sorry about your son, detective.' When Brogan merely nodded, she added, 'But I'm not sure I how I can help you? It doesn't seem that anything has changed, and you should have access to my expert witness testimony in Clayton Mace's court case.' She glanced down at her comms-watch.

'Well, we'd appreciate just a little more of your time. Please, tell us, why do you think it's only cybernaters dying, and not people who log in through a standard VR headset?' Brogan moved to sit on the edge of her desk. Standing was not a strong point despite the coffee.

'It's not entirely clear, as I said in my report. The brain is a very busy organ. Perhaps the brain of a conscious person is too active, or perhaps whatever happens to a cybernater is due to certain brainwaves that are only active when they're in stasis. It's all only a theory. I mean, only Mace really knows how he's doing it. You should ask him.'

'We have. Now, what about the fail-safes? I thought the systems prevented any harm coming to the cybernaters by bringing them out of stasis before any adverse effects occurred.' He spotted Tempest's gaze dart to something behind him. He glanced down and saw a photo of a young girl holding a birthday cake. He picked it up.

'Again, this is in my report. The person's biometrics are constantly monitored, an auto-extract is fired if they fall outside normal ranges.' Tempest moved, took the photo from Brogan, and placed it on the far side of her desk.

'What happens if the machines are switched off suddenly, like if there's a power cut or someone found a way to switch them off remotely?'

'It shouldn't happen. All the machines have a backup battery that lasts long enough for a safe extraction.'

'And if you just switch the machine off?'

'Well, it's the same as a power cut. You'd have to manually disable the backup battery first, then kill the main power. But that's not what's happened to the cybernaters, as I understand it.'

'So, what does happen if someone's machine is suddenly switched off, without backup power?'

'We're not certain. When the system was tested with the prison inmates, some survived with no ill effects, some died and… some had permanent brain damage.'

'You were part of that pilot testing, doctor. Can you be specific with the numbers?'

Crikey, Clarkson, you've done your homework. Brogan

returned his gaze to Tempest, who seemed to be thinking about it.

'I don't see what this has to do with the cyber deaths?'

'Then humour us.' Brogan stepped over to the shelves and inspected the dusty books, all of which were about neurology.

'Only about thirty per cent survived with no long-term damage.'

'So it might be possible that their machines are being switched off somehow?'

'That's not up to me to determine.' Tempest looked out to the landing, shook her head and waved someone off. Brogan turned to see a young man in a lab coat scurry away.

'This is strictly confidential, doctor, but our analysts still haven't been able to determine a true cause of death. The two most recent deaths are identical in every way to the eighteen murdered by Mace two years ago. But still, the cause of death remains unexplained.'

'Oh, really.' She tugged on her lab coat, neatening out the creases.

'As my colleague said, so far it's only affecting people who are hooked up. So could it relate to the specific type of technology used?' Clarkson studied a headset she'd found on a shelf. 'Do you have any thoughts on that, doctor?'

'Well, hard-lining into the Grid requires more bandwidth. I don't know, maybe the virus or whatever it is needs that to be able to function.'

'Okay, so more bandwidth. Then where would you start, doctor, if you were investigating the deaths?' Clarkson put the headset down and tilted her head, her gaze fixed on Tempest.

'I think I'd be interested to know what they were doing at the time of death. Where were they in the Grid? Gaming, chatting or looking for sensual thrills, that sort of thing.' She seemed to get fidgety, shifting her bodyweight and playing with her hair. 'Well, if that's all your questions, detectives, then…'

Brogan started to sweat, and the room seemed to sway. *Not now.* He balled his fist and dug his nails into his palm. *Mikey.* Clarkson opened her mouth to speak but Brogan cut her off. 'Yes, yes of course. Food for thought there. Thank you for your time, Dr Tempest. Come on Clarkson, we've kept her long enough.' Brogan strode over to the door.

'Please, let me know if there's anything else I can help you with. Maybe call ahead next time, though?'

'Of course.' He paused a few steps before the automatic sensor swooshed the door open, then turned and added, 'On the off chance, have you heard of something called "Project Metanoia" or the "Metanoia Code"?' And there it was, the sole reason for his visit, to see the flash of nerves that showed for a nanosecond in her eyes, his 'gotcha' moment. He knew she knew something. He let the silence grow because liars needed time to think.

'Metanoia?' She sounded the word like she was only just learning to talk. 'Hmm, no, no, it's not ringing any bells, sorry.' She fidgeted with something in her pocket.

'Oh, okay, thanks. And I'm sorry too.'

'Excuse me?' She was twitching. She buried both hands deep into her pockets, anxiety leaking from her like the stink of an old sock.

'About your daughter?' He'd seen the way she reacted when he picked up the photo and took a guess.

'She's not dead, detective,' her clipped tone surprised everyone.

'I'm sorry, my mistake.'

'Bye doctor, thanks for your help. We'll be in touch if we have any more questions.' Clarkson ushered Brogan out of the office. They were immediately collected by a securatron.

'She knows more than she's letting on.' Brogan knew it in his bones, and knew he was bloody well going to find out what it was.

'Sshh, all this technology gives me the creeps. You don't know what they might be recording.' Clarkson eyed the securatron and Brogan kept his thoughts to himself.

* * *

Tempest collapsed into her office chair as she stared at the two detectives making their way back towards the elevators.

'ANNA, activate Security Protocol 9.' *Why have we not thought to check their Grid locations?*

Although ostensibly the candidates were taken to a fake clinic room created by Novanoid, no one thought to actually check. Now she'd potentially tipped off the Peacekeepers. *Jaro isn't going to like this at all.*

A grey tick appeared in the corner of her visi-wall, showing that the security protocol was active.

'ANNA, call Elliott Parker, tell him it's urgent.' Moments later the visi-wall displayed the youthful face of Parker.

'What's so urgent?'

'Have you ever checked where the candidates are in the Grid while the metanoia script is running?' She held her breath.

'They're in the mocked-up clinic room, of course. It's secure and untraceable. You should know that.' He seemed quizzical with an edge of annoyance.

'But are they, are they actually? Have you ever thought to check? Is it possible that they could be in two places at once, like there's a back door or something?'

'No, there's no such function in the code. Back doors have to be programmed in.'

'Look, can you check, please? We've not got any other leads and our time is running out.'

'I can have a look this aftern—'

'No, this needs investigation now. I'll call a meeting for three p.m., get what you can by then.' She waved at the visi-wall and switched him off before he could protest. 'ANNA, send an urgent meeting request to all members of the Metanoia project, three p.m., the CAVE.'

* * *

Three p.m. Tempest ditched all her wearable tech in a box on the shelf and was the first one to arrive in the CAVE. She sat staring at her feet through the glass table.

'This better be good, Tempest.' The internal door to the CAVE barely slid open before Jaro Dax stepped in and took the seat at the head of the table, annoyance oozing from him like pus from an abscess. Elliott Parker arrived a moment later.

'Tempest, Parker. You'd both better have something for me?'

'I've analysed the event log. It's a mess of data and I haven't been able to identify any breaches. Whoever stole it has some serious skills. There isn't a trace.'

'Because it never happened and you were stalling for time?'

'No. No, not at all. I want Metanoia to succeed. I wouldn't put everything my father worked for at risk.'

'So it was you then, Tempest? Thought you'd copy the code for yourself?'

'No. Someone else out there knows. I was visited by a couple of Peacekeepers this morning, Detectives Brogan and Clarkson. He specifically asked about Project Metanoia.' She gulped as Dax's cold stare hit her. She had found that it was better to get straight to the point where he was concerned.

'And you said what exactly?' The coolness in his voice unnerved her.

'I said I'd not heard of it…' she left a tangible 'but' in the air and was more nervous about her next admission. 'But… he was asking questions about the deaths, and I fear I may have accidentally given them a clue.' She stared down at her feet. When the room remained silent, she raised her gaze. 'I don't know where the thought came from, but I suggested their analysts look at where the candidates were in the Grid moments before they terminated. It's not something we've looked into either.' Her throat was now dry. She looked through the table to the floor but could still sense his eyes on her.

'So what you're saying is that although you denied

knowing anything about Metanoia, you might actually have led them straight back to our fucking door?' His nostrils were flaring.

'If I may…' Parker pulled himself upright and leant forward on the table. 'To her credit, Dr Tempest called me this morning and I've been able to review some of the early data.' He paused but no one broke the silence. 'I've reviewed the two latest cases. It's scrambled and messy, like really messy. Grid tracers show they were everywhere and nowhere. Simultaneous appearances in chat rooms, games, videos, photo files, the lot. They were spread across the Grid like butter.'

'Is that even possible?' Tempest's heart fluttered.

'Well, clearly not, because otherwise they wouldn't be dead.' Dax stared at him.

'Tempest, if the finger of blame doesn't point our way then you got lucky. Very lucky.' The icy deliberateness of his tone resonated deep inside her. She would be scrutinised and watched.

'What about Brogan and Clarkson?' She really wanted to shift the attention elsewhere.

'Leave that particular obstacle to me.' Dax eyed them like he was deciding which one to eat. 'Parker, when will you have all the data?

'By lunchtime tomorrow.'

'Make it ten a.m. tomorrow. We'll reconvene here.' Dax got up and left the pair of them. Only when both doors had closed did either of them breathe.

'Thanks.' Tempest disliked Parker slightly less. 'You really didn't recruit or run the code on the Brogan kid, did you?'

'No. You?'

Tempest shook her head and sighed.

'What did you make of the early data? I mean, it's like I said, they're all over the shop, all at once. They're everywhere and nowhere. I've never seen anything like it.' Parker seemed more animated now, his geeky excitement having been unleashed.

'Are you sure that's what's happening?' Tempest moved forward, elbows leaning on the glass table.

'Yeah, positive.' He nodded.

'I'm not sure what it means from a bio-technical point of view, what that might do to a person.' She thought for a moment. 'Maybe they're overloaded, what did you say... "spread like butter". Maybe there's a loading limit on the synapses and beyond a certain point it causes death somehow. I can re-examine the integrity of the neuro-synaptic network. I've only ever taken a random sampling, but there's billions of connections in a human brain.'

'Overload... overload...' Parker tapped his forehead. 'What if we're blowing their fuses?'

'Pardon?' Tempest's brow creased.

'Well, basic electrical circuits have transistors, transformers, modulators, fuses and that kind of stuff to help maintain a steady flow of electricity...'

'Like a heart pacemaker regulates heart rate... So, all we need to do is slow the program down or regulate it somehow?'

'Yeah, I think so.' Parker's gaze drifted upwards, probably already trying to formulate an algorithm.

'It's brilliant. I mean, it's also the only thing we've got. We need to analyse the previous deaths. A sample size of two is not conclusive.' Her analytical brain was kicking in but it was too late, her hopes were already waving a flag from the top of a mountain. Partly because it might actually work, but partly because it meant that Dax wouldn't have her daughter taken off life support just yet.

'Right, I'll finish the analysis and get working on adapting the program.'

'I'll check if the recruiter has any new candidates ready for us.' Tempest practically levitated with renewed optimism as they left the CAVE. She grabbed her comms-watch and typed a message.

How much longer? We need another subject ASAP.

She was halfway back to her office when the reply came.

Do not rush this. She is close. A week. Maybe.

Chapter 17

Brogan followed Clarkson out of the elevator and onto the twentieth floor of HQ. In the corner of his eye he spotted the awkward glances and semi-smiles of those brave enough to make sympathetic eye contact. He fixed his gaze on a spot right between Clarkson's shoulder blades.

The office had been restored, even the damage to the plasterboard bore no reminder of his outburst. He sunk into his chair, staring blankly at the screen looking back at him. Only two weeks ago, life had been so different. His inbox was cluttered with the usual interdepartmental shite. Brogan deleted them.

There were a few hollow messages expressing condolences and empty promises of help with anything, the sort of thing you say when you can't think of anything else to say. Brogan much preferred the typed messages. He didn't want to have to see the awkward sympathetic looks of those that took the time, and felt the need to record a video message. One message caught his eye. Someone he had worked with years earlier, who had not spoken to him since Mikey was born sixteen years ago. He had come out of the woodwork to express his sorrow, and then in all likelihood would disappear back into the woodwork again.

A cough that sounded like someone treading on gravel alerted him to Kane's presence.

'What are you doing here?' Kane, whose physical appearance matched his name – the man wore his skin like a shrink-wrapped pencil – loomed over him like the rotten branch of an old oak tree about to snap.

Brogan sensed where this conversation was going. 'Nowhere else to be, sir.' He played the game.

'We're all sorry about your son, but there's no need to be a martyr and come into work.' He shifted awkwardly and adjusted his tie. 'You need time off to grieve.' Niceness and compassion weren't terms you'd associate with Kane. "Knob", however, was strongly affiliated with him. As was the nickname "Corpse".

Brogan's mouth twitched. His skin prickled just looking at him. 'Sir, I can assure you there is nowhere I would rather be than cracking this case.'

'No. I've given the Hausman case to Clarkson. As you said, it looks like there's a connection with the cyber deaths.' Kane stabbed a gnarled finger in the air. 'And after that stunt you pulled with the tramp at the bar, you can thank your lucky stars you still have a job.'

So much for the compassion. 'Well, I've just got a lead from Dr Tempest at Novanoid Corporation and I think we're close to a breakthrough.' Brogan's stomach started to growl, but not with hunger.

'You've been to Novanoid? You've conducted an interview when you're in no fit state? Oh for pity's sake.' Kane rubbed what little hair he had left.

'But, sir—'

'You'll hand over to Clarkson, then you're to go home. Understood?' It was really a rhetorical question. Kane turned to leave. Brogan sprang up from his desk, refusing to take this horse-shit.

'I don't see what the big deal is. Clarkson was there for the whole interview.'

'Good, then she's up to speed and you can go home now.' Kane stretched out a creaky arm and pointed towards the door. 'You're being stood down. First you left Hausman for dead, and now you've popped along for an unscheduled chat with a pre-eminent doctor. This investigation is at risk of becoming a farce.' Kane stared, his lips forming a pencil-thin line across his craggy face.

'Sir, with all due respect, I know when I'm onto something and—'

'Good, then you'll also know you're one signature away from losing your job, or going back down to the 1st Division.' Spit formed at the edges of Kane's mouth. 'And believe you me, you'd already be there if it weren't for Clarkson. I've had enough of your belligerence. Go on, out. You're signed off for a month. Leave your firearm with security on your way out.' Kane walked away.

'No. I've spent too many years taking dipshit orders from dipshit officers only to see good men killed. I can't stand by and see more kids being killed.'

Kane whipped his head round. 'Then don't stand, find somewhere to sit and leave it to Clarkson. Out. Now.' By now every head was turned in their direction. 'Do I need to have you escorted off the premises?'

'You're a fuckin' moron, Kane.' Brogan stormed out of the office, stabbed the elevator call button and headed up to the sky-trax platform. He was breathing like an enraged bull. His jaw was clenched and he'd balled his hands into fists, digging his nails into his skin. Tempest knew something, he was sure of it.

Brogan stomped up to the sky-trax platform. His watch buzzed. He was about to ignore it when he saw Clarkson's name roll across the display.

'Where are you going?' Clarkson's face appeared. Her gaze darting off camera, Brogan could see the back of Clarkson's head in a mirror behind her.

'Where are you?'

'I'm in the toilets. Didn't want Kane catching me chatting to you. Where are you going?'

'You heard Kane. Where do you think I'm going?'

'Not back down to the pub?'

'Tempting. Very tempting. No, I'm going back to my apartment. I want to try and do some digging on this Dr Tempest.' Brogan stepped out onto the cab landing area.

'So you're not going to listen to Kane?'

'No.'

'Good. Listen, I'm not sure what's going on around here, but there's something fish—'

A metallic noise came from an alcove to Brogan's right. He spun his head, expecting to see someone standing there. The hair on his neck prickled. 'I'll call you back.' He thumbed his comms-watch to end the call. 'Who's there?'

Silence.

'C'mon, I know someone's there, I can smell your fear. You might as well save us both the hassle of me ramming my fist down your throat.'

A foot swiped out from the alcove and was quickly retracted.

'Look, I'm getting in the next cab that comes. If you wanna piss about and try to attack me from behind, then get on with it.'

'I-I'm not here to attack you. I'm… I'm here to warn you.'

'Warn me?' Brogan's brow furrowed. 'Come out, let me see you?'

A figure emerged from the alcove, a ragged, dishevelled guy an inch shorter than Brogan. One eye swollen and purple. *I know that face.* Brogan racked his brains. He'd seen that chinless skeleton before. *Where, where have I seen him?*

'I… I've been trying to get your attention.'

'You weren't the guy that threw a stone at me, during last month's protest?' Brogan stood square on to the guy.

'And you gave me this,' the guy pointed to his eye, 'and a couple of broken ribs in the bar yesterday.'

'That was you?'

The guy rubbed his ribs. 'Yeah. Not my best timing.'

'Look, if you're after revenge, I don't blame you. Go on, you can have a free crack at me if you like?' Even through the guy's baggy clothes he could tell he had about as much strength as a maggot. It was a pretty safe offer.

'No, look, there's not much time.' The guy appeared uneasy. He kept glancing over Brogan's shoulder to the other door. 'They're everywhere, they're watching all the time.' His eyes darted around like he was watching a fly. 'I need to know what you remember about the day you shot Annika Estrada?'

'How'd you know about that?' Two paces and Brogan was in the guy's face, prodding him in the chest.

The guy inched backwards, his eyes darted to a waiting aero-cab. 'I know, okay? And I know you didn't pull the trigger, and I know that killing her baby is eating away at you. Now, tell me what you remember.'

'Come off it, I pulled the trigger. What's it to you, anyway?'

'There isn't much time. C'mon, think. What do you remember?' He was shifting about on his feet now. Twitchy as fuck.

Brogan rolled his eyes. 'I've been through this. I had command shouting in my ear that she was wearin' a bomb, but I stalled because of the way she was walkin', it didn't seem right. Then I had a seizure and accidentally fired my weapon.'

'That's all you remember? Are you sure? You had your first seizure at the exact moment you had a lock on her. Don't you think that's strange?'

'Why would I? Medics said it could happen at any time, and I'd racked up a shit-ton of flight hours.'

'What if I told you your weapon was fired remotely, that your headset was rigged to cause the seizure, and that you're part of a top secret experiment?'

'What? What the fuck are you talking about? Who are you, and why should I believe any of this crap?'

'I can't tell you my real name. Not yet. Not until I'm

sure. For now, call me Eric. And I was one of the scientists involved in developing the drugs.' Eric stepped forward and grabbed Brogan by the shoulders. 'You need to stop taking the anti-seizure meds. Trust me. Stop taking them. That stone I threw at you—'

The metallic crash of a door hitting the wall made Brogan whirl around. Four guys burst through, guns held ready. Brogan lunged forward into the waiting aero-cab as the first shot rang out. He scrambled into the back seat and risked a look out the back window.

Eric legged it to the open mouth of the platform. He'd been shot in the arm. More shots were fired as he reached the edge and leapt off into the air.

'Circle around the building, anticlockwise.' Brogan's heart raced. The cab took off and did as instructed. None of the men were gunning for him. They looked like mercenaries, soulless bastards with a license to maim and murder.

It took forever for the cab to circle around. Brogan pressed his head against the windows, scanning the ground below, looking for signs of a scene, a gathering crowd, anything. Then he spotted it. A black dot, but it wasn't falling, it was gliding. The guy, Eric, was wearing a wing-suit. *The jammy fucker.* Brogan rubbed his face.

'What is your desired destination, Detective Brogan?'

He checked behind him. No one looked like they were following him. 'I need time to think. Take me on the aerial city tour, silence commentary.'

'Commencing aerial city tour, silent mode activated.'

Brogan sat back. *What the hell was all that about?* His mind took him back to that fateful day. He saw the girl, the shoot-to-kill order being yelled in his ear. Then, nothing until the medics were in his face, and then the investigation, and then the pat on the shoulder – see you later soldier, you're on civi-street now. *I had a seizure and pulled the trigger.* He rubbed his temple. *How else could she have died?* He rolled his bottom lip between his fingers. *Nah, that Eric's a nut-job. But why would those goons try to shoot him...* He shook his head as if to dislodge the thought. *I don't need this right now.*

Brogan circled the city, his mind following the same pattern. Mikey, Novanoid, Eric, Estrada and her baby. He needed a plan, he needed to speak to someone, someone he trusted.

He jerked his arm out to reveal his comms-watch. 'Call Clarkson.'

A message came up: *Connection failed. No network access.*

'Computer, I want to make a call. Access the network.'

Access denied.

'What the hell?'

The cab jerked. The windows opened and closed of their own accord and the dynamic display began blurting out the usual detritus of ads at high volume. The annoying ones 'for single men of certain age', dinners for one, hair dye and 'have you got a will?'

Brogan covered his ears. 'Computer, switch off the entertainment system and close the bloody windows.' *Friggin' machines.*

Suddenly the aero-cab accelerated, throwing Brogan into the back of the seat. It dodged through the traffic, narrowly missing auto-pods, bullet-trucks and drones. Some managed to dodge out of the way, but older models were too slow to execute their emergency manoeuvres and ricocheted off the side of the cab. Debris rained down on the traffic and the street below as the aero-cab continued on its path of destruction.

The cab clipped another auto-cab. Brogan was thrown against the side window as they spun off in the opposite direction. He glimpsed the faces of a petrified family as their cab's stabilising boosters engaged and regained control.

The cab threw him round like a pea in a washing machine. He couldn't get into the emergency harness. Then he banged his head on the dash panel and blood clouded his vision in one eye as the cab pitched and rolled.

The cab turned on its side and the door slid open as Brogan landed on it. He clawed at whatever he could grab, but he fell out. Managing to grasp the doorsill, he dangled out of the cab.

The wind battered him.

The cab jerked like a bucking stallion.

He lost his grip, clinging on with one hand.

His watch bleeped a warning: *Pulse too high, blood pressure too high, warning, warning.*

His jaw clenched tight, his strength sapping away.

Suddenly the cab righted itself. Brogan threw his arm up and held on with both hands, his legs flailing like he was riding an invisible bicycle.

He sucked in air then yelled it out as he pulled with everything he had and hauled himself upwards, hooking his elbows inside the doorframe. He swung his legs forward, then back, and managed to heave his chest and belly into the cab. He was spent.

Cars and skyscrapers flashed by as the cab continued to disregard its programming, crossing lanes, dodging into and out of the oncoming traffic, which peeled off at the last second.

A message bleeped and flashed on the dynamic display: *WARNING: LIFE PRESERVER MALFUNCTION.*

Brogan lifted his head and his eyes widened as he read the message. The cab rose vertically, the G-force pinning him to the floor. Up went the cab, high above the sprawl of the city, high above the air-lanes and up into the no-fly zone. It continued on. Brogan was pinned. His watch bleeped another helpful warning: *Oxygen too low. Warning: oxygen too low.*

Everything was a haze.

The cab vibrated violently.

The engines cut out.

The cab hung momentarily. The crushing G-force stopped, and for a second he was weightless. Then he was slammed into the rear window as the cab plummeted.

Darkness descended over Brogan.

The dynamic display showed a new message: *SYSTEM REBOOT, SYSTEM REBOOT…*

Brogan's watch sent an auto-alert to the emergency response teams. A traffic exclusion zone cleared the skies. Onlookers gawped through various bits of tech while live-streaming the unfolding events.

The cab continued to plummet, Brogan a rag-doll passenger, fighting for consciousness.

The lights in the cab came on. Through blurred vision and turbulence, Brogan squinted at the dynamic display, it read: Hold on, it's going to be close.

An explosion threw him off the rear window and the emergency safety pod inflated around him, cocooning him. The thrusters fired up to the max but they were too late. The cab slammed into the ground and skidded off down the plaza like a pebble skimming across a calm grey pond. Brogan's body slumped, motionless.

CHAPTER 18

PRESENT DAY – SATURDAY, 3 NOVEMBER 2057

Something rustled by his head. Hushed voices passed through his ears, fragmented in his mind, then disappeared. His body seemed detached, and he was only vaguely aware that he was breathing. Slowly blinking, blurred shapes passed before him. More voices called his name. Darkness fell again.

* * *

'So Brogan survived?' Parker arrived in the CAVE last, as usual.

'So I hear.' Dax barely moved his lips.

'Was that the plan? To kill him off?' Parker seemed way too cocky.

'Not necessarily, but either way the outcome has bought us time. Now, what have you brought?'

'I think I've found a way to make the program work.' Parker grinned as he pulled his chair in under the glass table.

'That's what you said last time. And the time before that, and… you get my point.' Dax leant forward. Parker shifted awkwardly. 'You'd better mean it this time.'

'Well, thanks to Tempest's spark of genius I've added in some breakpoints to slow the program down. It'll either work like a charm, or at the very least it'll give us more data on where the thing's bustin'.'

Dax slammed his fist on the table. 'This better fucking work, you cocky little shit. If not, you'll be following in your father's footsteps sooner than you think.'

Parker shrank back.

'Tempest. Candidate status?'

'Er… The Ranger said he was close to having one ready. I…'

'If he doesn't come good within the week we will be using your daughter.'

Julayha. No. Heat burned through her heart to her mind. She sprang forward and leaned on the table in front of Dax. 'She's *your* daughter too.'

'Parker. Out. Now.' Dax kept his gaze fixed on Tempest. Parker scrambled and could not get out quick enough.

'How dare you bring that up.'

'Oh, I dare, Jaro. I dare all right. I've got the DNA tests to prove it.'

'We've been through this. They mean nothing.' There was venom in his tone.

'She even looks like you. Thank God she doesn't behave like you. I think there'll be many a news outlet interested in my story.'

'You're in no position to threaten me.'

'Likewise.' Tempest released her grip on the edge of the table and strode out. She sensed Dax's eyes on her back.

By the time she got into the elevator her body was trembling. Her lower lip quivered and she tried to steady her breath. She hit the button for the medical bay on the next floor up. It seemed to take forever. She hurried down the corridor, nodding politely but not stopping to speak to the two colleagues she passed.

She entered the medical bay. It was like coming home. *Julayha's okay.* She sat down next to her, pulled off the sensor-packed glove on Julayha's hand, and held her. She cried as she held her daughter's soft hand against her cheek. *We'll be together again soon, sweetie. I promise.*

CHAPTER 19

PRESENT DAY – MONDAY, 5 NOVEMBER 2057

B rogan stirred, climbing through treacle to reach consciousness. Before opening his eyes he did a systems check, checking for sensation, first in his arms and hands, then his legs and toes. All sent back signals that they were still attached.

Blinking in the light, he scanned the room, searching for an anchor to reality. He found her. Katie sat beside him, watching him. He tried to raise his head but immediately regretted it. Pain seared down his spine, his head throbbed and his mind was a fog of confusion. A slight squeeze drew his attention to his hand. Katie had it clasped in both of hers.

'Hi,' he managed.

'Hi.' She smiled. 'I'll tell the health care assistant you're awake.' She squeezed his hand again then vanished from his eyeline. The room started to come into focus. It was very clinical. A machine bleeped near his head, a hospital bed with a squeaky mattress, crisp white cupboards with a sink in the middle of the worktop. There was something familiar and homely about it. The shape of the room, the soft lighting, the photos on the wall. As Brogan's eyes focused on the images he realised they were of happier times in the Brogan family. *I'm at home.* The fortune they'd paid for the hospital-at-home suite to be installed a few years ago still needled him. *Never thought I'd end up in here.*

'Hi, I'm Jeana, your personal health practitioner. Dr Koops has been remotely monitoring your status via the medi-link and will be aware that you've woken up.' She pointed to the screen to Brogan's left and his eyes traced the plethora of cables back towards his body. He nodded back in acknowledgement. It was the best he could do as shards of pain shattered his thoughts.

'How are you feeling? Can I get you anything?' Jeana had a bright-eyed, youthful way about her that only seemed to highlight Brogan's mangled frame.

Brogan's mouth felt like something had died in it. 'Headache, chest hurts.'

'Well, you did crack your head pretty hard and you've broken four ribs. You're pretty badly bruised too, but you'll survive. We've injected you with oesteobots programmed to help with bone growth. They will create a hollow infrastructure in the fracture sites to allow faster bone fusion. In a couple of days the pain will subside, but the bruising and muscle damage will take longer to heal.' Jeana beamed in her best upbeat and perky-little-miss-perfect tone.

Brogan could see her lips moving but hardly a word entered his mind. 'Painkillers?' He needed to clear his head.

He needed to think. He rolled his head gingerly towards Katie. 'What day is it?'

'Monday.'

Brogan's face contorted.

'The crash happened on Wednesday. You were very lucky. They took you to St Martin's Hospital, and released you here on Saturday once you were stable.'

'Crash? Lucky?' The word stuck in Brogan's head, bouncing around like an echo.

'Yes, Marcus, there was a… you had a bit of an incident and there wasn't much left of the cab…' She looked away, wiping a tear from her cheek.

'I'm here, Katie, I'm in one piece. I wouldn't leave you.' His words hung in the air as they both realised the double meaning: she had left him.

'I'm sorry.' She sobbed. He let her cry a little, her head resting on his chest. She'd clearly forgotten about the four broken ribs, but he hadn't. He gritted his teeth as the sharp pain subsided to a constant throb. He winced as he moved his hand to her face and cupped her chin, pulling it up to meet his gaze. He hated seeing her cry and wiped her tears with his thumb.

'Katie, I'm pretty sure someone wants me dead!'

'What? Marcus, no. You're being paranoid.'

Jeana coughed to announce her return, then proffered a pot of tablets and a glass of water. Brogan downed the tablets. It wasn't until after he'd swallowed them that he wondered what they were exactly. Shortly after that, Brogan succumbed to the darkness once again.

* * *

Brogan groaned, the dim evening light a blessing to his eyes.

'Feeling a bit better?' Katie's voice pulled him into the light, as did the sensation of her stroking his hand.

He nodded. His body still ached but it wasn't as intense. He raised his right hand to scratch his face but something cold and hard bit into his skin. He pulled harder and the sound of metal clanking on metal filled his mind. His gaze whipped round to his wrist.

'Handcuffs?' His mouth fell open. He pulled at them as though it were a dream, then he reached over with his left hand and tried to free himself. The metal dug into his wrist. *Handcuffs?*

'Marcus, I'm sorry. Just stay calm, everything's going to be okay.'

'What's going on? Why am I cuffed? I've done nothing wrong.' He made another pointless attempt to free himself. When that didn't work, he banged his wrist against the metal framework of the bedrail.

'Calm down, Marcus, please?' Katie looked flushed.

The machine next to him bleeped in time with the rise in his heart rate. 'Tell me, Katie. What's going on?' He tried to push himself up on the bed but the pain and the cuffs pulled him up short.

'You don't remember?'

'Oh Christ, not this again. No. I don't bloody remember.' He racked his brains. *Remember, remember.*

'You… you took control of an aero-cab and—'

'No. No, I took control of nothin'. That aero-cab damn near killed me. I had nothing to do with it.'

'It was all over the news. People saw you driving

recklessly, hitting drones, other cabs, and then, well, you aimed it at a bunch of protesters in the marketplace.' Katie glanced at the cuffs.

'What? What are you talking about? That's not what happened at all.' Brogan rubbed his face with his free hand. 'Oh shit, someone is trying to kill me.'

'They said you might be like this. Look, no one is trying to kill you, it's all in your head. Let's face it, you've not been right since your discharge.'

Brogan sighed heavily. *I can't believe this. It can't be happening.* 'Show me the footage, Katie.'

'You're not allowed to see it.' She winced.

'Why?' He lifted his head despite the complaints from his muscles.

'Kane, the medics, the courts… it's a condition of you being here and not in the medical bay at the prison.'

'Oh, hell.' He let his head flop back down onto the pillow.

'Look, try not to worry about it. It's getting late, get some rest and I'm sure things will be clearer in the morning.' She gave him a weak smile, patted his arm, then stood.

He watched her leave. The cool bite of the cuffs on his wrist stopped him trying to roll away from the ache in his chest. He closed his eyes and took a deep breath. *Someone wants me out of the way. But who?*

CHAPTER 20

PRESENT DAY – THURSDAY, 8 NOVEMBER 2057

'Good morning, Detective Brogan. I have determined that you are sufficiently recovered to undergo an interview with the Peacekeepers.' Dr Koops stared out of the screen as though he'd been trapped in there for some time.

'Thanks, doctor.' Brogan winced as he got off the bed and Katie helped him dress. That was painful in more ways than the merely physical.

The two burly 1st Division Peacekeepers who'd been guarding the door came in. 'Time to go, Mr Brogan.' This guy had a scar across his forehead that made his head look like a tennis ball. He caught Brogan staring at his scar.

'Got it in mili service, on tour during the drone wars. Got caught, they damn near wiped out our unit before the flyin' circus arrived.'

'Oh really? I was a Skiff operator.' Brogan tried to recall if he'd been deployed to that mission.

'I know who you are, and it's an honour to meet you.'

'Alright, lovebirds.' Brute number two wasn't ex-mili. 'Let's get this show on the road. You play nice, mister, and we all get in the happy van as sweet as pie, right?'

Brogan rolled his eyes. 'Yeah, sure, whatever.'

Brute number two slapped on a pair of cuffs. Brogan was in no mood, or position, to wipe the damn smirk off the man's face, but he did memorise his collar number.

There was a media circus out on the lawn, and as soon as Brogan appeared they were like rabid dogs. They showed no remorse, not even for treading on Katie's pansies.

Brogan ignored the shouts of the media swine with their sensationalist questions and requests to pose for the camera. He kept his face deadpan as he stared ahead to the Maximum Security Transport Van, otherwise known as the 'happy wagon'. He'd been in one many times before, but only on the side where you were free to get out. He thought back to his time as a prisoner of war. This was nowhere near as bad as that, which was why he decided to go with the flow instead of making life difficult. Besides, he knew the truth, although he wasn't yet sure how he'd prove it.

* * *

Brogan stared at his reflection in the mirror of the interrogation room. *You've seen better days, kid.* The stark box room had the usual one-way mirrors behind which, Brogan knew, was recording equipment, a forensic analyst, and probably half the office knowing those nosey bastards. Sitting there, waiting, still achingly battered and bruised, Brogan's thoughts flashed back to the time he was captured and tortured. He woke up in a room the same as this one. He shuddered as though trying to shake the memories from his mind and body.

Kane strode in, followed by a man and a woman Brogan had never met before. There were plenty of women he'd never met, and some he'd regretted meeting altogether; this one, he regretted not meeting sooner. Brogan didn't budge, though. He watched and waited.

'These are Agents Green and Chang, they're from Internal Affairs.' Kane stepped aside and allowed the two agents to come forward. Brogan eyed them impassively. 'They are here because of your suicide mission.'

Brogan stared at Kane. He had no time for the stick man, and leaned forward.

'It *was not* a suicide mission.' His eyes drilled holes into Kane's soul, if he had one. 'Like I said, the cab was hacked.'

'Who set you up, then?' Agent Green's husky but gentle tone caught Brogan's cock off-guard and it did a happy little twitch. In those five words he knew how this was going to play out: the old good cop, bad cop charade.

'Well, if I knew who'd damn near killed me I wouldn't be the one wearin' cuffs. Would I?' Trying to hold back on his usual sarcasm was a challenge. *God, I sound like Mace.*

'You're sticking to your somewhat flimsy story, then?' Agent Chang sat opposite Brogan. His metal hand glistened in the harsh light of the interrogation room. He must have caught Brogan staring at it, because he stretched out the fingers curled them up one by one. 'Platinum carbide.' Chang smiled.

'How do you Metal Mickeys do it? I mean, keeping all

the fluff outta those little joints must be a right pain.' Brogan fixed his stare on the middle of Chang's forehead.

Chang rolled his eyes and sat back. 'So you're saying the cab was jacked? Despite the fact that no one's *ever* managed to hack a cab. This one was remotely controlled by someone who'd managed to override the encryption, take control of the vehicle and fly it like a maniac into oncoming air traffic, through the drone-zone and then the no-fly zone. The grand finale being to switch the bloody thing off and plummet to your death – but oh, lucky for you the system magically came back online and the surviva-pod engaged in time? Bit far-fetched, don't you think?' Agent Chang's face screwed up like he'd licked a lemon.

'Look, I don't know who or how, but yeah, that's about the size of it.' Brogan maintained his glare.

'Detective Brogan, your son has only just died—'

'Thanks for the reminder, I was at risk of forgetting for a minute there.'

Green hooked a lock of hair behind her ear. 'What I'm trying to say is no one blames you for not coping, you don't have to try and carry on working.' Good cop Green softened the tension, but Brogan didn't respond because it wasn't really a question, nor was it a statement of fact. Facts could be proven and justified, explained and understood. Yes, his son had died, that was a fact, but the rest of her sentence galled him. *Who is she to tell me what to do?*

'If I wasn't being blamed, I wouldn't be sat here now, would I, Agent Green?'

'Tell me, detective, your military service record states you were a drone fighter.' Clearly Agent Chang thought he was onto something here.

'Yeah, I was part of the flying circus. What of it?'

'So, you know how to handle a craft then?' Chang seemed like was trying to reel him in.

'Nope. I might know more than the average Joe, but any kid with an aviator-sim setup could do just as well.'

'So you're saying it's child's play?' Chang was the cat playing with a mouse before he ate it.

'Look, I'd probably stand a better chance, but piloting a drone – from the ground – is not the same as flying in the actual air.'

'So, you think you'd be a bit wobbly to start off with but you'd get the hang of it pretty quickly?'

'Probably.' Brogan held up his hands as though giving up and rubbed his tired face. He tried to rub away his mounting frustration. He knew they thought they knew something, but he didn't know what. He resigned himself to playing the game.

'The trajectory data and a drone cam show a period of instability, then more concise movements through the air-lanes.' Chang really wanted to be the one to dig the knife in. Brogan stared at them with the expression of a corpse. Not that he thought he was a dead man, but presenting yourself as such does have a way of unnerving folks. The unnerving silence worked and Green tweaked the controls on the stack.

'Detective Brogan, there's something you need to see...' She swiped and the holo-screen blipped into life in the middle of them. 'This is the internal video from the cab...'

The best degreaser in the world couldn't have wiped the smug-bastard smirk from Chang's face. If his forehead were an advertising board it would have said *Gotcha!* Brogan gulped, not because of guilt but because someone had gone to extreme lengths to rid him from the human infestation of Earth.

All four watched the playback. It started with Brogan sitting in the back seat, tinkering with his comms-watch. Smug Chang forwarded the clip.

Brogan's mouth fell open as he watched himself clamber forward, punch a few buttons on the cab's control panel and take command of the vehicle. He watched as his on-screen self tugged and jerked at the control sticks, getting a feel for the cab as he dodged traffic and getting more confident, maniacal laughter erupting from the speakers. He couldn't look away but couldn't make sense of it either. The video showed *his* face, in the front seat, contorting with the G-force as he powered the cab up into the no-fly zone. Then, the on-screen Brogan stabbed at the controls again and cut the cab's power.

The internal video ended, so Chang cut the playback to a drone cam. It showed him at the controls as the cab plummeted.

'This isn't right. This isn't me.' Right now, that was sounding like a weak argument even to him. 'Play it again.'

Chang, still smug, sighed and reset the video. As the shock of seeing the footage for the first time subsided, Brogan watched more closely. Eyes like crosshairs, taking small, shallow breaths as though the act of breathing was an inconvenience.

When the video finished for the second time Brogan sat back and folded his arms. 'That's not me.' He injected the words into the room, his usual confidence bubbling up through his feet once again.

'You do understand that this recording came from the cab?' Green glanced at Chang. Brogan sensed his sudden change in demeanour had caught both agents off guard.

'Who gave you the data file?'

'It was uploaded directly from the crash site, of course.' Chang broke his stare.

'By whom, who did the work-up? Who was on the ground?' Brogan pressed his index finger into the table.

Green flicked through the data files looking for the evidence log.

'Don't waste our time with this misdirection, Brogan. You're bluffing and you know it.' It was Chang's turn to sit back and cross his arms. 'This is you, we have the evid—'

Brogan lunged forward like an angry lion out of its cage. 'Stop wasting my time.' He leant across the table, the hologram reflecting off his face. His ribs hurt but he'd reached his tolerance for shite. 'This tape is so full of fucking holes it's like pissing through a sieve. Someone has been killing those kids, including mine. Someone tried to kill me and when that didn't work, they're framing me to get me off the scent. And *I'm* wasting *your* time?'

Brogan reached over to the controls and rolled back the video to the point where it showed him clambering forward in the cab. He froze the image.

'This is how I know.' He turned, yanked up the back of his shirt and pulled down his trousers. He looked back over his shoulder. Both agents tilted their heads to one side. 'Not got it yet?' Brogan zoomed in on the screen shot of the imposter's back and there it was: a fleeting black mark, a tattoo. A tattoo that Brogan didn't have.

Chang waved it away. 'It's just a shadow.'

Green zoomed in further and enhanced the image. It was no shadow.

'Need more?' Without waiting for a response, Brogan fast-forwarded to a clip of him reaching for the control panel, his right wrist in clear view. He froze the image and held out his wrists. It was Green who understood first. The two Brogans had their comms-watches on opposite wrists.

'More?' Brogan forwarded the recording again, this time to a red cab he'd seen. He froze the image, took a screen grab and moved the original footage on further. He paused it again. The exact same red cab appeared again. Chang slumped, defeated. Green seemed pissed but impressed.

Brogan sat back heavily. He turned to the one-way mirror and made a slicing movement across his neck, then pointed up to the CCTV camera in the corner. Universally understood as 'stop recording'. A little red light went off on the camera.

'Now, we have a problem.' Brogan glanced around at the three blank faces.

'We either have a mole, or there's some clever-dick fuck who's accessing our servers.' Brogan stared at Kane. The man looked paler than normal.

'Sorry. Whoever it was really did a number on you.' Green kind of winced and nodded at the same time.

'Yeah, I've sure hit someone in the nads. Now, we just need to work out who.'

'There's no *we* about it, Brogan. You're off this case and you're on suspension.' Kane creaked into life and out of his chair.

'What? You've got to be kidding me.'

'You heard. You need to stay out of this now. You've

rattled someone's cage and the media are all over you like a rash. Every move you make, your mental stability, your competence, will be watched and scrutinised. And then there's your physical health after the crash. No, I don't need any more cock-ups and the last thing we need is to investigate this with the media watching your every move.'

Brogan's mind flashed to Eric. *'You're being watched.'* He stared at Kane. 'No, I think that's exactly what you need. I've rattled someone's cage and spooked them into taking action. Plus, I'm sure if they wanted to kill me they would have done it by now, or maybe they didn't expect me to survive the crash and now they've had to rethink.' Brogan stared at the tabletop for a moment.

'Clarkson is leading the case now. She's made progress while you've been in recovery, and she's doing it without all the media fuss.'

'Lead? What lead?'

'It's not your case, so drop it, Brogan.'

'Damn it, Kane. Right now I'm the best lead you've got. Without me as a target we have no way of digging out the mole.'

'Hmmm, he's got a point.' Green turned to face Kane. 'Plus, if whoever's cage was indeed rattled then maybe Brogan can rattle it again, and distract them while Clarkson carries out her investigation unhindered?'

'Yes, Green.' Brogan stabbed the air in her direction. *Thank fuck for Green.*

Kane looked between the pair of them. His mouth twitched. 'Fine. But you're on your own. You report to me and me only, Brogan. I want to know what you're doing and when. We can't predict what they'll do once they find out you've been released.'

'Right. Are we done here?' Brogan stood to leave.

'I think so.' Green glanced at Chang, who looked like he was still sulking. 'We'll need to release a press statement about your release, but otherwise you're good to go. What's your plan?'

'I haven't got one, yet.' Brogan glared at Kane, who'd opened his mouth but closed it again.

Out in the corridor there was the usual hubbub of people being led into and out of the interview suites. No one seemed to pay much notice to Brogan as he made his way back up to his desk on the sixteenth floor. *Predict… We can't predict…* The word stuck in Brogan's mind.

He was on his own in this, no one to trust, no one to turn to. The feeling of isolation crept up on him, as did the sickening in his stomach. Clarkson was probably okay, she'd had his back in the unit on more than one occasion. No, he trusted her. She was a good guy. The beer called to him but he forced it from his mind like everything else.

Back in his office, there were a few glances and elbow nudges. Clarkson was deep in conversation on the phone. He sat at his desk and stared at the blank visi-wall.

'Paysos, how predictable am I?' The question surprised him as he watched the genderless face of Paysos appear in front of him.

'Very, detective.' An artificial smile spread across the computer's face. If the face of an AI could be anything, this one did smug very well. Brogan half recalled a memo about a recent upgrade, injecting more personality into a lifeless chip.

'No jokes, Paysos. Answer the question more fully.'

'All humans are predictable to a degree, detective. Current data indicates deep-stacking algorithms can predict with seventy-nine per cent accuracy. For example, your psychological profile predicted correctly that you would use alcohol as a coping strategy. That your discharge from the military caused a deep internal rift, and subsequently led to the break-up of your marriage. Resulting in your desire to be left alone. This gives a slight decrease in your predictability score because your response varies above the average curve depending on your state of mind—'

'Right, I've heard enough. So what about Amber Hausman's killer? What can you profile about him or her?'

'From my analysis, Amber Hausman was a cautious person. She cared what people thought about her and would therefore consider their reactions first. I think it highly likely that either Amber knew the killer directly, or that someone she trusted sent the killer to assist her in some way. Given that the killer had access to technology that is not currently available on the market, and that none of her known associates are likely to have access to that kind of equipment, I would suggest that someone she knew paid for the murder.'

'Hmm, interesting. Who would be on your list of possible suspects, based on that profiling?'

'I would say someone with wealth—'

'Brogan.' Clarkson appeared next to his desk.

* * *

'This place seems like a ghost town.' The Ranger strode over and sat next to Catsanga.

'Yeah. Everyone's got the jitters. I mean, if a Peacekeeper's son isn't safe…' She shook her head.

'No one's safe. Christ, half the galaxy's paused.' The Ranger logged in to a console.

'Yeah. Everyone's goin' analogue.'

'Not you?' He flashed a quick glance over to her but pretended to be more interested in his screen.

'Hmm. I was waitin', to be honest.'

'Oh?'

'Yeah, I wanted to speak to you.'

He turned to face her. 'Look, if I go on about my mum too much then I'm sorry.'

'No, no it's not that.' Catsanga flashed a palm in his direction. 'It's about the trial, I err…'

'Ah, that. Okay.' He looked around conspiratorially. 'I don't think I'm supposed to tell you this, but I think it's got something to do with the cyber deaths.'

'What?'

'It's top secret, but they're trying to find a way to stop it. I'm not sure how, maybe a defence program or something.'

'Oh. But it's safe though?' Her body seemed to relax.

'Of course. Minty's alright, isn't she?'

'Yeah, I suppose so. I could really do with the creds. Well, my family could.'

'Things bad at home again?' The Ranger gave a sympathetic smile.

'Mmm.' She nodded.

'Look, why don't I get you into the clinic, you can ask

the doctor any questions and if you're still not sure, well, you can pull out.'

Catsanga stared at her console for a moment. 'Alright.'

'Great. Give me a couple of hours. I'll sort it.' His body tingled. He'd get paid just for getting her there. 'I'll meet you back here in a bit.'

Catsanga nodded.

The Ranger exited the hangout, swiped his dash panel and sent a message to Dr Tempest.

Chapter 21

'Sel.' Brogan looked up at her. The big grin on her face told him she was onto something. 'Kane said you'd found a lead. What have you got?'

'Well…' She sat on the edge of his desk with her back to the office and lowered her voice. 'I've been doing some digging around, talking to some of Minty's online friends. Anyway, I spoke to a couple of kids who said there was this guy who started coming in, real regular like; then, after Minty died, he disappeared, they hardly saw him. They said he was a recruiter or something. Always sat with Minty and left either before she did or just after. Followed her like a stink, one of them said.'

'Okay, so did they get a name?'

'No, and I checked back with the gaming company. The guy's ID bounces around the Grid like a flea on a dog.'

'So no record, then?'

'No, it's impossible to trace. I had Anders take a look and he said he'd never seen anything like it.'

'Christ, what that kid doesn't know about programming isn't worth knowing. You're still smiling though, so what's the good news?'

'Well, apparently Minty used to sit with this other girl, Catsanga. She had a cat avatar. Anyway, she used to hang around with Minty and was there when this recruiter was around.'

'And what's she said?'

'That's the thing. She's said nothing. I can't reach her. She's in the Grid but isn't responding. Not even to a legal request.'

'Okay.' Brogan narrowed his eyes, the creases in his face fell together like well worn curtains.

'I've managed to get her full details and thought I'd head over to her place. Well, it's her parents' place, she's still a minor. I want to try a direct uplink, she can't ignore us forever.'

'Right. I'll come with you.'

'What about Kane, what about the media?'

'Screw 'em. I'm coming.'

'Okay, but I need to get Kane's approval to interview.'

Brogan rolled his eyes. 'Fine, do it by the book, but only tell Kane. No one else is to know.'

'Why is it top drawer?'

'I'll tell you in the cab – oh, and we're not going in an aero-cab. We're going old-school. There's no way I'm going aerial.' Brogan rubbed his ribcage.

'It'll take longer.'

'Fine. It'll probably look better if we leave separately anyway. I'll set off now, and by the time you get the warrant we should arrive about the same time. Don't tell anyone I'm coming with you.'

'Christ, you're paranoid.'

'Yes, for good reason. See you in a bit. Call me on a secure channel when you're in the air.'

* * *

Brogan grabbed his jacket and headed out to the street level. The taxi rank was a short walk across the plaza. The afternoon sun seemed like strobe lighting as the traffic stream passed above him. *Jeez, if that's not enough to bring on a seizure, I don't know what is.* He pulled out his shades and scanned the plaza, looking for Eric or anyone who looked like they might be tailing him. There were bunches of people enjoying lunch in the sun or scurrying about like ants on a doughnut. No one stood out. *What the fuck am I into? What secret bloody government agency? Why me? I must be a magnet for nut-jobs.* He hailed a cab and winced, his muscles and ribs still recovering.

A slick silver cab rolled its door open. Brogan flicked his comms-watch and the address details uploaded to the cab's nav system.

'Good afternoon, detective. Address verified. Journey time thirty-four minutes. Please help yourself to the onboard refreshments. What is your prefer—'

'Silence.'

'Silent mode activated.' The car moved off with only a slight hum from the tyres on the tarmac. Brogan fastened the lap belt then stretched out, to find the seats deep and comfortable. *What a morning.*

* * *

'I'm back.' The Ranger stood next to Catsanga. She'd zoomed in on a planet and was watching a turf war. 'Are you ready?'

'Yeah.'

The Ranger held out his hand. Catsanga took it and a little electric-blue light fizzed between them. The Ranger's avatar paused as he entered the Grid address. The hangout dissolved and the clinic room faded up around them.

'That's a sick transition, isn't it?'

'Yeah.' Catsanga let go of the Ranger. The clinic room was the same, a couple of palm-ports and an immense view. This time, it was a view of a gas cloud in deep space. The colours seemed unreal. 'Where's the doc—'

A woman in a white lab coat popped into existence. 'Sorry, I was only a few seconds behind you.' Her avatar had a warm, motherly smile. 'It's nice to have you back, Catsanga. We're so pleased you've decided to continue with the trial. We wouldn't be able to carry on without the help of people like you.'

'I'll leave you two to it.' The Ranger never stayed for this bit.

'See you later?' Catsanga tilted her head, her breath shallow and quick. *I wish he was allowed to stay.*

'Definitely.' The Ranger stepped back, and vanished.

'If you'll give me a moment to set the program. Do you have any questions before we begin?' The doctor tapped on a console in the centre of the clinic room.

Catsanga shook her head. *If Minty did it, I can too.* She put her hand on the palm-port.

Chapter 22

Brogan's cab rolled through a pretty decent area on the edge of the city. The houses were all detached, and a few even had aero-cars parked on the drives. As the cab turned the corner, Brogan clocked an aero-cab descending at the bottom of the street. A figure stepped out, paused, and then took a step towards the houses and the shade of a tree.

Brogan was almost there. *Nice timing, Sel.*

Sel was tinkering with her wrist. Her head jerked up like a prairie dog spotting a snake. She took several steps backwards. Brogan craned to see what she'd seen but the trees blocked his view.

Sel backed off further, stumbling on the kerb and into the road.

A red flash came from behind the tree, blinding Brogan. He blinked rapidly as Sel crumpled to the ground.

'Sel! No.' Brogan smacked the dashboard. A silver drone

flew from beyond the trees, hovered above Sel for a moment, then accelerated vertically.

Brogan's cab pulled up. 'You have arrived at your destination.'

Brogan leapt from the cab, his heart pounding. *Sel.* An explosion from above forced him to dive for the ground. His ribs crunched as he landed, winding him, his mind fuzzed with the pain. Little bits of plastic and metal tinkled to the ground, the smell of smoke reached his nostrils. He raised his head, scanned the sky and the street. There was nothing left of the drone except a lingering puff of smoke.

Sel groaned.

Brogan's military instincts kicked in. He kept low, despite the pain in his chest, and slid to a stop next to Sel. The laser-blade had sliced her open, a diagonal gash across her midriff. She was gulping for air, blood pooled at the back of her throat making each gulp more of a gurgle. Brogan grabbed her already pale and cold hand. He couldn't look away from her wide blue eyes as her body heaved for life. *The bastards knew she was coming.*

She moved her lips. '…ter, ters…' It was impossible to tell what she was saying.

Brogan put his hand on her cheek and stroked her. *She's going.* 'Sel, don't go, stay with me Sel. Don't leave me.'

Her hand reached up and grabbed his wrist. Her head tilted back as she gasped for breath. Her body jerked. Then sagged. Her grip on Brogan's wrist went limp.

Brogan stared at her. Numb.

The sound of sirens bounced up the street and into Brogan's mind. He glanced around to see the blue lights of the rapid response teams arriving.

He looked back down at Sel, slid her hand off his wrist and onto her chest. '*Alis aquilae.*'

He stood up and ran to Catsanga's house. The drive was pristine, the front garden immaculate. Two hollow faces stared back at him from behind the net curtain in the front window. He flashed his Peacekeeper badge then jabbed a finger towards the front door. The male of the pair had understood.

Brogan tapped his foot as the door was being unbolted.

'Detective Brogan, 5th Division Peacekeeper. I have reason to believe your daughter is in danger.'

The man looked blank, that look of shock that Brogan had seen many times.

'Sir? That woman on the street was my colleague. She was coming to see your daughter. Please. Let me in?'

As if suddenly prodded, the man nodded and stepped aside.

'Where is she?'

'Upstairs, first on the left.'

Brogan side-stepped the man and took the stairs two at a time, using the handrail to haul himself up. The landing doubled back to the right, and Brogan used the stair-post to swing himself around the corner. A white door faced him. A little panel on the door said 'AADYA'. Brogan pushed it open.

Brogan strode over to a small, motionless figure lying on the formatic bed – a souped-up dentist's chair. Cables hung like Christmas decorations from the girl and the chair, connected to a monitor to the left. Brogan followed the snake of wires down to the control unit.

The girl barely looked to be moving. *Is she dead already.*

Am I too late? His gaze scanned the monitor, the bottom third of the screen taken up by vital signs, brainwave activity and her heart trace.

He took a step closer, trying to find the console. He spotted the corner of it, tucked on a little shelf under the formatic bed. Leaning forward to get it, he stopped short. Her face began twitching. First it was just the corner of her mouth, then her whole face. Brogan flicked his gaze up to the monitor. Her brainwave activity was all over the shop.

Brogan looked from the monitor to the girl.

'What have you done?' barked a voice from behind Brogan.

'Nothing.'

'That's not normal. Aadya's heart is beating too fast.'

The machine started bleeping rapidly.

'We've got to switch it off. Where's the master switch?'

'No, you can't. It could kill her.'

'She'll die if we don't. It should be switching itself off, but it's not. Where's the switch, damn it?'

'Don't, don't pull the plug.'

'Stay back, this is Peacekeeper business.' Brogan pushed his palm forward to keep the man at bay.

Sirens howled outside. Blue lights flashed and bounced off the walls in the girl's bedroom.

Brogan crouched down, tracing the cables at the back of the control unit. *Backup battery. Shit, where's that?* He yanked a thick cable that looked like it could go to a battery source. Aadya's body started jerking on the bed.

He spotted the master switch, on the wall, under the bed. Glancing at the girl, whose face was still twitching and little beads of sweat had formed across her forehead, he dived under the bed.

'No, no, no!' The man pulled on Brogan's legs.

Brogan reached for the switch, and froze. For a moment he was back, back to the military, back in his unit. Explosions going off around him, bleeps and buzzers whirring through his mind, the shouts from command ordering him to pull the trigger. *'Fire now, soldier, fire, fire, she's got a bomb.'* His hand shook. Sweat dripped from his forehead. If he didn't flick the switch she would be dead, if he did she could still die anyway. *Tempest said thirty per cent survival…*

Another pull on his leg shook his mind free. His arm reached forward and he flicked the master switch off. In that moment, he knew. He knew he didn't pull the trigger on the pregnant terrorist. The woman hit the ground before his seizure.

The buzzing and bleeping alarms died instantly. The thrum of electricity silenced.

'No! Oh Christ, what have you done? What have you done?' The father was pulling off the headset that covered most of his daughter's head while Brogan stood up. 'Is she breathing?' The guy was trembling.

Brogan stuck his fingers on the girl's neck, pressing them into her jugular. He steadied his own breath and focused on the warmth of the girl. It was there. A pulse.

'She's alive.'

The father sobbed. 'But the brain damage…'

Brogan stuck out his wrist, pressed a button on his comms-watch. 'I need immediate medical backup at my location.'

Brogan stepped away and looked out the window. Clarkson was being parcelled up. Two medics were making their way up the drive. He stared out the window, the activity behind him barely registering.

'*Alis aquilae*,' he muttered as they took Clarkson's body away. He stared down at the only speck of dirt he'd seen, on the windowsill. *It wasn't me. I didn't kill that baby.* Brogan sensed a heavy weight lifting from his chest. Somehow it seemed a little easier to breathe. Brogan turned to see the parents clutching each other as the medics checked their daughter. One was holding a probe pressed to her temple.

'EEG looks good. She's wakin' up.' The older of the two medics removed the probe, and gave Brogan a nod.

The little figure on the bed began to move and groan gently.

'Aadya? Aadya, can you hear me?' The medic squeezed her shoulder and the girl's head lolled in that direction. Her mouth opened and closed as though she was tasting the air, then she yawned, a wide, deep yawn. She blinked in the daylight and Brogan followed her gaze as she looked around the room, confusion etched on her face.

* * *

Brogan was lingering on the landing, checking his messages, trying to distract himself from the whirlpool of thoughts bubbling up inside him. The two medics came out of the girl's bedroom. He took a deep breath.

'She's got the all clear. She'll be monitored for a few days but there doesn't seem to be any lasting damage. You got lucky.'

Brogan huffed. '*She* got lucky.'

'Messy job out there.' The medic nodded towards the street. 'You know her?'

'Yeah. I knew her.'

'Sheesh, sorry. You're having a right day of it.'

'You could say that.'

'I'd give them a minute before you go in. The mum's a bit fragile.'

'Thanks.' Brogan stared at the back of the guy's head as he made his way downstairs. He chewed his bottom lip. *Someone knew we were coming. No. Someone knew* she *was coming, otherwise we'd both be dead.* Brogan took a deep breath. His hand reached for his e-cig but his brain remembered where he was, so he patted it instead.

He took a step towards the door and listened. Silence. He knocked but didn't wait for a reply. He needed answers.

Three faces turned to look at him as he entered.

'What just happened? You almost killed our daughter.' The slender man, the girl's father, looked pale. Pale from shock, or pale from anger. If it was anger he wasn't pulling it off, the tremor in his hand gave him away.

'What do you know about the cybernating deaths?'

'That they've started again… and, and that your son was one of them…' The man glanced at his wife.

Ah, so he's angry, but he can't be angry with someone who's just lost a child. Brogan gave a slight nod. 'I couldn't let it happen again. Mr Hussein, we had intelligence to suggest that your daughter was the next target. My colleague lost her life out there—' he thumbed towards the window, '—to come here and tell you.'

Mr Hussein opened his mouth to speak but Brogan

waved him off. He couldn't afford to allow the thoughts about Sel into his head, not now anyway.

'There isn't much time. I need to speak with Aadya, I need to know everything she knows.'

'She's weak, the medics said to—'

'Dad, stop. I'll speak to him.'

'Aadya, dear—'

'No. What do you wanna know, mister?'

'Call me Detective Brogan.' He stepped closer to the formatic bed and got a better look at the girl. She was young, younger than Mikey by a year at least. Her hair had been scraped back but he could see now it was thick and brown, like her mother's. 'Let's start with why you didn't respond to my colleague's legal requests for an interview?'

'I-I didn't get one.' Her eyes widened and she glanced at her parents.

'Are you sure?' Brogan raised an eyebrow.'

'I'm sure. I would have responded. Honest.' She nodded.

Brogan made a mental note to get Anders to check. 'So, your friend, she went by the name of Minty…'

'Only knew her online. We hung out from time to time. She had her strife, I 'ave mine. We'd chat, you know, girl stuff.'

'Right. Did she ever mention someone who went by the name of "The Ranger"?'

'Sure. I knew 'im too. He was the guy, at least I think he was a guy, that got me into the experiment.'

'Experiment?' Aadya's mother reached forward and grabbed her daughter's arm. 'What experiment?'

'Mum, let go. You're hurting me.' Aadya had a childish, whiny tone.

'What were you doing? What were you thinking? You're banned from this contraption for life. Do you hear me?'

'But Mum—' That whiny tone again. Aadya rolled her eyes.

Brogan coughed. 'I need to know everything you can remember about this guy. Where you met him, how you met, what he told you. And I need to know about the experiment.'

'Right, well, I was checkin' out the latest in *Xenon Fire*… it's a multiverse game,' she added when she saw the blank expressions around her, 'when I find Minty chattin' to this guy. Minty hardly chats to anyone so I wandered over. I thought if she was chatting to this guy then maybe she already knew him or something. So I wandered over—'

'How long ago was this?'

'Hmm, a couple of months ago maybe—'

'What did his avatar look like?'

'Pah!' She grinned. 'A cheapo vintage thing. I mean, it looked pretty slick 'n' all but boy it was glitchy, or his tech was glitchy. He'd fuzz out every now an' again. Jeez it was annoying, but I never said anything cos I knew he was short of creds. Anyway, once you got past that he seemed alright. He knew naff-all about the game, though.'

'So you taught him?'

'Nah, Minty did, I mostly just laughed at him. I thought he was croonin' for Minty.'

'Croonin'?'

'Yeah, you know, like he fancied Minty.'

'How does the experiment fit into all of this?'

'Well, he didn't tell us he was a recruiter. Not at first. We probably would have told him to do one if we'd known. He didn't try to recruit us so we thought he was cool. Thought he was just hangin'. Then he came in all flustered one day, said he was going to be in deep shit—'

'Aadya!'

'Sorry, Dad. He said he would get into trouble because he had no money. He said he needed to buy his mum some medicine but he'd not been able to recruit anyone for a medical trial. He said he needed the creds and that anyone who participated would get fifty creds and so would he, so Minty offered to help. Then when she came back and said it was easy-peasy, well, I thought why not and I had my turn.'

'Oh my gosh, Aadya. Why would you?'

'Because, Mum, you're always sayin' how tight money is, I thought fifty creds would help.'

'So, you both helped him out. What did the trial involve?'

'Nothin' really, as far as I could tell. They ran a bunch of tests, said they'd like to run a game so all I had to do was try and think the opposite of what I was seeing. Like if a ball rolled, I had to think about it whizzing through the air or something. It was well random but easy as, and I got the creds the same day. The woman running it said I was exceptional. She said I could qualify for the next round of testing if I wanted.'

'Who was she?'

'I don't know, she told me to call her Doctor. Her avatar was pretty neat, like it was so clean, not one pixel out of place.'

'Where did you go for the test?'

'That was pretty slick too, they had access to some high-end jazz, like the graphics were better than real life. It was funky, they'd built a hospital room, it had windows all around that looked out over a city. The view was immense. The clouds drifted past and everything. They changed it every time, this time it was deep space. Like I said, that's some top-whack tech.'

'So you went back?'

'Sure, not for a bit though because the Ranger didn't mention it again. It was Minty. She needed the creds, so she asked him. They went and she came back with two hundred creds.'

Aadya's mother gasped.

'When she told me, and she'd come back in one piece, well, I went too. How could I not? Christmas is on the way and I wanted to surprise everyone.' Aadya glanced at her parents and pressed her lips into a tight smile, then gave a little shrug. Her mother rubbed her arm.

'Then Minty got a bit greedy and she wanted to go again, because the doctor offered ten thousand creds. She reckoned she'd be stupid not to take it.'

'And then she died?'

'What? No. Minty's not dead.' Catsanga pulled herself up the bed, then glanced at her parents.

'I'm sorry. She is. Minty's real-life name was Florida Graham. She died six weeks ago.'

'She couldn't have. She's been messaging me.'

Brogan's brow furrowed. 'You received messages from her? After she died?'

Tears rolled down Catsanga's cheeks. 'I don't understand. She sent me messages, honestly. Only short ones. Minty never did long messages. I thought all was cool. Then I heard Mum and Dad arguing about money again and—'

'Now, honey—'

'No, Dad. I heard you, both of you. Arguing about the mortgage and sellin' the car, and I thought I knew a way to solve all our problems. I went to where we hung out and the Ranger was there. We chatted. There was a lot of talk. Everywhere was buzzin' about it. The Ranger said it could be a software virus and that's what the medical trial was about, finding a cure. He said he wasn't supposed to tell me because it was top secret and if I knew it could screw my results. He made me promise not to tell anyone. He said they needed more participants, so more data could be collected and help save lives. I said I wanted to go through to the next round of the trial. He told me it was a bit more risky because they had to run a program—'

'While you were cybernating?'

'Yeah. I didn't care at that point, I thought if Minty could do it then so could I, and I wanted the creds so we'd all be happy again.'

'So did you go to the same place? Was it the same doctor?'

'Yeah, every time.'

'Do you have the Grid address?'

'No, the Ranger always took me via a palm-port link.'

'And what did the doctor tell you this time?'

'Just that they were very grateful of my participation. All I had to do was allow her access to my stack and stay linked up by the palm-port. She said she'd run the program and do some tests afterwards. Well, she ran the program and I'm not sure what was going on, I was being whizzed from one memory to another, like all the things I'd ever seen or heard were replaying all at once. I was about to scream but then everything went blank and the next thing I know the medics are all up in my face.'

'What else can you remember about the Ranger? Any little detail, did he tell you where he lived or worked or anything?'

Aadya shook her head and shrugged. 'That's all I've got, sorry.'

'Okay, you've been really helpful. If you remember anything, anything at all, even if you think it's a little thing, then you let me know, okay?'

'Sure.'

'Can I quickly copy your stack data? Will that be okay?'

'Do I have much choice?'

Brogan shook his head and hooked up the drive scanner. He drummed his fingers on the windowsill while he waited. The guys were still outside, tidying up. A little bleep was the loudest thing in the room. Brogan stuffed the drive back into his pocket. 'Thanks for your help. I am sorry about your friend.' Brogan felt the heaviness of loss. The sadness in her eyes reflected his own.

He headed back out onto the street and stared at the empty spot where Clarkson's body had left its mark. Her blood, thick and claggy, stained the pavement. *Fuck.* He hailed a cab, not sure where to go. *The mole must have been at work. But they didn't know I was here. Kane? That scumbag bastard.* HQ is compromised. *How does someone send a message from the grave – unless it was a setup. This Ranger is the key, but how to find him… And this Eric. I need to find that guy.*

Chapter 23

A terra-cab rolled up beside him and he ducked in.

'Good afternoon, detective. Please state your destination?'

Brogan sat for a moment, trying to pinpoint a safe location. 'Take me back to the city centre. Go the long way around.' *I need time to think.*

'Route confirmed.'

Brogan patted the flash drive in his pocket. He needed to find out what was on it – and interpret it. *What the heck did Catsanga mean, 'whizzed from pillar to post'? How's that possible?* Chewing his lip, he stared out the window. The blue streaks flashed by above him. *Kane must be working with someone, he could never pull off an aero-cab hack. And Eric, what the fuck.* Brogan rubbed his mouth, his stubble pricked at his skin. When was the last time he'd shaved? *Tempest. When I saw Tempest.*

'Approaching the city centre, detective.'

'Change of plan. Take me to Novanoid.'

'Certainly. Estimated journey time twenty-five minutes.'

They were on the edge of the city when the cab jolted to a stop and the electrics went dead.

'Computer?' Brogan leaned forward and stabbed a finger at the system restart button. Nothing. *What? Not again.* A flash of movement caught his eye from across the street. *No one there, but…* He was sure he'd seen something. He felt his brow crease. The street was pretty empty. That's when it started. The tingly, churning feeling deep in his gut, the hair on the back of his neck prickled. *Time to move out.*

He punched the emergency exit button and the doors hissed open. He glanced quickly skyward. *No drones.* Four bulky Metal Mickeys rounded the corner, their stares locked onto Brogan. He launched himself out of the cab, heading down the street and away from the mob. The guys started laughing but the sound wasn't getting further away. They were coming for him.

Two more guys rounded a corner in front of him, penning him in. Brogan pulled up automatically and reached for his gun. It wasn't there. *Fuck.* Kane had made him hand it in. *Six Mickeys against one of me.* He sucked in air through his teeth, and scanned the old offices lining the street. His options were limited. Up ahead was a small side road. He needed an advantage, a weapon, anything.

He bolted towards the gap between the buildings. The two guys clocked his plan and legged it to intercept. Maybe he got lucky, maybe they had old legs, cheap tech, and they weren't as fast as Brogan, but he made it to the side road first.

The tall buildings to either side damped the daylight. A chain-link fence glistened in a chink of sunlight at the end of the road. A dead end. Brogan glanced back. The mob had congregated. *Dickhead.*

He passed a row of windows that then became a solid brick wall with a metal door at the end. A padlock dangled pretentiously. Brogan's gazed darted around, looking for hope. The echoes of his pursuers bounced off the buildings. *I could scale that fence...* Then he saw it. The back of the building opened out onto a car park. The delivery entrance had a roller-shutter door and it was open. Not wide open, but enough to roll under. *Thank fuck for squatters.*

The last few strides to the door seemed to take forever. He skidded to a stop, dropped to the floor and rolled underneath. A spike of pain from his ribs made him clamp his jaw and suck it up. He couldn't afford to stop now.

The place was dark and smelt of piss. He scrambled to his feet, his lungs aching for more oxygen. He tried to push the shutter doors down and they gave a squeal of resentment. It was two inches off the bottom when it jammed. *It'll have to do.*

Brogan flicked on the little LED light on his comms-watch. The darkness sucked it up like a black hole. He caught a glimpse of a couple of rows of tall industrial shelving. *Cover.* He headed that way as he heard a shout: 'He came round 'ere, so where's 'e gone?'

He edged his way to the back of the warehouse, keeping half an eye out for an exit and the other half for a weapon. Empty shelves, bits of discarded paper and boxes were all that caught his eye.

The squeal of the roller-shutter doors made him hunch his shoulders and clench his teeth. *They're in.* He spotted a door with the frame hanging off where it had been smashed open. He pulled at a spike of wood. With a twist and a yank, a broken piece of the doorframe came off in his hand. *Yes.* He gripped the wood, his chest broadened. *Right, you fuckers.*

A gruff voice echoed in the darkness. 'Split up. He can't have got far. Wingnut, see if you can't get the power on.'

'Righto, chief.'

Brogan headed down the dim corridor. Dust and the unmistakable putrid smell of death clogged his nostrils and scratched at his throat. He ducked through a doorway on his right. Given that most people are right-handed, he planned to attack from the right and disable their strong side. The stench seemed to amplify, then a crunch underfoot made Brogan jump back. He pointed his little torch downwards. A rotting corpse was slumped against the wall and he'd trodden on its hand. He ditched that plan and dashed further into the bowels of the building.

He scoped out another room to his left. Not ideal, too much light. A stairwell – he was in the core of the building now. All the ground-floor windows had bars on them. No escape there. The front doors that led out to the main street were boarded up. No escape there either. *Up. Buy some time.* The door to the stairwell creaked on it hinges. Brogan cursed the age of the place.

The little light on his watch offered enough illumination to let him see the cracked lino on the stair treads. He got to the half-landing. The fluorescent lights winked into life. Brogan squeezed his eyes shut, then blinked. *Shit.* Darkness was his second weapon. Stopping at the first floor would be obvious, so Brogan dashed up to the second. The sound of a creaking door echoed up the stairwell. He froze.

'Ha. The idiot don't know he's left footprints in the dust.'

'Shut up, ya flamin' moron.'

Brogan looked down. *Carpet.* He shuffled his feet a little to get rid of any dust. He pushed slightly on the door to the corridor, bracing himself for its hinges to sound his presence. They didn't, so he slid through and breathed a sigh of relief. He found himself at a T-junction of corridors. Left or right was the short option. If there were two guys they'd probably split up, take the short corridors by themselves then re-join and check the long corridor together. Two against one might be doable, but one on one would be better.

Brogan went right and slunk into an office second from the end. He was faced with the side of a large metal store cupboard, and another next to that. Anyone checking the room would have to come right in, and would probably expect an ambush from behind the door. The second filing cupboard provided some cover.

He checked out the window. *Balls, no fire escape.* He managed to open the window wide enough to make it look like someone had escaped. Then he scuffed up the dust on the sill. An old office chair caught his eye, so he grabbed it and put it by the window. *This might just work.*

Brogan took up position in the nook by the cupboard, his back military straight and flat against the wall. The wood gripped in both hands, raised and ready in front of him. Grey electrical cable, from an old light fitting, dangled like a crooked tree branch in the centre of the room. He closed his eyes, listened to the rush of air into his lungs, and forced his body to take slow and steady breaths.

'Here fishy, fishy, fishy, c'mon. I've got some juicy maggots for you. Five shiny metal ones, in fact.'

Brogan heard the sound of a door being smashed open, then a moment of silence. Time hung in the air like he was in an old photograph.

A knocking sound vibrated through the thin walls and travelled towards him. It wasn't the hollow sound of knuckles; it was thicker, harder, dense. *So the guy's got metalwork for a right hand.*

The knocks crept closer to the door. Then paused. Brogan waited.

The door flung open, clattered against the wall, then sprang back. Another pause.

Then a quiet swish as the door brushed the carpet. A guy rushed in and headed straight for the window. The guy was a good four inches taller than Brogan, a tight blue T-shirt hugging his finely honed torso. He was halfway across the room when Brogan launched himself off the wall. He swung the wood back and threw everything he had into whacking the joint between man and metal. The weak spot. The most painful spot. The spot most likely to disable the mechanics.

The wood cracked against the guy's arm as he turned, connecting below his shoulder, and split in half. The guy staggered but kept his feet. His right arm fizzed then dangled limply. Brogan's momentum took him towards the chair, but he pivoted and raised the remaining bit of wood like a baseball bat. That's when a glint of metal flashed in front of him. *Fuck.* The guy's left hand was metal too. The punch came as a hammer blow to the side of his head.

Brogan's head spun, his body followed, and he found

himself on all fours. He blinked and shook the daze from his mind. His fingers scrambled blindly for the splinter of wood that wasn't there. A boot to the stomach knocked the wind out of him and he keeled over, gasping for breath.

As Brogan dragged himself away on the floor, the Metal Mickey followed, grinning. It took Brogan a fraction of a second to realise he'd moved himself into a corner. The metal man's smile unzipped further, revealing a few metal teeth. He raised his arm, ready to strike. Brogan, sapped of strength, turned his head away from the direction of the blow and braced himself.

A crack of bright white light pierced through his closed eyelids. Pulling his legs in, Brogan risked opening his eyes. The metal man was toast. Electricity charged through the dangling cable, lighting the guy up like a firework, sparks snapping and crackling from his metal appendages.

It seemed like it was over in a second, but the image would burn forever in his mind. Smoke and the smell of burnt flesh wafted into Brogan's awareness as his opponent crumpled to the ground.

Certain that the guy wasn't getting up again in a hurry, Brogan slumped against the wall. The dregs of adrenaline drained from his system. He'd taken a beating, again. Ribs aching, ear bleeding, every breath a painful reminder of life. He closed his eyes and let the fuzziness take him.

Chapter 24

'GET UP!... GET UP!... DAD, GET UP!' The fuzziness in Brogan's mind gave way to Mikey's voice. It couldn't be him, though, he was dead. The voice shouted again. 'GET UP, MOVE NOW, GO!' Still Brogan didn't move.

'CORPORAL BROGAN, STAND TO ATTENTION!' Brogan's body responded to a command it had heard countless times before, his mind still clambering through a swamp of disorientation.

'CORPORAL, EVACUATE IMMEDIATELY. TURN LEFT DOWN THE CORRIDOR, THEN RIGHT AND TAKE THE STAIRS DOWN ONE FLOOR. GO THROUGH THE DOOR ON THE RIGHT AND WAIT IN THERE. GO NOW!' The order had ignited some deep reptilian part of Brogan's brain, the bit that housed his military training and the autopilot switch. His feet followed the command and carried him down the corridor, one hand stemming the flow of blood from his ear, the other outstretched and steadying him against the wall.

Heading down the corridor, he passed what looked like disused office space. He heard shouting and heavy footsteps, his mind struggling to fit the jigsaw pieces of the moment together. He wasn't sure if he was being led into another trap, but there wasn't much of an alternative. Metal Mickeys were motherless bastards. Besides, he'd had an order and he preferred to be moving than to wait around for another beating.

He reached the end of the corridor and headed right and down the stairs. Stumbling down them, only just remaining upright. He stopped dead. Voices echoed around him but he couldn't work out if they were floating upwards or came from above him.

Controlling his shallow breathing, since deeper breaths caused pain, he sidled around the quarter-landing and carried on down the stairs. At the first floor there were two doors. With his back against the door, he leant on one. It moved with little resistance, and peeking around the door he stumbled in. The door closed behind him and there was an audible click as the lock engaged.

Brogan's heart sank as he took in his surroundings. There were a few odd desks, some old bits of computers strewn about, and graffiti on the walls. He heard voices out in the stairwell and froze. *I won't survive another beating.*

'He's in 'ere somewhere, check that door…' A loud metallic *clang* rang through the floor. Brogan was not breathing, not moving, not blinking, as though the act of it would be as loud as a jackhammer and give him away.

'Damn it, locked. 'E was headin' this way.'

'Maybe he went up? Come on, let's go, I wanna try me new knuckles out.'

Brogan listened as heavy feet thudded away. He sighed like a deflated balloon. He'd barely survived a beating from one Metal Mickey, but fending off two while injured was a big ask. He looked around. He had expected, or at least hoped for, an emergency exit or a sky-trax platform. He needed the relative safety of the street. If it was help he'd had, it wasn't very good help. If it was a trap, why had the Metal Mickeys been locked out? This was an empty room, there wasn't much here. What was he supposed to do now? Where did those orders come from? *Did I imagine it?*

He took a few steps into the room. It was dark, only a few chinks of light managed to squeeze through the gaps in the boarded-up windows. Slowly, his eyes adjusted to the dim light. A small bleeping noise made it through his good ear, rode over the waves of gushing blood and registered its presence.

Listening carefully, he followed it towards a soft glow coming from a door in the corner of the room. In no rush for another pounding, he decided to investigate it. He needed to know where the orders had come from. Tentatively, he stepped towards the door, scanning the room for anything that resembled a weapon. There wasn't much except a pile of paper, and no one had ever heard of death by paper cuts. He neared the door and stood with his back against the wall. Steeling himself, he took as deep a breath as his ribs would allow. He had considered bursting in like a firework because he always liked the element of surprise, but the noise might draw attention to his location so he opted for a quick shove and wait. He managed a quick glance inside the room and didn't see anyone. He hoped that if anyone was in there, they'd take the bait and pop their head out. Clasping his hands together and raising them above his head, he waited. No one came. No sounds other than the gentle bleep that had drawn him there.

He pushed the door right back on its hinges. If there was someone hiding behind it they would push back, but there was no resistance. Satisfied, Brogan moved into the dingy room. It looked like a small office area, but more recently it looked like a squatter had used it. Shoved against one wall, a shitty mattress and bedding, discarded food cans and a bag of God-knows-what lay abandoned. A desk in the corner appeared relatively tidy in comparison. Brogan could see a whitish glow emitting from a plastic box on the desk. He strode over to it.

He'd only seen photos of vintage monitors; they'd been phased out before he even went to school. Someone had been taking care of this one, though, a relic of early technology complete with a bulky box next to it, presumably the CPU.

He lowered himself into a wobbly office chair and studied it. The monitor glowed blue-white, wires left the back of it and led to a vintage keyboard, hard plastic keys with faded letters. *I need to add this to my collection.*

Brogan picked up the keyboard almost reverentially and turned it over in his hands. These were relics from the days when people had to drive their own cars and died of curable diseases. As Brogan stared, the monitor blinked a message: *We haven't got long…*

What the hell? Brogan blinked back at the screen, put the keyboard down, glanced at the keyboard then back at the screen. Awkwardly, he began to type. He was used to compressed one-handed boards with predictive sentencing. This thing was awkward and slow.

Who's we? he typed.

Time for that later. Right now, you have to trust me. I'm your best chance of getting out of here alive, blinked the screen.

Trust you? I'm not trusting you until I know who or what you are. Brogan spat the words from his fingers.

Right now, there are eight Metal Mickeys in the building, there'll be more on their way. I stopped one upstairs and two more on the landing. They want blood. Either trust me or die.

Brogan stared at the screen for a few moments. There was no arguing with that, he was very definitely in the shit here. The metal-heads were intent on killing him, you didn't need many brain cells to work that out. He wasn't particularly in the mood for dying today, so given the options he typed his reply.

Okay, I'm in.

Good. There's an old server room next door. I need you to go and switch it on.

Why? typed Brogan.

It controls the elevators. When you've done that, go down one flight and through the left door.

Brogan sighed. His body ached and his blood sugar levels were in his boots. He gripped the desk, hauled himself to standing and headed out the door. He peered around in case a Metal Mickey had slipped in. They hadn't. He headed back to the door that led to the stairwell. Leaning against it he listened, trying to even out his breathing and steady his heart rate. It sounded clear. The lock unclicked as he reached to pull the door open a crack. He peeked out onto the landing and edged out, looking up and down the stairwell. He made a quick dash for the other door. Pushing it open, he stumbled and landed heavily on the floor, knocking an old chair that clanged like a church bell. Gathering himself and cursing, he closed the door and took in his new surroundings.

This place looked like a disused parts warehouse, shelving units and boxes abandoned and empty. Brogan made his way over to the door at the far end. Sure enough, it was a server room. A plethora of dusty cables snaked their way in and out of boards and sockets. His eyes were wide, taking in the sight, trying to locate his target: the 'on' switch.

When his eyes fell on a big lever that looked like a door handle he took a gamble and flicked it up. He waited. Nothing.

Trying to keep panic at bay, his eyes searched further and found a thick cable tucked into the cornice. He followed it to a metal box. A handy upturned bucket served as a step and he reached up, grimacing against the pain in his ribs. The box turned out to be a fuse box and immediately he flicked the master switch.

In an instant the room was full of electrical life, an illuminated pond of LED eyes winking at him. Satisfied, he stepped down and made his way out.

He was crossing the room when the sound of voices stopped him. His stumble must have alerted the Mickeys. He dashed into the darkness behind some shelving as the door began to open. Brogan's heart rate leapt as adrenaline coursed once again. He forced the images of being turned into minced meat to the back of his mind.

'Here pussy, pussy…' the mocking voice carried across the silence, 'now come on, we know you're in 'ere…' The voice sounded like it was heading towards Brogan. There was only one set of footsteps, which meant the other dude was either standing still or creeping about. The latter would leave the exit clear for escape, while the former would lead to instant death.

A noise behind him caused his head to whip around towards the back of the room, his eyes scanning wildly for signs of movement, but his view was obstructed by the shelving units and the dim light. He forced his body to bended knee, a position so familiar to him during the war, but it felt alien without a weapon in his hands. That, and at least five other guys who'd have his back.

Although he was only outnumbered two to one, it was more like six to one when facing a Metal Mickey, and that's not including the others lurking in the building. Those were odds he didn't like.

He stayed low, biding his time, trying to think. Whoever or whatever he'd been communicating with on the damned computer certainly didn't appear to be helping him right now. He felt a pang of stupidity and a bigger pang of anger for believing it. He'd wasted time turning on the server when he could have been away on his toes.

Brogan crept to what felt like the centre of the room, between two rows of shelving, his body obscured by a few boxes. He glimpsed the giant pacing the room, trying to wheedle him out. The other guy, he was fairly sure, was blocking the exit.

Still searching for ideas, Brogan groped inside a box next to him. It was empty. Adjusting his footing, he reached into another box, hoping that it contained at the least a stun-gun or a laser-blade. Hope turned into disappointment when he found that box empty too. *One more box.* He reached in and jumped as though stung by a bee. Flesh. There was something in there that felt like flesh. Carefully reaching back in, his desperation for a weapon overwhelmed his trepidation, hoping for lady luck's favour. All he could do was grin. Lady luck was absolutely taking the piss as he pulled out a double-ended dildo.

He almost laughed at the thought of defending himself against a score of Metal Mickeys by flailing around a sex toy like a floppy light-sabre. He took the dildo anyway. As he felt its eye-watering girth and weight, he thought he might be able to at least whack them around the head and make a run for the door.

It was a plan. His only advantage was the element of surprise. With time against him, he inched his way to a few rows nearer the door. He waited, watching the big guy in the glow of light from the doorway. He only had one shot. If he cocked it up, he'd be fucked.

Still crouching, he adjusted his grip on the dildo, took a deep breath and launched himself at the back of the man's head. The dildo swung like lead and connected with its target. He went down, out for the count. Dropping the dildo, Brogan ran full-pelt at the door. He was readying to push it when the other Metal Mickey swung it open.

Brogan had no choice, he'd committed. He rugby

tackled the guy, the metal embrace squeezing the air from his lungs as he pushed forward towards the stairs. The big guy staggered backwards. Brogan kept pushing against the wall of man. Suddenly the resistance relented, the floor disappeared, and the pair fell down the stairs.

Metal hands grabbed and flailed about. Brogan clung to him.

The floor came quickly. The man's skull cracked on the concrete. Brogan lifted himself as a pool of blood seeped across the stairwell. The guy's glassy-eyed, dilated stare looked straight through Brogan. *Definitely dead.* His life-extinct alert would give away their location. Brogan had to move.

He rounded the quarter-landing, then flinched as the whole building seemed to come alive. Lights flashed, doors opened and closed, the sprinklers came on, sirens howled. Loud bangs and pops of light were followed by the sound of shattering glass. Brogan glanced up the stairwell and made eye contact with another Metal Mickey, who shouted something inaudible at him. He glanced down and saw the shadows of more men running up towards him.

On the landing he pounced through the left door.

A long corridor confronted him, seeming to go on for miles – it was like being in a nightmare. All the doors were on the left. He staggered his way forwards, checking a few doors. Offices mainly.

He approached a junction in the corridor. His gut told him to go straight. He glanced back but there was no one in the corridor, only the sound of banging.

All the lights went off. *Shit.*

Then the lights in the left corridor began to flash like

strobes. Blinking in the light, he couldn't ignore the sense that he was being beckoned that way. The electric Mexican wave continued, pulling Brogan along. Another *clang* echoed and Brogan picked up his pace. As he followed the lights, he checked over his shoulder. The lights behind him weren't coming back on, encouraging him to push onwards.

At the end he found another stairwell. He could hear voices and the ominous clunking of another Metal Mickey. He was about to head for the stairwell when a pinging sound made him swing round. The lift doors *swooshed* open and a crackly electronic voice said, 'ABOUT TIME. GET IN.'

Brogan dashed inside. He threw himself against the back wall of the elevator and held on. Expecting the lift to go down, his heart sank as he felt it going upwards. *The sky-trax platform.* What had he done, why was he trusting an unknown quantity? He knew why, though. He was desperate, and desperate men do desperate things.

As the lift slowed to the twelfth floor, Brogan pressed himself to one side, out of direct firing line. He needn't have worried. There was no one there. Well, no one alive anyway. Four of the mob lay motionless along the corridor. The smell of burning flesh filled his nostrils and the crunch of shattered glass filled his ears as he stepped over them.

A sign saying '*Sky-Trax*' flashed at the end of the corridor. Brogan wasted no time in heading towards it. The fresh air was a welcome change from burnt flesh and dust.

As Brogan stepped out onto the bay, an aero-cab landed and he hesitated. *More Metal Mickeys?*

The gull-winged cab door opened. Empty. The last time he'd got into one of these he had almost died. More banging released his body and he dived in, looking back, expecting to see the mob tailing him. But they hadn't caught up yet.

The aero-cab took off and he sagged into the seat. Drained of energy and badly bruised, he felt only slightly safer.

Chapter 25

After a few moments, Brogan realised he hadn't given the cab any instructions, yet it was flying out into the traffic stream, dodging some of the older vehicles and overtaking others. He sensed his ordeal was not yet over, and he'd still not come to terms with his last experience in an aero-cab. If he didn't hate them before, he did now. This one seemed to have a mind of its own, flitting between the upper and lower traffic streams.

'State your destination,' Brogan ordered the cab. No reply. That shouldn't be possible, cabs were programmed to respond to this question. He said it again, and this time the cab replied.

'Hang on, will you, I'm concentrating. I'm scrambling the landing platform codes so no one else can land. Your blood sugar is low, drink this.' The cab released the latest nootropic concoction shake from the onboard comfort station. Brogan took it, annoyed that the cab was right but not sure how it knew. His body tingled with gratitude as he gulped down the drink. He could have done with ten more of those. As his blood sugar rose, the old mental engine began to fire back into life.

'Right, I want to know who you are, why you're helping me and where the bloody hell you're taking me?'

'I'll answer your questions once we're safe.'

'You'll answer me now, thanks. We're safe in the traffic stream, they won't try anything in full view.'

The cab seemed to consider this for a moment.

'Call me Milestone. I'm heading to Peacekeeper HQ.'

'No.' Brogan made himself jump. 'HQ is compromised.'

'Where then?'

Brogan was silent while his addled brain tried to hatch a plan.

'You'd better think fast. We're being followed.'

Brogan stared out the back window of the cab. They were in the mid-level traffic stream, nothing appeared particularly out of place. He glanced to the stream below. 'Grey Volat, a hundred metres back?'

'More like eighty-four metres, but yeah, that's the one.'

'Shit, are you sure?'

'Yeah, watch.' The cab accelerated and moved up to the third-level traffic stream. The grey Volat moved up a layer and sped up too. 'I can try and lose 'em?'

'Oh Christ, no. That's all I need, another joyride in the sky. No, stick it out a bit. Honestly, they won't try anything while we're in the stream.'

'Well, we can't wait forever, fuel cell's running low.'

'What? Didn't you check before you jacked the cab?' Brogan turned to face the front as if the cab had an actual driver.

'Well, there wasn't much time to, I dunno, save your skin.'

'Fair point, well put.' Brogan rubbed the side of his head. His ear had swollen where it had connected with the metal fist. 'We need to buy some time to think.'

'I've got an idea. There's the old Vortrax test tunnels, out by Cambourne. It's been abandoned for ages. We could lose them in there. You can get out and hide in the tunnel while I draw them off. Then I'll jack another cab and pick you up when the coast is clear?'

'Hmm. Will the juice last that long?' Brogan looked out the window. *It's a long way down.*

'Just about.'

'Just about? Would we make it to the tunnels or not?' Brogan had an urge to put his seat belt on.

'Well, we'll definitely make it to one end of the tunnels.'

'That's reassuring.' Brogan tugged on the seat belt.

'Alright, Captain Chaos, let's hear your plan then?'

How did he know my nickname? Brogan's brow furrowed. *A coincidence. Gotta be.* Several scenarios ran through his mind. None of them ended well. 'Fine,' he sighed.

The cab veered off to the west. Brogan braced himself against the sudden change in direction and the tingling sensation in his gut. A glance out the back window confirmed they were still being tailed.

'Take your comms-watch off.'

'What?' Brogan stared down at his watch.

'That's how they're tracking you, via the geo-locator. Take it off and leave it in the cab.'

'Do you know how much these things cost?'

'Yeah, but it'll be no good to you if you're dead, will it?'

'Jeez. Fine.' Brogan unclasped the watch. It was like parting with a limb. He'd worn it for so long that the skin was pale underneath. It was the same when he'd taken his wedding ring off.

'Good. We're almost at the tunnels. Look at the TV screen.' Milestone pulled up the tunnel schematics. A curved X shape appeared. It reminded Brogan of the kind you see in algebra.

'There's a porthole on each leg of the tunnel, about halfway down, before the tunnels intersect. We'll enter by this tunnel.' The bottom left arm of the tunnel pulsed red on the screen. 'There's the access porthole. It's an airlock, so you'll have to unscrew it quickly, and get inside before those guys catch up with you.'

'How long have I got?'

'Fifteen, twenty seconds max.'

'You make it sound so easy.'

The car dropped altitude.

'Are we there?'

'Nearly. Had to drop lower because, well, the fuel cell's dryin' up.'

Brogan peered out the window. They still looked pretty high up to him. 'So, you drop me off, then what? I walk home?'

'No. Climb the shaft. I'll see you in there.'

'So you're in the tunnel already?'

'No. If I can't get another cab to you, I'll meet you there.'

'How do we know these tunnels aren't blocked?'

'We don't. Not for sure. They were decommissioned in the thirties. I need to preserve the power. I'll let you know when it's time to jump.'

ANGELA ARCHER

'Oh great, this plan is getting shittier by the second. We might not make it to the tunnels, which may or may not be blocked. And then I have to jump? No. No way. I'm not jumpin', you're crazy.'

'Look, this ain't no bus ride. I can't stop to let you off, granddad.'

For a moment, Brogan swallowed down the lump in his throat that was telling him he'd never be a granddad.

'I'll be able to slow down enough that you don't hurt yourself, but you gotta get up and get moving. Anyway, didn't they teach you how to land in a parachute? Think of it like that.'

'Yeah, I am thinking of it like that, and it fuckin' hurts if you get it wrong.'

'So don't get it wrong then.'

Brogan closed his eyes for a moment. *This day needs to be over.* He took out his e-cig, rolled it in his fingers. *Fuck it, useless thing anyway.* He slipped it back into his pocket.

The cab lowered further then dropped down over a chain-link fence. 'Tunnel entrance looks clear.'

'Oh joy.' He might have preferred smashing into a wall at high speed than what he was about to do.

Then everything turned black as they entered the tunnel. The cab's headlights didn't come on and pretty soon the light from the entrance was swallowed up by the darkness. Brogan sensed his mysterious driver speed up the aero-cab. Behind him a little dot appeared in the middle of the tunnel mouth. The idiots had followed them in. Their headlights were on full beam. *They're gonna see me jump.*

As the tunnel curved, the headlights of the trailing car disappeared. The cab slowed suddenly, jerking Brogan

216

forward. He put his hand on the dash panel to brace himself.

'I'll get as low as I can. Get ready.' The cab's door hissed open. The blast of air ruffled Brogan's hair. His mouth went dry. *Shit. What am I doing?* He unbuckled his seat belt and edged to the door.

'You've only got about a three-foot drop. I'll count you down, jump on my mark. The porthole will be a yard or so ahead, on your right. Right?'

'Right.' Brogan gulped. It wasn't the first time he'd jumped from a moving vehicle, but it wasn't an experience he'd been hoping to repeat.

The cab tilted, and Brogan braced himself against the doorframe. *Feet first, knees bend, roll.* He visualised his landing.

'Three... Two... One... Jump.' The cab dipped a little as if to help him out, and Brogan leapt. Eyes scrunched closed, he could see bugger all.

His boots hit the concrete hard and slid on the curved surface of the tunnel, so instead of absorbing the impact the momentum dragged him and slammed his shoulder into the wall. He gritted his teeth and sucked up the pain as his body rolled to a stop. His body was overloaded with pain but the order in his mind was clear. *Get to the porthole.*

Scrambling to his feet, squinting in the pitch black, he kept his right hand on the tunnel wall, in part for balance and in part to feel for the door. A glow came from behind him. *The Metal Mickeys.* They'd done him a favour, though. The porthole door was only few steps away. He lunged at it, grabbing the handle to stop himself slipping but slid anyway. The light was getting brighter.

The lock was like a small steering wheel, it squeaked as he twisted it. Heavy bolts slunk out the way. The headlights were getting brighter. *They're gonna see me...* He pulled on the wheel, a little suck of air released and the little round door opened. A dim green light spilled out of a small chamber only big enough for two men, if that. He hauled himself in, pulled the door shut, locked it again and then waited.

Chapter 26

Brogan's eyes adjusted to the dim green light in the chamber. *I thought this place was decommissioned. Why's there juice?* He pulled in a deep breath and became more aware of the pain in his shoulder. He felt heavy.

Something hard smashed into his head from above. He yelled and ducked, then a second blow came and he raised his hands protectively. Another blow came and he dodged to the side. Managing to glance up, he saw the sole of a trainer as it scraped against his face.

He grabbed the foot with one hand, his other hand grabbed the ankle. He pulled, then twisted it, hard.

An agonised groan from above turned into a yell. 'Stop it, stop, you're hurting me.'

Brogan yanked on the streaky piece of piss like it was an old church bell. It tumbled down. He caught it and swung his arm around its neck, and pressed his weight against it.

Brogan's voice was clipped and low like distant thunder.

'What the fuck is your game, tall boy?' Brogan was almost on his tiptoes. The kid looked about twelve.

'You ain't s'pose ta be 'ere.' The kid gasped and pawed at Brogan's arm.

'You know you've assaulted an officer of the law?'

'O-oh, shit. Sorry, sorry, I-I was just doing my job.'

'Job? What job?'

The kid gulped. Brogan gave his bicep a squeeze. The kid squirmed.

'I-I'm on watch.' He nodded upwards. Brogan's gaze followed the ladder up to the top of the shaft. Green light filtered down.

'Who's up there? How many?' He made sure to breathe on the kid's neck. The kid shifted his weight.

'There's five of us but four are hooked up, they're all cybernating.'

Brogan stood for a moment. The kid wasn't a threat. He released him but gave him a shove towards the ladder. 'You fucking try anything like that again and I'll see you're fed through a tube for the rest of your life. Understood?'

The kid nodded.

'Right. Up you go.' If the thugs had spotted him, his only advantage was up. He was about to climb when an explosion echoed through the tunnel. *Aero-cab's gone, then.*

'Shit. What was that?' The kid looked down at Brogan.

'None of your business. Now, up.'

The climb to the top seemed relentless. Brogan focused on one rung at a time. His left shoulder was properly fucked, his ribs felt like he was being stabbed in the lung and his ear was ringing like he had flat-lined. As the green light above grew stronger, Brogan grew weaker. When he looked up again the kid had disappeared. He was at the top already.

The ladder went through a hatch and the space opened out into a slightly larger chamber than the one below. Stepping out onto the platform, Brogan walked round to a metal door. The source of the green light came from a sign above the door that glowed with the words '*Zone 1*'. The doors themselves had been defaced with graffiti. The most prominent was a menacing blue skull, its eyes heavily shaped like an infinity loop.

The kid reached for the door. Brogan grabbed him. 'You'd better be being straight with me, kid.'

The boy nodded like his head was going to fall off. 'I-I am. They're under, they won't even blink. I promise.'

Brogan let go of the kid's arm and watched him press his palm against the security panel. A small bleep followed by a click, and the kid pushed the door open.

The same dim green light filled the next room. Brogan stepped inside. Five pods formed a semi-circle on one side, only one was unoccupied. Their bodies seemed motionless, only the slight rise and fall of their chests gave any clue that life remained. They were all hooked up to high-tech gear. One had a Plexus Pro-G, like Mikey's.

Brogan's gaze arced around the room, following a bundle of cables through to another door at the end. A row of cupboards and a desk, piled high with food wrappers, cans and the odd cable, lined the opposite wall.

'What's through there?'

'That's the livin' area. We take it in turns to look after the place, sort supplies, and well…' He glanced down at a tube on the floor.

'You keep the shit tubes from blocking up?'

'We prefer to call it flow-metric management.' He puffed out his pigeon chest.

Brogan smirked, shook his head and strode over to the other door. 'Is there another way out through here?'

'Nah, it's the livin' area, the toilet and an air shaft that you'd have to be a cat to get up.'

Brogan shoved his nose through the door, winced at the smell of stale body odour, then shut it again, satisfied there was no one else lurking in the dark. 'Right, now it's time for questions, kid. What's your name?'

The kid chewed his lip.

Brogan raised his eyebrows.

'Telescope. They call me Telescope on account of my height, see.'

'I'm not calling you that. What's your real name?'

'We don't use our real names. It's against our code.' Telescope hugged himself.

'Give me strength. Do I look like I give a shit about your code? Just tell me your real name, then we can move on.'

The kid shifted, twisted his foot on the floor like he was putting out a cigarette. 'It's Kennington Kennedy, sir.'

Brogan laughed. 'Christ, I don't know which is worse.' He shook his head. 'Right, Ned it is then.'

Ned opened his mouth to speak but Brogan cut him off. 'Who are these four?' He jabbed a thumb toward the cybernaters.

'Well, I don't know their real names, but that's Moomins on the end, then there's Yard-dog – Yardy for short – Pastolla in the middle, and on this end is Bluewolf – Bluey.'

'How long have you been here?'

'Couple of years, I guess.' His little mouth twitched. 'C-can I ask you a question now?'

'Shoot.' Brogan stared at Ned. He'd be the type that spilled everything in the interrogation room.

'Have you come to arrest us?

'No, should I?' He tilted his head to one side.

'Well, I thought cos… er… well, how did you know we were here?' Ned looked down at his toes.

'I'm meeting someone.'

Ned looked like he'd swallowed a stone. 'But… w-who? No one knows we're here.'

'Guy called Milestone. You've got security cameras set up. Where are they? I want to see him coming, or if anyone else is coming for that matter.'

'Milestone?' Ned's neck stretched up. No wonder they called him Telescope.

'Yes, that's what I said. Cameras?' Brogan looked around.

Ned opened a cupboard door and a display screen came to life. The screen was split into three, each of them showing infrared images of the tunnel below. One faced the porthole door that Brogan had scrambled through earlier. The other two pointed in opposite directions into the tunnel void.

Ned dipped his head into Brogan's eyeline. 'Milestone? You sure that's what he said?'

'Yes. That's what he said.'

'*The* Milestone?' Ned scratched his head.

'Look, I don't know if he's *The* Milestone you're talking about, but that's what he said his name was.'

'But Milestone's dead.'

Brogan shrugged. 'Look, I don't know how many ways I can tell you. He said his name was Milestone and he sure knew about this place and said he would meet me here.'

'Holy hell.' Ned's face lit up. 'It must be 'im. I've gotta tell the guys.' Ned hopped around like a happy frog and rummaged in one of the cupboards. 'You won't be needin' the cameras, you'll need this.' Ned shoved a headset towards Brogan.

'Nope. I'm not puttin' one of those things on my head. The guy definitely said he'd meet me here.'

'The guy dusted like three weeks ago… And now you rock up 'ere…' Ned extended his arm a little further. Brogan took the headset and turned it over in his hands.

'It ain't gonna bite ya.' Ned swiped a load of rubbish off the desk to reveal a small stack underneath. He flicked a switch and it whirred into life. Then he reached under the desk and hauled out an old camping chair. 'Sit. I gotta tell the crew.' He grinned. 'Somethin's going down.' Two lanky strides and he was over at the empty pod, swiping at the console then sitting down. His headset was on in one slick motion.

Brogan twiddled with the straps on his headset. The last time he'd geared up shot through his mind. The pregnant Estrada. The epilepsy. The trial. He looked at the security camera. Nothing, not even a rat. He steeled himself. *This isn't like last time.*

He slipped the headset on.

His world went blank, again. Then a metallic fuzz swept across Brogan's mind like he'd licked a battery. His body shuddered away the sensation. The blue skull logo from the door appeared in the centre of the screen. Its eyes pulsated.

LOGGED IN AS GUEST… OPENING CHATROOM… PLEASE WAIT…

He didn't have to wait long. The black screen faded and he was suddenly standing in a room with a fireplace and a red armchair. It seemed familiar, somehow. He looked down at a pair of grey, badly rendered trousers and a white shirt. *The carpet, the curtains, the fireplace… Why is this familiar?*

Five avatars materialised in front of him.

'If he's going to turn up anywhere, it's gonna be here.' Ned's avatar was a pretty close replica of his real-life self, except that he was the same height as the rest of them.

'Sure thing, Telly. You'd better not be shittin' me, cos I was killin' it over in the… Hey, who's this guy?'

'Yeah, Ned, who's this guy?' Everyone stared at Brogan.

'Detective Brogan, this is Bluewolf. Bluey, this is Detective Brogan.' Ned was almost bowing to Bluey, whose avatar looked like Elvis with blue hair. Real vintage but with a crisp edge.

'Brogan, you say?'

'Yes, that's what he said.' *This kid's thicker than treacle. I'm wasting time here.* Brogan's jaw tightened.

'Why's he callin' ya Ned?'

'Because his real name's Kennington Kennedy.' Brogan grinned.

The whole room gasped. Everyone except Ned laughed.

'Milestone said you were a dickhead.' Ned seemed braver in the chatroom.

'C'mon, Ned, it suits you.' Pastolla's avatar was an anime-style sorceress with purple hair and matching eye colour.

'What do you mean Milestone said I was a dickhead? I've never met him.' Brogan glared at Ned's avatar and the chatroom fell silent. Ned's eyes widened, the prickle of tension transcended the electronics.

'Well, this is awkward.' Yardy rocked on his beefcake of an avatar's toes.

'What's awkward?' A new figure appeared, dressed in black combat gear.

'Hey, Milestone?' Bluey was the first one over. They fist-bumped and a little sign above their fists appeared saying '*BOOM*'.

'See, see, I told you.' Ned was almost singing.

'Where the heck 'ave ya bin? We thought you dusted, man.' Moomins moved in next, they high-fived and another sign appeared saying '*SLICK*'.

'Well, clearly not.' Milestone did a twirl then clenched his fist and thumped it twice against his chest. The others copied in reply and smiled. Brogan shook his head and hoped he'd never been such a twat at their age.

He'd seen enough. 'Right, well, now the niceties are over, let's start the explanations shall we? Like who are you, and why are you calling me a dickhead?'

'For that, right there. No "Oh thanks for savin' my life, *twice*, I really appreciate you getting me out of that shit." I mean, could you be any more ungrateful?' Milestone sat in the red wing-backed chair like it was a throne.

'I could try.'

'God, no wonder Mum left you.'

'What? What did you say?' Brogan couldn't really move his avatar, but he sure wanted to grab the kid.

'Oh my God, Dad. Look around you. Haven't you

worked it out? This is Grandma's old place and you know, it's me, Mikey, your son.'

'Don't you dare. My son is dead.'

'Oh, I'm dead to you now am I? Jeez, I knew you hated me, but hell.'

Brogan's jaw fell slack.

'No, Mikey, he's right. You are dead. We all went to your funeral. Well, we watched the stream anyway. You died while you were hooked up. Watch this…' Pastolla's avatar froze for a second then a vid-screen appeared where the living-room window was. She hit play. A drone camera had followed the funeral procession. It zoomed in on a coffin, then on Brogan's pale face as he stepped out of the hearse. His name flashed across the screen as the drone-cam followed them to the entrance of the crematorium.

'Enough. Stop it.' Brogan could hear his voice crack. *Not here. Not now.* He swallowed hard but the pain in his chest throbbed more than his shoulder.

'Dad? I—'

'Don't call me that. You're not my son. Somehow you've stolen Mikey's identity and—'

'No, Dad. No. I don't understand. I left a note for Mum and hooked myself up. I jacked in to a game, found a back door into Novanoid and poked around.'

'Wow, you got into Novanoid?' Yardy's avatar shone with amazement.

'Yeah, it was pretty neat. Bagged a P9 file and got the hell out.'

'P9? No way you did.' Pastolla sat on the floor next to Mikey, her big purple eyes all doey.

'Yes way.' Mikey puffed out his avatar's chest.

'Err, if you really are my son, what did your last note say to your mother?'

'It said something like, I'm sorry mum, I'm someone in the Grid, the analogue life isn't for me. Please don't be mad, love Mikey.' He looked pleased with himself.

'Ha, close, but Mikey would never say that, he'd say—'

'LM, like I said. Love Mikey.'

'Mikey?' Brogan struggled to find any other words. His gaze fixed on his son's avatar.

'Yes, Dad?'

'But you're dead. We buried you.' Brogan swallowed. His mouth had gone dry.

'Yeah, so you keep sayin', but I don't feel dead.' Mikey raised his hands like he was surrendering. 'And I don't look dead.'

'You do in real life, mate.' Bluey glanced at the frozen vid-screen.

'Milestone, what the hell did you do?'

'I dunno. I grabbed a look at the P9 file. The code was immense, like I'm tellin' ya, I've never seen anything like it. I added a slow-mo-algo so I could see what it did while I ran it. I was only trying to work out what was.'

Brogan struggled to keep up. His head was a mess. 'Would someone mind telling me what a P9 is?'

'They're highly classified, highly encrypted Novanoid files, security Protocol 9, P9s. They're the stuff of legend. You have to be an absolute genius to even have a snatch at one. Incredible.' Bluey's grin stretched from ear to ear.

'Jammy sod.' Ned stood shaking his head.

'So you hacked into Novanoid and stole classified information. Do you know how many laws you broke?'

'So what you gonna do, ground me? Oh, hang on, you've already done that.'

That was a punch to the gut. 'That's enough, Mikey.'

'So where've ya bin hiding?' Pastolla cut through the ice. 'It's been what, two, three weeks?' She swiped off the frozen vid-screen and the window returned to the view of the countryside.

'No way? Three days tops.' The rest of the crew shook their heads. 'What? I was in a weird place. I thought it was a software upgrade or something. I got your email, Dad, and tried to track you down. That's when I found you on a collision course with the tarmac in that dodgy aero-cab. Then it was weird, I felt like I was scattered in a thousand pieces, but the next minute I was back together again. Things made sense again. I cycled through that a couple of times at least, I think. Then you were in trouble, *again*. I managed to force a power surge and fried some Metal Mickeys.' Mikey's eyes widened, he glanced at his friends.

'Sweet.' Bluewolf was the first.

'Micheal Brogan, that was you? You electrocuted real people. You're not in some flamin' shoot-em-up game now. It's real life.' Brogan entered parent mode.

'I know, cool, right?' Mikey's friends were all nodding at him.

'No, not cool.' Brogan raised his eyebrows.

'C'mon, Dad, it was pretty cool? It did save your bacon.'

Brogan rolled his eyes. He was still alive, after all was said and done. 'Okay, a little bit. But only because you saved my hide.'

'Ah, an acknowledgement.' Mikey's avatar did a one-sided smile.

'That's all you're going to get.' *That's Mikey's smile. Can it really be him…* Brogan stared at his son's avatar. He looked like an army recruit fresh out of training.

'So what happens now? You gonna go in there and bust 'em?' Moomins boxed the digital air in front of him.

'Bust who? Novanoid?'

'Yeah.' Moomins nodded. He looked like a hopeful puppy.

'With what evidence?' Brogan's avatar jerked awkwardly. It was supposed to be a shrug.

'Me. I'm the evidence, and I've still got the P9 files.' Mikey stood and moved towards his dad.

'A file that you stole. Do I need to remind you that stealing is illegal? We can't risk the case being thrown out of court. So no, I'm not going to go in there and "bust 'em". We need watertight evidence.'

'So this Metanoia Code that's taking up a bazillion bytes of data storage is worthless?' Mikey put his hands on his hips.

'You didn't say the file was named Metanoia…'

'Yeah, that's it, that's the one. The Metanoia Code. I've never heard the word before.'

Brogan shook his head. 'Fuck. Those slimy pieces of shite.' *Mace was framed.* 'Right, we can't just go waltzin' in there and arrest them. We've got a file, sure, and we've got you, Mikey, but it was illegally obtained and it'll get chucked out. We need something more and we need it to connect the cyber deaths with Hausman's and Clarkson's murders.'

'And they tried to kill you, too. Twice.' Mikey paced the room. Brogan clocked the others all staring at Mikey.

Brogan felt a little taller, and a warm fuzzy feeling grew in his stomach.

'Could we leak the file?' Pastolla sat on the arm of the chair.

'We could, but we'd lose the advantage of surprise. What else is on the file?'

Mikey's avatar glitched, flicking off then on again. 'I've not had time to look. Moos, you've got an eye for detail, if I send it to you will you have a dig around?'

'Happily.' Moomins rubbed his hands together, then his avatar vanished.

Mikey stared out the window for a moment, then turned and grinned. 'Are you lot up for this?'

'Are we ever. Tell us what you need?' If Ned had a tail it would be wagging.

'Right, we need to get Pops here as much data as we can. We can't use the back door I found because some other dweeb found it and cashed in on the finder's creds.'

'What about the scavenger bot, the one you built to bring down Primedia?' Pastolla followed Mikey to the window.

'That's only good if we know where the root server is. Novanoid's massive, they've probably got data stored across the globe. Besides, it took months.' Mikey glanced over at his dad.

'Have we got anyone on the inside?' Yardy, the quiet one asked. His avatar for the day appeared as a fighter pilot.

'No, not any more, a security upgrade wheeled them all out.' Bluey rubbed his face.

'C'mon, think guys. There must be a way.'

They all glanced around at each other.

Brogan coughed. 'I have an idea.'

'What you gonna do, just walk in and ask 'em to come clean?' Ned sneered. His digital persona really was braver than reality.

'Well, maybe I'll call someone first.'

'Eh?' All four heads tilted to one side.

'Look, Clayton Mace—'

'Nope. No way. Don't even mention that name in here.' Bluey shoved his palm towards Brogan.

'Hear me out. Mace got in. Recently, too. I don't know the nuts 'n' guts of it, but he got in via a phone call to someone who was inside the building at the time.'

'He's a blinkin' murderer, Dad.'

'And an arse,' Ned chimed in.

'I'm pretty sure he's been telling the truth about Novanoid framing him.'

'So what, you sayin' we bring him in on this?' Mikey glared.

'I'm sayin' it's worth a shot. He knows the Novanoid system.'

The crew looked at each other. Pastolla shrugged, Bluewolf shook his head, Ned stood on the fence.

'Do you trust him?' Mikey glanced from his dad to his friends.

'Not much, there's something about him that niggles me. But we're low on options and low on time.'

'Okay, we'll ask him, but he's not comin' here.' Mikey looked to Bluey, who was still subtly shaking his head. 'We'll meet him at the Vault.'

Chapter 27

'How do I put a call in on this thing?' Brogan's avatar started moving its head as though it were watching a fly.

'You can't. As soon as you do, they'll know you didn't die in the cab. You need to stay dead for as long as possible.'

Brogan shook his head. 'Nah, they'll know by now. They'll have seen there's no body.'

'Then we've gotta move.' Mikey turned. 'Pastolla, you call Mace, pretend to be his mum or something. Get him to the Vault.'

'And how am I supposed to do that?' Pastolla's anime eyebrows rose above her head.

'He's been taken out of the network, but he has a legal right to family contact. Call the hospital, tell him I said if he's looking to be atoned, he's to follow you. He'll understand.'

'Right. Gotcha.' Pastolla's avatar blinked out.

'Now, how do I get to the Vault?' Brogan looked around.

'I'll come get you.' Mikey's avatar strode across the room and put his hand on Brogan's shoulder. A little sign appeared on the edge of Brogan's vision: <CONNECTION SUCCESSFUL>.

A moment later they were all standing in a black void. Their avatars remained the same, but the nothingness around them caused Brogan's stomach to churn. He was standing on nothing but sitting in an old camping chair at the same time. He shook his head to shake away the sensation.

'It'll pass.' Ned grinned.

Brogan's stomach was coming right when Pastolla appeared with Mace. They were all stood in a circle. *That was fast work.*

'Detective.' Mace's avatar was an exact replica of his real self. Prison-issue avatars didn't allow for mods.

'Mace.' Brogan eyed him. *Do I trust him?*

'Pastolla filled me in. Milestone, I've heard a lot about you. Sorry you're dead, but holy hell on a stick. They've sussed out how to upload consciousness. That's as trip as... How come it worked on you but not the others?'

'It didn't. I am dead, apparently.' Mikey glanced at his dad.

'No way, you'll live forever. You're a conscious machine. That's so cool.'

'Mace. We don't have time for this. We've got to stop them experimenting, who knows who or what they've got lined up next. We need a way into Novanoid's database.'

'Can't be done. Tried it. For two years, remember?'

'You got in with a phone call to Hausman?'

'Yeah, but they'll have closed that gap… But—'

'See. I knew he couldn't help us.' Bluewolf tutted.

'I was about to say that was from an incoming call. If we got in there and made an outgoing call… maybe, maybe I could tweak the program, maybe they won't have got around to changing the protocols for outgoing calls… I dunno.'

Mikey's avatar froze, then turned to static, twinkling like Christmas tree lights. Everyone stared.

'That's one unstable 'gram. Looks like he's defraggin' while tryin' to run at the same time. He's gonna burn doin' that.' Mace sucked in air and nodded sagely.

'Burn? Defraggin'? What are you talking about, Mace?' Brogan didn't take his eyes off his son.

'It looks like his system is trying to… let's see how to put this… essentially, he's unpacking his suitcase before he's got to his destination. He'll need a load of storage capacity to run smoothly. Without the storage, he'll keep doin' that.' Mace gestured to the frozen, twinkling Mikey. 'He'll end up with corrupted bits of data all over the shop.'

'Storage, you say? Like a big tech company?'

Mace nodded. 'Yup, something like that.'

'So you think you can horseshoe your way in and give Mikey a piggyback at the same time?' Bluey folded his arms.

'Not if he's like that.'

'Fine. Yardy, let's try an' work out how to boost him.' Bluey glanced from Yardy to Mikey.

'Cool. Then I just need someone on the inside to make the call.'

'I guess that'll be me, then?' Brogan looked to Mace, who was nodding. 'I'll need a comms-watch.'

'He can use mine.'

'Thanks, Ned.' *Maybe I'm being too hard on the lad.*

'Right. I'll need to work from the cabin. Flick me the addy for the watch, and I'll be in touch.'

Ned's avatar froze momentarily.

Mace nodded. 'Got it.'

'I thought your cabin was shut down?'

'Ah, always the detective. It was.' Mace's face stretched into a smile. 'I'll send the link, you boys and girls can join me there.' Mace vanished.

'Someone should stay here and keep an eye on Mikey.'

'I'll stay.' Pastolla didn't hesitate.

'Right. Keep us posted. Fingers crossed he's back with us soon.' Ned thumped his chest twice. Pastolla, Yardy and Bluey did the same. 'C'mon, take your headset off, detective. It'll log you out.'

'Hold on, Ned. Give him the modded visor. He won't get far without it,' Bluey said.

'You sure?'

'Yeah, give it to him. We've gotta get him there somehow if it's Milestone's only chance.'

'Okay.' Ned and Brogan logged out.

Brogan blinked in the green light of reality. He moved his muscles tentatively. He hadn't realised how tense he'd been. Ned stood immediately, the twig of youthfulness to Brogan's log of age. His body felt so wooden. Ned bounced over to the cupboard.

'Here's my watch.' He fiddled with it, then a blue-white light appeared on the screen as he passed it to Brogan.

'Now this, this is very special.' Ned reached to the top shelf of the cupboard. 'Bluey made it, it's one of a kind and I think he'd really appreciate it if you could bring it back in one piece.' It looked like a pair of sunglasses. He tinkered with the settings on the side arm and handed them to Brogan.

'Why do I need a pair of sunglasses?'

'This, my friend, is your way across the city without being identified. See the rim? Micro-projectors, you can project any image across your face, look like anyone you want to, to the human eye and to electronic eyes.' Ned brimmed.

'I can look like anyone I want?'

'Well, yeah, your face will, but not the…' Ned looked up and down at Brogan, '…not the rest of you, though.'

'Right. Now all I need's a cab.' Brogan raised his wrist and was about to stab at the comms-watch when Ned grabbed him.

'Are you crazy? You're not callin' a cab to pick you up from here, you'll give away our location. Places like this are hard to come by. You've gotta walk out of the tunnel, cross under the border fence and get picked up at the mall.'

Brogan sagged. *Walking, great.* 'I need you to do something for me.'

'Anything.' Ned was eager to please, or eager to get Brogan out of there.

'Call my headquarters, ask for Agent Green in Internal Affairs. Speak to her and only her. Tell her Kane's the mole and ready a team to get down to Novanoid.'

'You *are* gonna go and bust 'em! Cool.'

'Agent Green. Got it?'

'Yeah. Green, got it.'

Brogan nodded then made his way out, back down the access ladder.

* * *

He trudged through the darkness of the tunnel, slipping on God knows what and ducking to a crouch with every clink or rattle. His mind wandered in the darkness. Clarkson, Eric, Mikey... how was he going to explain that one to Katie? *I could do with a beer.*

As he rounded the endless curve, the chink of light from the entrance seemed impossibly far away against the weight of the tunnel smothering him. With a few yards to go, Brogan put the sunglasses on. A tiny blue dot of light came on in the corner of his right eye. Fingers crossed Ned was right. Fingers crossed it was working. He stepped out of the tunnel into the dwindling afternoon sun.

The border fence was a few hundred metres away. Brogan scanned the sky. Nothing was above him. A concrete block framed the mouth of the tunnel. Brogan edged his way to the left with his back against the wall. He stopped and listened. Silence. He dared a glance around the corner. *Clear.*

He lumbered towards the back of the mall, his pace hampered by the rough grass and his knackered body. He stopped for a minute under cover of a copse. Ned's comms-watch buzzed on his wrist.

Mikey's back, was all the message read.

Spurred on, he saw the gap in the fence Ned had told him about. He crouched down and shuffled through it, and stood quickly on the other side. He was so unfit. He leant against the fence, trying to look casual but really trying to catch his breath. Panting, he took out his e-cig. *Like that's going to help.* He stuffed it back in his pocket and started walking. He avoided looking up at the security cameras and hoped the visor covered everything, including the sweat dripping off his forehead.

A constant stream of aero-cabs landing and taking off in front of the mall meant he didn't have to wait in the open for long.

'Please, state your destination.'

'Novanoid Corporation Headquarters. Activate silent mode.'

'Silent mode activated.'

In the back of the cab, Brogan sank into the comfy seat. He could have easily fallen asleep. Instead, he took a power-shot from the cab's onboard refreshments. A strawberry gloop filled with every kind of legal drug, vitamin and mineral slid down his throat and leached into his body and mind.

Chapter 28

B rogan caught sight of himself in the glass doors as he got out of the aero-cab. Ned had given him a nose like a door wedge and a thick rug of a moustache. He smiled and a gold tooth glinted back at him. *Jeez, I look like a right tool.* He was ugly, but the tech was impressive.

He strolled through Novanoid's foyer. The securatrons didn't seem to be paying him much attention as he made it to the reception desk. His heart was beating fast. The comms-watch hadn't buzzed with the number to call. He needed to stall for time.

He bent down and fiddled with his shoelace, and as he looked down the visor slipped down his nose. *Shit.* He scrambled to put it back in place. The little blue light that was in the corner was now red and flashing. *Shit. Shit. Shit.* He kept his head down, not daring to look up. He spotted the bottom half of a securatron heading his way. The little light turned blue and Brogan sprang to his feet.

'Excuse me, sir.' The securatron's manly voice still kept a slight electronic tone. 'Sir?'

Brogan half-turned to the machine. 'I'll deal with the receptionist.' Then he hurried towards the desk. A little bead of sweat formed on his temple.

'Hi there.' He grinned at the receptionist, a brunette with a pixie face, and turned on the charm. 'I have a meeting with... oh, damn it, sorry, I've forgotten his name already. Sorry. I need a memory upgrade or something, honestly.' The girl tilted her head to one side but continued to stare blankly, not even trying to hide her contempt.

'Oh, you have beautiful eyes. What are they? Hazel? Green?' Brogan fumbled in his pockets.

'Green.'

'Lovely, lovely.' His comms-watch buzzed. 'Ah, sorry. Do you mind if I...' Brogan pointed to his comms-watch. The girl couldn't be less interested.

'Ah, it's my boss. Probably wants to know how the meeting's going. Can I use a phone? I much prefer to do things the old-fashioned way.' He winked.

If the girl didn't roll her eyes outwardly, she certainly did inwardly. 'The phone at the end of the desk's for visitors.'

'Oh, thanks, thanks very much. I won't be a minute.' Brogan bobbed his head in inept gratitude. He grabbed the receiver, glanced at the number on his watch, and dialled.

'Hi Deena, it's me, the big cheese left me a message to call. Any chance he's still free?' Brogan glanced over at the receptionist. He flashed his eyebrows and the gold tooth and she looked away.

There was a pause on the other end of the phone. Brogan drummed his fingers on the desk.

'Hello, you. I'll see if he's available. Please stay on the line.' The woman's voice took Brogan by surprise. He checked he'd dialled the right number. 'He's on another call right now, can you wait a moment? I'm sure he's almost finished.'

'Okay, I'll wait. Thanks Deena.' Brogan tutted to no one in particular, then shifted to lean his back against the desk and looked out across the foyer. Two securatrons flanked him. His comms-watch buzzed: *Almost in.*

'Deena? Would you mind checking if I've got any other messages while I'm waiting?'

'Certainly… hmmm, no, not that I can see.'

'Oh, okay. Ohh, this is really embarrassing but can you remind me of the name of the gentleman I'm scheduled to see here at Novanoid. I'm dreadfully sorry, I thought I'd written it down…'

'What are you like? Your diary says it's with—'

Someone tapped Brogan's shoulder. *Shit.*

'Sir, we're going to have to ask you to come with us.'

Brogan followed the voice and his gaze fell on a human security guard. A big one. *Jeez, where do they find these guys?* Brogan held the phone against his shoulder. 'Sorry, what? Why?'

'If you would just come with us please?' The securatron standing next to him extended its taser.

'Oh. Oh. There's no need for that. I'm just a salesman…'

'Not yet, not yet,' yelled a voice in the receiver.

Brogan flapped his hand at the securatron. 'Alright, alright, I'll come. I mean, I don't understand what this is all about but…' He tutted and turned sideways away from the guards. 'Deena, love, I'll have to call you back. There's some mix-up with security, I've got to go with them apparently. Tell Mr Milestone I'll have to call him back, and no, I don't know how long I'll be.'

'Come on, Detective Brogan. Enough of the theatrics. You're fooling no one.' The big security guard put his hand on Brogan's shoulder and squeezed.

Damn it. Brogan turned and put the receiver back on the desk. He put his hands out to the sides and stepped forward.

'Take the visor off, detective.' The security guard held a finger to his ear, dropped his gaze, then nodded. 'Follow me, please.'

Brogan heard a little gasp from the receptionist as he removed the visor. The securatron circled around behind him and herded him forward.

'Well, it was nice chatting to you, young lady. Novanoid are *really* lucky to have you.' Brogan grinned, held her gaze a little longer than necessary, then turned his attention to the security guard. He sensed the girl's eyes were still on him and crossed his fingers that she hadn't noticed he'd not replaced the phone properly. His hand clasped the comms-watch on his opposite wrist. It hadn't buzzed.

'How did you know it was me?' Brogan stayed a couple of steps behind the security guard and the securatron brought up the rear.

'You're in the most high-tech building in the world, it wasn't that hard.'

'Where are we going?'

'You'll see.'

This guy's a jobsworth. Brogan followed him to the elevators, clocking several cameras on the way. He was being watched from the moment he got out of the cab.

'Basement level three,' the jobsworth instructed the elevator.

Brogan raised his eyebrows. 'We're not going up?'

'I'm just following my instructions.' The descent was rapid. Brogan's stomach was still at the atrium level when the elevator glided to a smooth stop.

'Out you get.' The guard stood to the side.

'What? You're not coming with me?'

'No. This lift's the only way in or out of here, and you don't have the clearance to summon it. Now, go on, through those doors like a good little detective.'

Prick. The elevator doors hissed closed behind him. The place was deathly silent. A single white light above his head shone down on him like a street lamp, illuminating the small anteroom of stark magnolia walls and polished concrete floor. Brogan looked at the slick black-glass doors. His comms-watch buzzed. His body tingled. He didn't know if he was being watched or not, so he tried to keep his cool. Instead of looking down at the message, he stretched out his arm as though to push the door open.

We're in but Mikey's glitchin' again, he's AWOL, read the rolling message bar on his watch as the automatic doors *swooshed* open.

'Welcome to the CAVE, detective.'

Brogan's eyes flashed up to meet the steel gaze of Jaro Dax.

'Dax.' Brogan stepped into yet another small room. This

one had two rows of shelving with neatly placed baskets the size of shoeboxes on them. A sign above the shelves read: *Please remove all electronic devices before entering the CAVE.*

'To what do I owe the special welcome?' Brogan couldn't bring himself to shake the man's hand.

'I'd prefer to discuss matters inside. Now, if you would divest yourself of any technology you have on you. There are storage baskets for your convenience.' Dax gestured to the shoeboxes.

'Fine. I mean, it's a bit paranoid of you, but sure.' Brogan unhitched the comms-watch. A quick glance at the screen showed no new messages. *C'mon Mikey.* He removed the visor from his pocket and slipped it into one of the baskets with his watch.

'Clever bit of kit you've got there.' Dax nodded towards the visor. 'How did you come by it?'

'Hmm, I'd prefer to discuss these matters inside.' Brogan's gaze darted to the next door, a thick metal one that wouldn't have been out of place on a battlecruiser.

'An alarm will sound if it detects a signal. You can try it if you like, but I wouldn't recommend it. The siren is awfully deafening.' Dax gave a wry smile then pressed his palm on a little black panel next to the door.

'That's a bit needless down here, isn't it?'

'I like to know if I'm being deceived, detective.'

The metal locks clinked as they disengaged, followed by a suck of air as the door slid open.

Brogan's mouth dried up and his stomach gurgled. *What's going on with Mikey…* He clocked the thickness of the doors and it took his mind back to the blast doors at a nuclear storage facility he'd been stationed at once. *Best posting ever.* He sighed.

Dax stepped through the scanner and turned to watch Brogan. No alarm sounded as he stepped through the door and into the third box of a room. A circular glass table and matching chairs took centre stage. Nothing else. The air felt dead. There was more life in a morgue. Dax took a seat on the far side of the table as the door slid back into place and clunked shut.

'Come, sit. Don't let's make this awkward.' Dax sat back in his chair, crossed his ankles beneath him and spread his knees unnecessarily wide.

If you want a dick-off, I'll give you a dick-off. Brogan sat opposite and mirrored Dax. The guy oozed slime like a slug leaving a trail of detest in Brogan's mind.

'This is the CAVE, detective. Buried in these walls is a network of EMP emitters, and beyond that… nothing but concrete.' A grin slicked across his face. 'No signal in, no signal out. Whatever is said in this room will not escape this room.'

'Nothing that gives off a signal, you say?' Brogan nodded, trying to feign being impressed. 'Do you mind if I…' He reached into his jacket pocket and pulled out his e-cig.

'The sign said no electricals.'

'I'm not much one for signs, and besides, it's only an e-cig with a suck'n'go dynamo. No batteries needed.' Brogan took a long, long drag. When his lungs were about to explode he blew the vapour into the middle of the room. He spotted Dax's lip twitch a little before he lurched forward, coughing and spluttering. He rose from his chair and carried on clearing his throat loudly, fumbling as he tucked the e-cig back in his jacket pocket. He sat back down and blinked back the water in his eyes.

'You're biding your time, detective. I can smell it a mile away.'

'Ah, there's nothing like a good drag on an e-cig to clear the lungs. You should try it, Dax. Too much clean livin', that's your problem.'

'What are you doing here, detective?'

Brogan shrugged. 'I don't know. You tell me. I mean, I was passin' through and then out of the blue you invited me down here to your lovely little snug.' Brogan coughed a bit more then undid his jacket. 'It's a bit warm in here.'

'Stop pissing about and tell me what you think you're up to.'

'Now, I'm the detective, I should be the one asking the questions. Why did you have Amber Hausman killed?'

'That one wasn't us. You're playing in the wrong park, detective.'

'*That one*? So the others were? Clarkson? Minty? My own son? They were you, were they?'

'Your son's death was nothing to do with us. This is all slander.'

'Oh, I don't think it is. Because, you see, I have a witness. Two, in fact.'

'So what if it was us. Good luck proving any of it. A mentally unstable detective against the richest company on the planet. I've got the finances to bankrupt the government, any poxy legal case will be thrown out like a fart in the breeze.'

'Tell me about the Metanoia Code, then.'

'You haven't the vision to understand,' Dax scoffed.

'Ah, come on, teach an old dog new tricks. Is it some sort of new, oh, what's it called… a multiverse game?'

'Ah, you're having a joke.' Dax oozed smarm. 'Metanoia is the new hope. Metanoia is the transcendence of the human mind into a limitless digital universe. Imagine the possibilities, no longer tied to decaying flesh, where death is no longer the end. We'll be able to live forever in an infinite realm of possibility, opportunity, free of the responsibility of a tawdry existence—'

'Not to mention the royalties and the spin-off creds. I mean, no doubt you'll charge for storage. Oh, yeah, yeah, I can see why you'd think it was worth it to kill off a load of kids.'

'Those kids were truly the brave pioneers of the modern age, each one a willing sacrifice to the greater good of the evolution of mankind. Without them we wouldn't be as close to perfecting the algorithm as we are today. The Metanoia Code will change everything, for everyone, forever. It is the future of our species and it will save us from the climate disaster.'

'So you're playing God now, are you? What about Mace? Did he get in the way of this… this great vision of yours?'

'He was a clever kid. Too clever. He was the perfect fall guy.'

'So now it's just me standing in the way?'

'Not for much longer,' he sneered. 'I mean, you don't expect to be getting out of here alive, do you, detective?'

'Well, you've tried to kill me twice already and look where that's got you.'

'Even cats run out of lives eventually.' Dax had a smirk that was asking to be smashed in.

'Are you seriously saying you'd kill me in order to carry on perfecting the Metanoia Code?'

'Progress is inevitable, some must fall by the wayside for that to happen. It's nothing personal, it's a fact of life.'

'You don't value life, Dax, you value fame and fortune.'

'You have me all wrong, detective. I value lives, but the lives of the many and not the few. I serve a greater good and a higher purpose.'

'Who died and made you God?'

'God did. Now, if you don't mind, it's time to adjourn to your final resting place.'

'Pardon?' Brogan's face creased, then the sound of the door locks disengaging made him spin around.

'Ah, here they are now. Like I said, you didn't think you were getting out of here alive, did you, detective? You're a bit old as far as test subjects go, but you never know, we might get lucky.' Dax grinned. Two security guards stepped inside. 'Take him up to the test lab in Tempest's office.'

Chapter 29

The two security guards grabbed Brogan under the arms and gave him little choice but to move with them.

'Can I at least get my watch and the visor?' Brogan tried to dig his heels in against the pull of the guards.

'Fine. Not that you'll need them.' Dax wafted his hand as he headed for the elevator. Brogan jerked his arm free of a guard and grabbed the visor and his watch. He rammed the visor into his pocket and fiddled with his watch, risking a glance down at the screen. Four messages rolled across the little display:

Mikey's back.

Mikey's gone rogue. Where are you?

Detective?

Help?

Brogan kept his gaze down, his mind racing with possibilities. *Shit, what's been happening?* Dax got into the elevator first, then Brogan was shoved in, between the two guards.

Then he saw it: a little insignia tattooed on the guard's right wrist. It was partially covered by the guy's comms-watch, but it was unmistakable. Eagle's wings. The symbol of his unit. The symbol of his brotherhood. An ex-drone fighter. Brogan pulled against their grip on his biceps, twisted his own comms-watch back and revealed the same insignia on his left. He glanced sideways. The guard seemed to clock it.

'*Alis aquilae.*' Brogan kept his voice low, but in the quiet of the lift he might as well have shouted.

'Be quiet, Brogan.' Dax reeked of impatience.

The guard with the insignia gave Brogan's arm a subtle squeeze before relaxing his grip.

The elevator slowed to a stop. The doors softly *swooshed* open. They took a few steps forward. People were standing around. Staring. Motionless. Then they saw it too and stopped.

Every screen, every display unit, every visi-wall, every console displayed images and videos of faces, of people laughing, people arguing, of a pretty girl leaning in for a kiss, of a toddler's dumpy hand reaching for a rattle, an old woman in a red armchair, a younger version of Katie scooping up a child's body while singing, of two little arms and legs running towards a man in a military uniform. Every screen a different snippet of life, of Mikey's life.

Brogan's mouth fell slack, his mind a jumbled mess of the memories playing out in front of him and a lump swelling in his throat.

Then every screen blinked out to a small white dot in the middle of the blackness.

No one moved.

No one made a sound.

As if someone had changed the channel, Mikey appeared on every screen, sitting in his favourite red armchair by the fire at his grandma's house.

'Sorry I'm late.' He smiled as wide as the screen.

'Liar,' Brogan managed, the edge of his mouth curling into a smile.

Dax pushed past Brogan. 'It works?' His eyes wide, the excitement of possibility shone from his face. He laughed and spun in a circle as though he were dancing in the rain. 'It works. My God.' He laughed.

'Don't get too excited, Dax. You're goin' where the sun don't shine, for a very long time.' Brogan's lip twitched, and his eyes narrowed.

Dax raised his wrist. 'ANNA, run the Icarus program.' Dax's smug, arrogant charm returned. 'You've got no evidence. It's being fragmented as we speak, it'll take you years to put all the pieces back together.'

'Mikey, can you stop it?'

'I'll try.' Mikey disappeared off the screen.

'With or without the data files, I've got your confession. That's all I need.'

Dax's laugh echoed into the expanse of the building. 'Give it up, Brogan. You've got nothing.'

'Nothing, you say?' Brogan reached into his jacket pocket and pulled out a little metal oblong. 'Ever see one of these? It was my great-granddad's. Still works, too. I mean, alkaline batteries are a bugger to come by, but she's totally worth it. This nifty little dictaphone recorded everything you said in the CAVE.' Brogan pressed a little button and two cogs spun round in the middle. Then he pressed another and Dax's muffled voice began repeating their conversation. 'It's amazing what people tell you when they don't think they're being recorded. Don't you think?'

'I've stopped it, Dad.' Mikey flopped down in his chair.

'Nice work, Mikey.'

'Guards, take him down and destroy the piece of junk recorder he's holding.' Dax pointed to the two men who'd escorted Brogan in the lift. The tattooed guard stepped forward and halted his colleague with a shake of his head. Neither of the men moved.

'Didn't you hear me? Take him down. Now.' Dax's gaze flitted from one man to the next. When they still didn't move, he turned and ran across the concourse. Brogan gave chase.

A bolt of electricity exploded through the glass office windows. Pane after pane shattered and rained down on Dax as he dashed towards the central staircase. He skidded but somehow managed to keep his feet, losing enough speed for Brogan to catch up, leaping and ploughing into the back of him, sending them both crashing to the floor.

A shard of glass punctured Brogan's hip as he landed, the pain searing his mind for only a moment as he wrestled Dax's arms behind his back and cuffed him.

'Dad? He wasn't working alone. Parker and Dr Tempest were working with him.'

'Shit. Where are they?'

'Dr Tempest is in the medical bay in the basement.

Parker is… hang on… he's getting into an aero-cab on the 25th floor.'

'Do you think his cab could take a detour to Peacekeeper HQ?'

Mikey's face lit up. 'Sure.'

A flurry of noise rose up from the lobby.

Brogan looked to the two security guards who'd restrained him earlier. 'Watch him for a minute, will you?' He dipped his head towards Dax, who'd gashed his forehead on a piece of glass.

Brogan looked down to the foyer. A stream of Rapid Response Peacekeepers filtered in and spread out around the perimeter. Bringing up the rear were Green and Chang from Internal Affairs.

Brogan whistled at them and beckoned them up. Green nodded then spoke into her radio, and six guys peeled off and headed up the central staircase. Green gave some more orders and made her way upstairs with Chang.

Brogan looked down at the throbbing in his thigh. Blood trickled down his leg, causing his trousers to stick to his skin.

Green and Chang arrived at his location. 'We need to get a team down to the basement. Dr Tempest has some explaining to do.'

'Yeah, Mikey told us.' She flashed the radio at Brogan. 'There's a team picking her up now. That leg looks dodgy.'

'I've had worse. Did you get Kane?'

'Yeah, he's back at base under lock and key. Anders is on his way down, he was right behind us. So how did you work out Kane was the mole?'

'He was the only one who knew where Sel was going. He gave Dax the heads-up.'

'Hmm, no. No, he wasn't…' Green chewed her lip and furrowed her brow. 'I saw her talking to Anders just before she left.'

'What?' Brogan's eyes grew wide as he searched for the answer that his gut already knew.

'Anders… Not "Ters"… An-Ders.' *Oh fuck*. 'That's what Sel was trying to tell me before she died.'

Green gulped, then swiped at her comms-watch. 'Paysos, where is Agent Anders?'

'I'm sorry, detective. There is no one here by that name.'

'Paysos? Check again. James Anders, tech division. Where is he?'

'I'm sorry, detective. There is no one registered by that name.'

'What? That's an error. Paysos, have your files been corrupted? Locate James Anders.'

'Dad?'

'Not now, Mikey. Paysos, review the security cameras. He was in the building when Detective Green left. He had to leave somehow.'

'Dad?'

'What? Can't you see I'm in the middle of something?'

'The Metanoia Code. It's gone.'

'What do you mean? It was wiped out by the Icarus thingy? I thought you stopped it.'

'No, it was deleted before Dax initiated it and… Mace is gone too.'

'What? What the hell is happening? Brogan's eyebrows were as far up his forehead as they could go.

'The cabin's gone. I tried the linkup, it's a dead-end. So I checked his location. This is the thing: the prison records show Mace was transferred to the hospital, but the hospital records show he was discharged back to the prison the same day.'

'When?

'The eighteenth of October, from what I can tell.'

'What? That can't be right. What about Dr Simms? I spoke to him only last month.'

'I'll check. Hang on… Okay, so there was a Dr Simms, but he died fourteen years ago.'

'What the hell? There's got to be a mistake. Are you in the right system?'

'Check for yourself.' Mikey split the screen in two and brought up the prison hospital files. A picture of the doctor appeared.

'Yep, that was him. That was the doctor I spoke to… But… he can't be dead.'

'We'd better release Kane. He should know what's going on.' Chang stepped away and started tapping at his watch.

'He's gonna be so pissed at me. I don't even know where to start.' Brogan shook his head.

'Dad?' Mikey had that drawn-out tone that instantly pushes any parent's buttons.

'For cryin' out loud Mikey. What now?'

'Well, there's also this…' Mikey nodded and beckoned for someone to step forward. Brogan looked over his shoulder, thinking Mikey was talking to someone behind him.

A young child scurried over to Mikey and clung to him.

She peeped out from Mikey's hug then buried her face into him again.

'Dad, this is Florida Graham, otherwise known as Minty.'

Brogan rubbed his stubble as he stared at the scared child.

'She's a fragment of consciousness. The program must have stopped before reaching Minty's full age. There are others too, they won't come out, they've been trapped in the system and they're scared.'

'When's Mummy coming?' Minty looked up at Mikey.

'Soon, I promise.' Mikey stroked the girl's hair then looked up at his dad.

Green stepped closer to the screen. She reached out and touched it. 'Haven't some of them been dead for two years?'

'Yeah.' Brogan's nostrils flared. He strode over to Dax, grabbed him by the collar and hauled him over to the balcony looking out over the atrium. Brogan pushed Dax hard against the railing, forcing his top half out over the drop.

'See? Do you see what your fucking tinkering has done?' Brogan flung an arm in the direction of a screen. His eyes narrowed. Froth formed at the edges of his mouth, his muscles rigid and ready. 'Give me one reason not to drop you down there, right fucking now?'

Little beads of sweat formed on Dax's forehead. He licked his lips, then glanced at Green.

'Brogan. Don't.' Green's husky voice had a sharp edge that cut through the red mist in Brogan's mind.

A pair of Rapid Response officers stepped either side of

them. Brogan kept his glare on Dax as he released the man.

A cocky smile slicked over Dax's face. 'You'll pay for that transgression, my lawyers will see to it.'

Brogan glanced at the floor, pulled back his arm, and punched Dax in the stomach. A gush of air left Dax and he keeled over, gasping for breath.

Brogan leant down to Dax's ear. 'Keep the fucking change.' Brogan stood up and stepped back. 'Get him out of here.'

The two Rapid Response officers hauled Dax away while he was still wheezing.

'Feel better?' Green raised an eyebrow.

'A bit. This is a right mess.'

'You're a right mess.' She smiled.

'Mikey, how you doing?'

'I've found seven kids, so far.'

'Hang in there, Mikey. Do your best to find the others, we'll get Family Liaison to deal with it. This is way above my pay grade. I mean, who owns you and the others? Are you intellectual property? Is it us parents, are we still responsible for you? What do we even call you, we have no word for what you are.'

'I quite like the word *Metanoia*. I think we should get to choose how we are defined, and for now at least I think *Metanoid* is a good choice.'

'It's as good as any. Your mum won't be happy no matter what you call yourselves.'

'Oh yeah, will you tell her?'

'Nope.' Brogan saw the disappointment in Mikey's eyes. 'Tell you what, seeing as how you've save my skin a few times, how about we tell her together?'

'Deal.' Mikey smiled, and for a moment it seemed as though the screen got brighter too.

'I'll get my leg seen to, then I'll see you at your mum's in a bit.'

'Cool.'

Brogan turned to Green. 'Any luck tracking Anders?'

'None.' She pressed her lips together in a tight line. 'He's vanished. Every file. Everything. Gone.'

'I knew he was good with computers, but holy hell. And to think of the files he's had access to.'

'Oh no, don't. I dread to think what classified information he's accessed.'

Brogan smiled. 'You'll be busy for a bit then.' He limped away to the sky-trax platform. His leg throbbed, his trousers were caked in blood and had stuck to his skin. The medical van's doors slid open and a strong pair of arms helped heave him inside. Brogan lay on the gurney and shut his eyes.

'I need to cut your trousers?'

'Fine, fine, whatever.' Brogan flapped his hand in a just-bloody-well-get-on-with-it kind of way as his body sank into the depths of fatigue.

'You have to stop taking the epilepsy tablets.'

Brogan's eyes flew open. The medic pulled down his facemask. Eric glanced at him, replaced the mask, and carried on treating Brogan's wound. 'Eric.'

'You are a subject in a classified military experiment. The drugs you are taking are not for epilepsy, they turbocharge your immune system. In the event of a bio-attack, they want soldiers to be resistant to any, if not all, lethal substances. You have to reduce the dose slowly, half a tablet at a time, and for heaven's sake don't kiss anyone.'

'What experiment? What are you talking about, don't kiss anyone?'

'They're testing a weapon. That weapon is you, but the drugs are backfiring. Anyone exposed to your antibodies can't fight them off. On the surface they look like they get the flu, and then they die.'

Brogan rolled his eyes. 'Why should I trust you? Who are you?'

'I was on the team that developed the drug. It's dangerous. We... we didn't understand the long-term effects.'

'What, so now you've developed a conscience and you're trying to make up for it?'

'This is bigger than just me. Project Hammerhead has to be stopped.'

'You've got the wrong guy. I've had enough of mad scientists and experiments. Find someone else.'

The side door clicked open and another medic appeared. 'Hey, who are you? This is my rig.'

'I got shipped in on supply. My crew left me here to clean up the minors, only this guy's leg needed a bit more work.' Eric nodded down to Brogan's gashed leg, which had now been cleaned and neatly glued back. 'It's all sorted, it only needs a dressing.' He glanced down at Brogan. 'I'll leave it with you. Remember, I'm only a *stone's* throw away.' Then he peeled off his latex gloves, stepped past the other medic and disappeared from Brogan's view.

A stone's throw? Exhaustion crept like ivy through Brogan's body and into his mind.

Chapter 30

Brogan didn't remember falling asleep, but he did remember waking up. He was in the hospital-at-home in his old place. Katie was sitting next to him.

'Hi,' he croaked.

'This is getting too regular, Marcus.'

'I'll try not to make a habit of it.' He half smiled, half winced.

'I don't know how to tell you this. Mikey's alive… sort of…' He searched her eyes for a reaction.

'I know.' Her head bobbed slightly. 'It was all over the news feeds.'

Brogan sighed. 'What do you think?'

'I don't know. Is it really him? Can it really be him?' She glanced away, her eyes glistened with the swell of tears.

'Honestly? I don't know. It sounded a lot like him and he knew things only Mikey would know.' Brogan pushed himself up in the bed, his muscles fighting against him. 'Has he contacted you?'

She shook her head and wrapped her arms around her. 'Novanoid's been on some kind of lockdown. I don't know what's going on.'

'Okay. Where's my watch?'

'Here.' She twisted, grabbed his watch from the cabinet beside her and handed it to him.

'How long have I been out?' He fiddled with his watch, swiping past a load of messages.

'Only a day.'

'Feels like longer.' He raised the watch towards his mouth. 'Call Kane.'

Katie sat back.

'Brogan.' Kane's face hovered in the air above Brogan's watch. 'It's a bit busy down here.' He stepped aside, the golden N of Novanoid's logo filled the screen.

'Where's Mikey?'

'He's helping with our investigations and supporting the other Metanoids. We're close to finding remnants or partial uploads of all the victims, and I must say your son is doing an excellent job.'

'Metanoids?' He smiled. 'Mikey got his way then?'

'Yeah, him and the media circus.'

'Sorry I had you pinned as the mole.' Brogan almost looked around to see who'd said that. The words seemed to come out by themselves. Not that they weren't true.

'I can't say I'm not pissed at you, but you've not done a bad job here.'

Brogan gave a single nod. 'Get Mikey to call his mum, would you?'

'Sure.' Kane looked away from the camera and shook his head at someone.

'Sir, about that time off…'

'Take as long as you need.'

'Thanks. There's something I need to do.' Brogan cut the call. He turned to Katie. 'I'm sorry I've been such a wanker.'

Katie's lips trembled.

'There's some kind of conspiracy going on and I need to find some answers.'

'I don't understand.'

'I didn't kill Estrada, or the baby. I don't have epilepsy. I was unknowingly recruited into a secret military experiment and I'm going to find out who's behind it.'

'Are you sure?'

'Positive. I'm going to start with a trip back to Porton Down.'

'But—'

'Look, it'll be okay. Mikey's, well, he's not totally gone, we still have a piece of him. We might not be able to touch him, he'll never grow old, but at least we'll be able to talk to him. That's more than some people get.' He pressed his lips together and reached out to touch her hand.

Her body sagged. 'This is all too much. I can't get my head around it. Can't you let someone else investigate?'

'No. You know me, Katie, I'm always fighting a battle somewhere, it's what I do.' He hauled himself up against the pain and pulled her into his arms. *Fighting a battle is one thing, winning is another.*

* * *

A man in blue jeans and a khaki jacket walked out the front door of Peacekeeper HQ and into the plaza. His thick black hair was swept to one side above a pair of vintage sunglasses. He took a deep breath, let the low sun warm his face, and strolled off towards Lions Gate.

Casually leaning against a tree, he inhaled a waft of weed drifting over from a bunch of students huddled nearby. He glanced around him before flicking his comms-watch. 'Open a secure line to the ambassador.'

'Do you have it?' The woman's voice was curt.

'Yes, ma'am. Copied from the Brogan kid's stack. I couldn't risk deleting it, the kid had it ring-fenced. I did manage to delete it from Novanoid's system.'

'Fine. And it works?'

'Yes. I assumed Mace's identity. The Brogan kid told me exactly how he did it.'

'Excellent work, Ranger.'

'Thank you, ma'am.'

'I'll send you half the credits now and the other half when you've uploaded the code.'

'Agreed.' Anders glanced up as a couple walked hand-in-hand past him.

'Are there any loose ends?'

'Not that I'm aware of, ma'am.'

'What of Clayton Mace?'

'He's still at the safe house. He'll be moved to another secure location tomorrow.'

'Good. I may have a use for him. His prison records?'

'Squared away, ma'am. The prison security codes you gave me were very helpful. No one suspected a thing.'

'Very well. Your transport is on the way. Your new name is Dominic Bochenko, access the details in the usual way. Understood?'

'*So ka*. Understood, ma'am.'

The call disconnected. Moments later, the man who used to be known as James Anders climbed into a slick white aero-cab. Its door gave a little sigh as it closed behind him. The destination? Classified.

DID YOU ENJOY THIS BOOK?

I really hope you enjoyed reading this book as much as I enjoyed writing it.

If you really, really liked Cyber Cell then why not sign up for my newsletter? Just head over to my website at **www.alarcher.com**.

You'll get exclusive freebies, insights, and you'll be the first to know about new releases or special offers.

Otherwise, if you'd like to leave a review that would be amazing. You'll be helping other readers find my book and decide if it's worth a read.

Thanks very much!

Angie

FUTURE RELEASES

Detective Brogan Series

Destination: Classified

James Anders assumes his new identity and gains access to some of the government's darkest secrets. Meanwhile, Brogan heads into the unknown as he tries to track down those responsible for Project Hammerhead.

Standalone Novels

The Rig

As the polar ice caps melt, the hunt for the last remaining pockets of untapped ocean oil is on. When the rig is taken over by pirates, only one man is left to stand in their way.

ACKNOWLEDGMENTS

Writing this novel has been a journey of discovery. It's harder than I thought to write a whole book. I couldn't have done it without the support of my family and friends – and by support, I mean the constant nagging about 'how's the book coming on?' Still, it all helped get me to the finish line, so thanks guys.

My thanks also go to my editor, Dan, who had to do a lot more polishing than perhaps he first bargained for – for that I am very grateful and I have learned a lot. Secondly to my beta readers, Bob and Jerry (no relation to the famous ice-cream makers). Their valuable insights helped complete the picture.

Finally, my thanks go to you, the reader, for reading this far. I hope that the fruits of my labour have entertained you, or helped to kill some time at least.

Printed in Great Britain
by Amazon

45174204R00166